Perpetual
Gloom

Shelah A Johnson

A two rut-road along
The Boloney Trial

*"A real book is not one that we read,
but one that reads us.*

W.H. Auden

1907 - 1973

For information and contact:
www.theboloneytrail.com

Cover designed by: COLONFILM
Map and chart: Leonardo Rubio
Author photo: Paul Thacker

Library of Congress Cataloging-in-Publication Data has been applied for.

ISBN
978-1-7377008-0-7 pbk
978-1-7377008-1-4 eBk
978-1-7377008-2-1 aud

DISCLAIMER

These are not my personal memories. Rather, they are firsthand events and stories shared decades after they occurred by some of the greatest storytellers I have ever known. These accounts were offered to me humorously or in a vaunter, especially when someone got their comeuppance – and I have tried to deliver them to you in the same manner.

For
Toril – my North Star
Christopher – always my teacher

Special Thanks
Kevin (Omaille) O'Malley

Contents

Perpetual Gloom,

a two rut-road along The Boloney Trail

Monroe's Travel

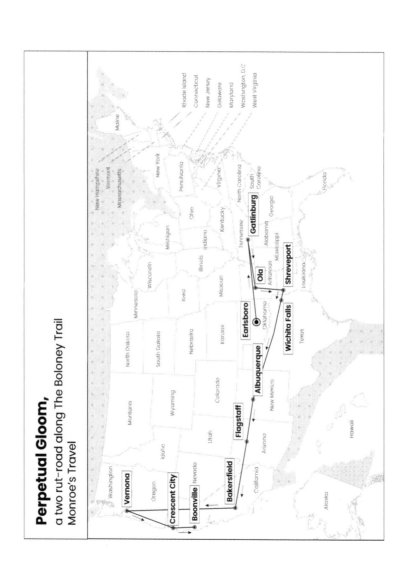

Mazie Isbell
Born 1875 – ?

Marta Isbell Hornbeck
Born 1914 – 1984

Monroe (Roe) Hornbeck
Born 1926 – 1999

Shelda Hornbeck
Born 1954 –

Wyatt Hornbeck
Born 1928 – 1950

Adilia (Lil'bit) Hornbeck
Born 1876 – 1970

Vergil Hornbeck
Born 1931 –

Jane Hornbeck
Born 1875 – 1970

Jedediah Chester (JC) Hornbeck
Alias: Jeb Dupree
Born 1900 –1986

Orson (O'd) Hornbeck
Born 1933 –

Mr. Dunks
Jane's common law husband

Floyd Dunks
Born 1913 – ?

Noreen Hornbeck– Massy
Born 1913 –?

Clyde Massy
Born 1931 –

Hester Hornbeck
Born 1934 – 1936

Gary (Slice) Dunks
Born 1931 –

Jessie Hornbeck
Born 1876 – 1970

Landry Hornbeck
Born 1942 –

Ona Hornbeck – Jackson
Born 1876 – 1970

Brady Jackson
Born 1923 –1980

Effie Hornbeck
Born 1943 –

Hollis Hornbeck
Born 1944 –

Poppy Hornbeck
Born 1949 –

Part 1

"Poverty is the parent of revolution and crime."

Aristotle

Chapter 1:

Preach it, Daddy

Arkansas, 1936

PERCHED ON AN OLD leaky galvanized bucket in a darkened corner inside a dirty coop, Monroe hid from his father and picked his guitar. The G string had snapped months ago, but he had replaced it with a long piece of kitchen string and ignored the flat thump it now made. The lone Dominique chicken did not seem to hold it against him.

Monroe tried to recall the chords he had heard only once when his father's truck blew a tire after a late-night church gathering outside a *hootchy kootchy* joint on the outer edge of Harrison—a joint where the coloreds hung out just beyond the sundowner law. It was the kind of place where even a big-mouthed sheriff with a posse of beat-up trucks driven by broken-down drunks with rifles would think twice before walking into. Monroe moseyed across the road and stood in front of the joint's single neon light that illuminated a billboard advertising the special appearance of a Detroit snake dancer by the name of Shimmy Shammy Shelley. Around the billboard of the almost naked girl, moths fluttered their wings to the beat of the swing jump music that made the walls vibrate.

The dreaded humidity was still a month off, yet Monroe was in no hurry to head back to the field. When his daddy sent him on an errand to grab a roll of wire to mend a shovel handle, Monroe knew all he had to do was wait out his old man, that if he lingered long enough his father would call it quits. It was, after all, a Sunday, the day of rest.

JC leaned on the cracked handle of his shovel, letting his hand glide up and down the wood that years of use had worn smooth. As he scanned the few acres he'd been able to clear, his eyes paused on his two sons as they pried rocks loose with picks and long pieces of wood, then pulled them out of the ground with the piece of rope that had been tied to a mule to help hoist the heavy rocks onto a short wagon and an old flatbed truck. He wished they were older, stronger, and would pull together like his two old jennies, Ruth and Esther. Though long in the tooth, they were not ready for the glue factory[1] yet, and at least they were able to come together as a team one could rely on.

I be lucky to get five acres plowed at the rate they's goin', JC thought as he picked up the shovel and rammed it back into the stubborn soil in frustration only to hear the wooden handle crack further and rip apart.

In desperation, he had written to his mother Jane in Shreveport to ask if she would pack up his younger brothers and sisters and come to Arkansas. But she would not budge, even though they were still living in a tent beside a small creek that fed into the Red River. He could hardly blame her. She walked a dirt rut worn deep by her daddy's people, the Kortright clan, who helped settle Louisiana along the Red River. Handy with a gun, they followed Jackson, firing the first shots on the British in 1814 from an R. Johnson flintlock. One even claimed to have shot one soldier twice between the eyes before he fell.

JC's heart softened as his thoughts lingered on his mother. *She shore 'nuff got spit enough for us all,* he thought as he remembered how she could jump to her feet after picking her guitar, sing her children to sleep and then, just as quick, pull off a shot through the canvas opening of the tent into the dark while screaming, "That'a teach ya sons of bitches! Keep to ya own patch!"

---

1. Horses have loads of collagen, which is turned into glue.

Fishing through the upper pocket of his dirty bib overalls, JC pulled out a crinkled letter, the markings made by his sister's lead pencil now worn down into tiny shadows. But he did not need to read the words; he had already memorized Noreen's reply:

Shreveport, Louisiana
May 21, 1933

Dear Brother,

Mamma asks me to wite ya as her roertism been actin' up for a spell. Somethang affel and wez gotta collect her herbs and barks. Ya nos how she don't like nobody doin' it fer her. It seems like it git bad after Mr. Dunks took off last time. He left his boy Floyd, so it ain't so bad as last time. He's been hep'n' a lot. So she specks we ain't be comin' over to Arkansas no time soon.

With love to yaw,

Your sister, Noreen

Crushing the letter in one hand, JC pulled the shovel out of the dirt with the other and slammed it down once again. Just thinking about Mr. Dunks made his blood boil. JC wished his mother would have let him die. But no, she was a healer, a woman looked to by others to mend their guts, birth their babies, and put broken men's bones back together.

Mr. Dunks was shot in the jaw by a .22 long[2] by a railroad yardman in Robelin. He claimed he was taking a shortcut across the yard when he caught the lead, but the1930s were desperate times, and there would not be one out of work family that would have blamed him for breaking into boxcars looking for something to eat or sell.

Jane later found Mr. Dunks sitting in a waiting room chair at the tiny eight-bed hospital, pressing a bloody shirt against an open hole in the side of his face. After she removed the shirt, she

---

2. A .22 long (L or LR) refers to the length of the bullet.

could see the bleeding had slowed to a trickle, and the coagulated blood was building a dam along his jawline.

"What yaw waitin' fer, gangrene?" Jane yelled at the chubby nurse who was wearing a stained, tight-fitting white uniform and sitting behind an oak desk, doing her best to avoid eye contact with the sick and needy.

Peeking up from her paperwork, the nurse asked, "Are you going to pay for the doctor?"

The Kortrights had a well-earned reputation, a lethal combination of both mulishness and cantankerousness. It only took one determined look from Jane to adjust the nurse's attitude. After that, Mr. Dunks was stitched up by the area's only *bona fide* doctor—who stayed drunk most of the time.

Within days after returning to the tent along the creek, Mr. Dunks developed a high fever, and his face swelled like a wild pig's bladder that had been left out in the hot sun. And it gave off a stink that smelled like a dead chicken rotting its way into crab bait.

"If ya wont some'm done right, ya gotta do it yaself," said Jane. Then she called to her youngest son. "Jesse, drag over a chair and run down and fetch a fresh bucket of water from the creek."

"Yes, Mamma."

"Noreen, cut up a bedsheet!" she yelled.

"Ain't got no bedsheets."

"Then get an old shirt," she said in a disdainful tone. "Yaw know how to make do."

So Jane gathered her jars and pouches filled with wild honey, garlic, and oregano.

"Floyd," began Jane, "sharpen the knife and build a fire. Then boil the water that Jesse's brang'n up. I ain't gonna be but a flash." Then she headed down along the creek side.

When she returned, she had a small cloth pouch filled with fresh goldenseal. "Come on," she said, and she motioned Mr. Dunks onto an old oak kitchen chair. "I need to see what I'm a gonna be diggin' into."

Jane opened Mr. Dunks' wound, snipping through each stitch with a pair of small scissors that she dipped in jar of whisky, letting the stench and the purulent drainage flow freely onto an old shirt.

"If it weren't for bad luck, you'd have no luck at all," she said as she gave Mr. Dunks a piece of willow bark to chew on while she assembled a small assortment of instruments.

"That dagum doctor left a mess of bone fragmentations," hissed Jane as she poked around the hole in Mr. Dunks' face with her tweezers. As she took her time fishing for small splinters of bone, she started humming, partly to ease Mr. Dunks, but mostly to comfort the children who had gathered around her. Once she felt their breathing relax, she started one of the children's favorite songs, *"Ya Gotta Quit Kickin' My Dog Aroun' "*[3], one whose meaning would not get lost on its way to Mr. Dunks.

Mr. Dunks did not flinch but sat quietly as Jane's tweezers drew out small remnants of bone and cartilage, one after the other. He had lost much of the feeling in his face years before after he poured kerosene on hot coals and created a big explosion that severely damaged his face and upper torso. As Floyd watched Jane fling fragments across the dry dirt, he concluded that his father's face would be no worse for wear.

With Jane's herbs and constant care, Mr. Dunks soon recovered, and one day, with a face hard to shave, he walked out of their camp. Some say they saw him working for wildcatters[4] somewhere in East Texas. Others claimed he died outside of Abilene. Whichever the case, Jane inherited Mr. Dunks' boy Floyd, who always earned his feed.

---

3. *"Ya Gotta Quit Kickin' My Dog Aroun'"* was first recorded by Gid Tanner & The Skillet Lickers in 1926.

4. Wildcatters are speculators who drill in areas not known to have oil.

Smoothing out the letter he had just crushed, JC gently folded it along its deep creases, pushed it deep into his chest pocket, and yelled, "Boys, time to knock off and git the wagon and the truck unloaded! Let's get on up to the house and git'er done!"

Monroe could hear his father's bark all the way up to the chicken coop. He gently leaned his guitar against the bucket and picked up the roll of wire that he had carelessly tossed on the ground and made his way back into the field.

"What in Sam hill took you so long?" asked JC as he smacked Monroe alongside the head before grabbing the wire.

Rubbing the sting his father's hand left on his head, Monroe climbed into the cab of their 1929 Chevrolet International truck, claiming his firstborn rights to the steering wheel. He pulled himself up close to the push-out windshield, pulled on the choke, and gave the throttle a few hard pumps with his worn-out boot before he turned the engine over. It failed to turn, so he pushed himself further down into the seat and stomped on the throttle.

"Don't go a-floodin' it, Roe!" Monroe heard his father yell, then he turned and saw his daddy's face pushing its way through the open driver's-side window. "Give it little taps."

"Okay," answered Monroe as he pushed himself back into the seat and flipped a lock of his wavy black hair from the middle of his forehead.

"Trouble with ya dagum younguns is ya always in a dang rush—sep' when it comes time fer work."

Monroe nodded smugly, hoping his father would get off the pulpit so he could pull out the truck. He was about to turn twelve, and there was nothing he loved better than his guitar, the picture show, and having complete control of a one-ton machine.

"And don't ya go gunnin' it. We ain't got enough gas to be wastin'. Ya hyeer me, Roe?"

"Awraht," acknowledged Monroe as he fixed his eyes straight ahead through the cracked windshield.

With the engine sputtering, Monroe popped the clutch as he squeezed the handbrake and pulled away while his daddy still had his arm resting inside the window.

JC took a dirty blue bandana out of his back pocket and, after removing his gray, sweat-stained fedora, wiped his brow. Then he shoved the bandana back into his pocket and shook his head. "What yaw waitin' on, an engraved invitation to a debutante ball?" he yelled. "Get them mollies movin' up to the corral and get 'em watered and fed like I done told ya!"

"Yes, sir," Wyatt and Virgil replied in unison.

"And don't furget ta get yourselves washed up. Get on with it. Ya know how Lil'bit gets when we'z late."

"Come on, Miss Ruth, and you too, Miss Esther," called Virgil as he gently pulled on their harnesses, careful to keep his bare feet away from Miss Esther's hooves. Virgil was going on six and was often teased about his small frame, but he could run a team of mules better than his two older brothers, and he guided them and the wagon up to the house.

Before leaving the field, JC paused one more time, looked over his thirty-nine acres, and tried to visualize a crop of high cotton, but it was hard to see beyond the mounds of rock that still made much of the land impossible to plow. He should have known better, but he was both stubborn and desperate, which is an explosive combination for a man with a hungry family. "At lease we ain't got dust blowin' in all which-a-way," he concluded. Then he hustled up the small incline to catch up with the wagon and yelled, "I ain't goin' back a broken man!"

Wyatt, JC's second oldest boy, and Virgil could see a small trail of smoke winding its way from the stone chimney of their small sled-roofed, wood-framed house. More a shed than a house, it balanced itself on rock pilings like a blindfolded tightrope walker with a broken leg, afraid to look down and too afraid to look up for fear of losing his balance.

JC and his wife, Martha, had been in a hot hurry to get back to Louisiana after he got into a fight with his wife's cousin while trying to make a go of it in Tennessee. They had never intended to put down roots in Arkansas, but JC let it slip one day while loading up on canned goods at a corner store that he had come into a little money, and before he knew it, he owned thirty-nine-acre rockpile twelve miles off a two-rut road.

They quickly displaced a family of racoons who had taken up residence in the one-room structure. Not only was it sitting on a crumbling stone foundation, but nearly every windowpane was busted out. The well had caved in, and the tin roof leaked. Now, eight months later, they had mended the roof by overlaying metal advertising signs salvaged from retail businesses that had not survived the early days of the Depression. "Drink Big Boy Beverages," "Beech-Nut Chewing Tobacco," and "Snow King Baking Powder" signs had all been ripped from the sides of deserted buildings. "Get 'em before they git melted down for ammo," JC had instructed his children.

Martha plugged the window openings with pieces of cardboard to help keep the flies out. Their water came from a year-round creek nearby, and as for the racoons, to Virgil's delight, they had found their way into an iron Dutch oven nestled under a layer of wild onions and spring greens.

"They's bout up ta the house, Mamma!" yelled Adilia as she adjusted her nine-month-old sister on her slender hip. With her free hand, Adilia reached down and grabbed her naked, towheaded brother Orson, a four-year-old who had been practicing his aim by peeing into the loosened foundation rocks below the porch. "Come on, Daddy, we'z gonna be late!" Adilia yelled down the hill.

"Yaw heard her!" hollered JC. "Get a hassle in them there bustles!"

"He means you, girly!" teased Wyatt as he ran up behind Virgil and stuck his foot out in an effort to trip him.

"Ya think you's some kinda hotshot, don't ya? Well, ya ain't!" Virgil shot back.

"Mamma musta taken out that old hen by the smells of it," JC said to the boys as he kicked a few pebbles that had fallen from the wagon.

"Mamma don't fool around," laughed Wyatt. "If ya ain't a layin' bird, you's a Sabbath bird!"

"Don't yaw forget that boys. She don't take to freeloadin'," chuckled JC, "so get that wagon unloaded before Lil'bit crawls into a hissy fit."

Adilia came third, just after Monroe and Wyatt. She was a tiny thing with hair the color of a raven and a nose that looked as though it was a middle finger pointing up to the heavens. Each time the family moved on or a new child was born, she seemed to leave a bit of her childhood behind until, at eight, she rarely moved beyond the shadow of her mother.

As his eyes adjusted to the darkness in the small house, JC snuck up behind Martha as she stood over the potbelly stove the prior owners had left behind. Then he grabbed her by the waist, leaned over, and kissed her on the neck. "Dang if that girl ain't got a voice that could chip paint," he said as he heard Adilia yelling at her brother to hurry.

"Oh, sugar, she's just shy," Martha explained.

"Shy?" snickered JC in disbelief as he moved to the far end of the kitchen where Martha had set up a large, galvanized No. 11 tub with hot water that had been boiled on the stove.

"When we'z late, everybody turns and watches us get situated, and she just don't like all that attention," explained Martha. "I set out yur clean clothes. Hung 'em up on the nail. Ya see 'em?"

JC and the other boys took their baths in birth order behind the quilt Martha had strung along a rope in a corner of the house. With JC and the two older boys washed and dressed, Virgil slowly made his way to the back of the kitchen.

"Go on now, Virgil, and get warshed up," insisted Martha. "Quit draggin' those feet, boy. Orson's gotta get warshed up too."

"We gonna be late, Virgil!" hollered Adilia.

"Lil'bit, take the day off," snapped Martha. "It's the day of rest."

Once he pulled the edges of the quilt tight against the wall, Virgil stood and stared down at the now cold, dark gray water in the tub, and even in the dim light he could see a thick coat of soapy residue floating on the surface. He took a step closer until his toe touched the edge of the small, chipped, floral-patterned saucer his mother had placed next to the tub to hold the home-made bar of lye and grease soap, a "new and improved" recipe sent from a cousin now living in Nebraska.

For a moment, Virgil felt selfish about complaining. No one else seemed to mind dirty, chilly water or the bar of soap covered with body hair. But moments are short by their very nature, so he turned back toward the curtain and made sure there were no gaps, then he picked up the saucer and let the soap slide into the tub, which made a loud splash. Using the soap saucer, he created sounds to mimic someone bathing, occasionally letting the water spill over the side of the tub and onto his bare feet.

"Don't let that water run all over the floor, Virgil!" Martha called.

"Awraht, Mamma," he calmly answered.

Taking the tattered wet wash rag from the side of the tub, Virgil lightly dabbed his face and hair, giving the appearance that he had bathed. After gawking into the small, cracked mirror that hung on the wall, he was pleased with his facade. And when he appeared from behind the curtain, fully dressed in clean over-alls, he saw that everyone was seated at the table.

"Roe and Wyatt, go dump that tub," instructed Martha. "And bring it back in so little baby Hester can be up at the table with us." Then looking over at Orson, "I'll give him a spit bath later on."

Monroe and Wyatt jumped from their chairs, each grabbing one of the tub's two handles, slopping water over the sides as they navigated around the kitchen table.

"Make sure you don't throw the baby out!" joked JC.

"The water's so dang dirty you couldn't tell if there was a baby in there or not," Virgil said, and then he laughed.

"Dirty water ain't nothin' to be ashamed of," Martha said proudly. "Some folks ain't even got water to get dirty."

Monroe carried the wash tub back into the kitchen and set it on the floor next to a table leg. Adilia grabbed the quilt from the rope and lined the tub before placing Hester gently inside. Hester sat upright and grabbed the rim with her tiny hands, then bounced on her cloth diaper like a joyful jackrabbit.

"Make sure that diaper pin is fastened good," Martha told anyone within earshot.

Martha was a one-pin mother. She knew mothers who used two, but she had already given birth to six children, five of them all the way up through diaper stage. After the first child, for her, it was all about efficiency.

"It ain't about to come loose," said Monroe after he checked the yellow duck diaper pin.

"Now that we got everybody at the table," began Adilia, "let's say grace so as we can..."

"Bless this meat, bless this skin," blurted Wyatt before she could finish.

"Lay back my ears and stuff it in.

Amen!"

"Ya's blasphemin', Wyatt!" yelled Adilia.

"Yaw stop it now," said Martha. "Go on, Daddy, say grace."

JC began his simple, never-altered entreaty to the Lord on behalf of his family, but only after he checked to make sure all heads were bowed and all hands were clasped:

Bless us, oh dear Lord,

And these Thy gifts,

Which we are about to receive from Thy bounty,

Through Christ our Lord.

Amen.

"Pass up yaw's plates," instructed Martha, "and I'll dish ya up."

"Sho smells good, Mamma," Wyatt said.

"Thank ya, son. But it might be a spell 'fore we gets another meal like this'n. All we got left is the one bird that lays the eggs."

The boys at once began laughing and started devising ways they could have both. One suggested the chicken could have its legs amputated and given wooden ones to jump around on. Another said that since chickens really don't fly unless chased, take the wings.

"That there's enough," said Martha as she extended her left hand and ruffled Virgil's hair before asking, "Did ya take a bath?"

"Yes, em," he answered.

"Lean in some and let me take a look," said Martha as she tugged his ears. "Lord, have mercy! What you got goin' on here!"

"Ouch!"

"If you took a bath, how come ya got all this dirt in yur ear?" Martha asked as she grabbed the end of her apron, spit on it, then twisted it inside Virgil's ear until it turned flaming red.

"That hurt, Mamma!"

"Ain't nearly hurt as bad as it's gonna when I scrub you down when we gets back!"

"Might be outta chickens, but we'z got ourselves a tater patch," laughed Monroe.

"I'll grab the hoe," said Wyatt.

"Shut your mouth before I come over there and whop the tar outta ya!" yelled Virgil as he rubbed his ear. "I know'd ya pissed in the water, Wyatt!"

"Did ya, Wyatt?" demanded Martha. "Cuz I can tell."

"It just come out," said Wyatt with his head bowed in an effort to hide his snickering.

"That'll teach yaw!" yelled JC from across the table so loud that Hester started to cry, "cuz I pissed in the tub first!" Then he let out a devilish laugh as he leaned his chair back on its spindle legs until they splintered, causing him to crash onto the floor, leaving the last decent chair they owned a pile of junk beneath him.

"See what yaw done!" yelled Adilia as she leaned over and tried to hush Hester. "Now we'z gone be late."

Irritated, Martha yelled to her children, "Git on up from the table, and if yaw's got shoes, get 'em! It's time to be gettin' on down there."

"But we ain't done et yet," said Wyatt as he pushed his fruit crate back across the bare pine plank floor.

"It'll be here when yaw gets back," Martha told him. Then she picked Hester up out of the washtub, carried her to a nearby bed, and gently pulled her small head and delicate arms through a doll-sized dress sprinkled with tiny yellow flowers that had been fashioned from a cotton flour sack.

Monroe glanced at his father who was struggling to get up off the floor. *I ought to spit on ya, ol' man,* he thought. Instead, he grabbed a biscuit from his plate and strutted onto the porch, letting the screen door slam hard behind him. The thought of sitting in his father's piss lit a fire in his gut as he leaned his head against the house. Holding the biscuit in his left hand, he rolled his right fingers into a fist that he slammed into the side of the house, just next to where he had cracked a board only days before.

With their brood trailing behind them, Martha and JC walked arm in arm down their dirt road for about a quarter mile until they reached a tight cluster of black hickory trees and short-leaf pines. There they cut onto a small trail that easily could have been mistaken for a mule deer path.

"Mind yaselves, boys. Ya got on your best britches," Martha cautioned, "and Lil'bit, make sure a branch don't come on back and poke that baby's eye out."

"It ain't my first time luggin' her through these woods," Adilia mumbled under her breath.

"I heard that! Adilia, remember: a girl who whines stays on the vine. Now, who's got Orson?" asked Martha as she turned around to count her brood.

"I got 'im," answered Monroe in barely more than a whisper.

"You hold on to 'im, Roe. He's a runner."

"I'm gonna be runnin' soon *myself*," Monroe vowed under his breath.

JC reached out and cleared low-hanging branches and vines so Martha could safely pass, then he let them swing back just in time for the branches to smack Monroe in the face, creating a small scratch on his flushed cheek. There was little doubt in Monroe's mind that JC knew exactly what he was doing.

"I thank I hear 'em, and it sounds like we ain't late yet," Adelia joyfully called out as she pushed forward, trying to walk faster.

When the family members emerged from the grove, they found themselves next to the creek that ran down their property line, and there, in a small clearing, stood about a dozen men and women dressed in their Sunday best. And sitting on a floor of pine needles were rows of colorful quilts lined up as though they were church pews, and Martha laid her crazy patchwork next to a log cabin.[5]

Once the "How yaw doins" and "we'z gettin' alongs" were exchanged, Martha guided her family onto the quilt she had laid out, and there her family sat, quietly in a row, elbow to elbow, patiently awaiting the word of God to be transmitted from the mouth of the presiding overseer.

Brother Isham Toomey instructed his small flock to bow their heads in prayer in a voice warm like a favored sweater that had been worn until the yarn was so frayed and thinned at the elbows that a harsh, betraying chill slipped in. He led his congregation through a long and rambling diatribe that rivaled Moses' plea to the disparaging Israelites at the beginning of what would be their forty years of wandering through the wilderness, full of hope. And it was a reminder that their perseverance was a test designed by God, and to win Yahweh's favor, although steamily unbearable, they were obliged to endure it under the guise of gratitude.

Without opening his eyes, Toomey could visualize the faces of his flock, sunburnt and craggy, missing teeth or limbs, bent backs, club feet, and all sorts of unnamed afflictions, but he was

---

5. Log cabin quilt designs are the most easily recognized quilt patterns. Beginning with a center shape, usually a square, the traditional design is made by sewing strips in sequence around the sides of the square, varying the values between light and dark. This pattern was widely used in America in the 1800s, but it also has been found in ancient Egyptian tombs.

entrusted to lead them into the "New World Order,"[6] and he would not fail.

After dark, in the privacy of his own home, Toomey often prostrated himself naked on a bare wood floor with arms and hands stretched in front of him as though stranded on the desert plains of the Sahara, reaching for water through a mirage. There he stayed for hours, seeking direction and guidance. Like his congregation, he battled with his own doubts. When the church splintered into three sectors, he vacillated between them. He ultimately chose a side, not based on doctrine but on the leadership and the financial resources required to build a *bona fide* religion, one that could take on the Methodists, the Baptists, and someday even the Catholics.

Seven years later he hid amidst the Ozark pines, preaching a Sunday sermon to a small, newly-formed, ragtag congregation, many of whom could not even read.

". . . And in summation, dear Lord, we ask you for your blessing and offer you our deepest gratitude for the gift you provided us through the sanctuary of Brother Hornbeck's farm so you might nourish us with your word and protect us from the evils of this old world. In the name of your son Jesus Christ, Amen."

This offshoot needed divine protection from the townspeople who thought the congregation was nothing more than a small group of religious zealot colporteurs, peddling their books and pamphlets door to door. And as one local Baptist minister pointed out, those dogmatists were violating local Sabbath laws that, in turn, prompted a number of church-going sheriffs to act quickly. As a result, many within Brother Toomey's congregation faced stiff fines they could ill afford. In protest, the congregation created a firestorm by joining nearby congregations and flooding main streets throughout the Ozarks. There they carried signs and wore sandwich boards hinged at the top with kitchen string that proclaimed in large black lettering, "RELI-

---

6. Jehovah's Witnesses believe that Armageddon will destroy all the non-witnesses and leave the faithful to welcome resurrected believers who will join in making a "New World Order."

GION IS A SNARE AND A RACKET." Thus, the townspeople had been warned: their churches would not be a sanctuary in the approaching end of days.

Well, all that proved too much for the Baptists and the Methodists, so those religious zealots soon found themselves flung out of every public house and taunted in every private dwelling. Many were put on trial for sedition. A handful of witnesses were even burned out of their homes, tarred and feathered, beaten, and run out of town. Hated even more than the Catholics, the congregants then began to proclaim themselves martyrs, which attracted society's dispossessed and oppressed.

Brother Toomey began his Sunday lecture with a reminder of their covenant with their God, Jehovah, and asked the congregation to turn to Exodus 20:4-5.

Martha pulled out her black leather King James Bible with Jesus' words printed in red, a gift from her parents on her twelfth birthday.

"Brother Hornbeck, would you please read the passage for us?"

Martha passed her open Bible to JC and whispered, "Don't fret. I'll hep ya out."

[4] *"Thou shalt not make unto thee any graven image," JC began reading, "or any likeness of anything in heaven above or that is in the earth beneath, or that is in the water under the earth.*

[5] *"Thou shalt not bow down thyself to them nor serve them: for I, the Lord thy God, am a jealous God, visiting the iniquity of the fathers upon the children unto the third and fourth generation of them that hate me."*

"It is only a matter of days, a few months at most, until this country enters the conflict overseas," began the elder. "Make no mistake: every one of us, especially these here younguns," and he pointed to JC and Martha's children, "all of us will have our obedience tested as this country plunges into the abyss of patriotism. As the Apostle John wrote in Chapter 18, Verse 36, *"Jesus answered, 'My kingdom is not of this world.'"*

"I ask yaw," continued the elder, "is your heart longing for where there ain't no end of days? If so, then you will pay heed to John's Gospel." Then the elder read the organization's position on the flag, national anthem, and military service before reciting God's position on the giving and eating of blood, as explained in the pages of *The Watchtower.*[7]

---

7. *The Watchtower* is a Jehovah's Witnesses magazine that is published by its Watch Tower Bible and Tract Society of Pennsylvania.

Chapter 2:

Better Dead Than Red

Arkansas, 1936

GUIDING HIS RUSTED '29 Chevrolet International along the three-mile dirt road that featured ruts deep enough to bring a baby on early, JC glanced at the *Arkansas Gazette* lying next to him, the one he had picked up off a bench while in town to collect the mail. The headline read: "WAR! GERMAN TROOPS INVADE POLAND".

He felt a burn rise from his belly and run all the way up his throat. Then he tucked the paper behind the set, thinking it wouldn't take much for Monroe to jump ship and sign up with the French Foreign Legion.

Rolling to a stop, JC gazed at the freshly-plowed dirt across the road as Brother Isham Toomey's words echoed in his ears: "Ain't no part of this here world."

His eyes narrowed as he scanned the acreage for his boys. And there they were: Virgil, he could scarcely see, was hoeing weeds between the rows of waist-high cotton in the back field, and Wyatt was clearing rocks from a patch for next spring's planting. And Monroe—*Is it pure rebelliousness that he challenges me every chance he gets?* JC wondered. He knew the boys had kept an eye out for the dust from his back tires so they could put their backs to it. But Monroe had not even bothered to hide the fact that he was playing his harmonica, and JC swore that Monroe was now playing it harder, and he wanted to beat him, but he had already beat the fear right out of him.

So, JC sat quietly, listening to Monroe play *"Cool Water."*[8] He did not fault the boys—not much, anyway. He would have done the same. He just prayed he would have them long enough to clear the next nine acres. Before he realized it, he was mouthing the words to the song.

Then he laid on the horn.

"What's up, Daddy?" asked Monroe as he ran and jumped into the cab of the truck and tucked his harmonica into his bib pocket.

"It's about dinner time, and Sod should be up at the house by now," JC began. "Go on and git Virgil. I don't thank he heard me blow the horn."

"He'll figure it out fer himself," Monroe shot back. "It's every man fer himself."

"Well, ya ain't no man—yet! Get on up outta here and carry him up to the house. And since you know so much about water, pour some down the radiator before ya go."

Monroe jumped back out of the truck, pried the wooden peg from the radiator, and poured water into it from the canvas water bag that hung from the bumper. Then he shot his father a dirty look before he trudged back toward the field.

Sod Higgerson had recently taken early retirement from his job as a federal marshal and purchased a little over a hundred acres that shared the water rights to the creek that ran between his property and JC's. It was generally understood among the locals that Sod was going to lay in cotton when he felt the market was right, but they also knew he was more of a desk man than a

---

8. *"Cool Water"* is a song written in 1936 by Bob Nolan. Members of the Western Writers of America chose it No. 3 on the Top 100 Western songs of all time.

farmer, so while he waited for the commodity market to light a fire under cotton, he busied himself counseling local citizens in the unincorporated areas on civil and legal matters and offered support to his brother, a sitting judge in Hot Springs.

After letting the dust settle, Sod opened his car door and slowly walked back toward the turtleback.[9]

"Nice to see ya back, Mr. Higgerson," called out Martha from the porch as she stood and wiped her wet hands on her apron.

"Thank you, Miss Hornbeck," Sod answered. "It shore's good to be back in what I would consider the comfort of friends."

"That there is a fact, Mr. Higgerson. Times can be troublesome, especially down in Hot Springs," Martha said as she gave him a knowing eye. "Come on up to the house for a cool glass of tea."

"Yes, ma'am."

Turning to Adilia, Martha said, "Child, run on over to the stream and fetch the coolest jar of sweet tea. Run, now!"

Adilia, barefooted, ran alongside the house and through the grove of trees that lined the stream. When they first arrived, she and her mother created a small alcove to store canning jars filled with perishables like butter and milk. Adilia fished around for the coolest jar she could find and carefully dried it with the hem of her dress before heading back to the house. Cradling the jar like a newborn, she softly handed it to her mother.

"Thank ya, Lil'bit," Martha said as she took the jar of sweet tea. "Now bring them there glasses on out to the porch." Adilia's shoulders drooped as she reached for the two glasses. Martha, seeing Adilia's disappointment, said, "No need to get all long in the face. Yaw be gittin' some, but not in the nice glasses and, for heaven's sakes, suck that lip in before a mad dog comes along

---

9. The turtleback was a popular design used by many car manufacturers whereby the roof sloped down to the rear fender in what resembled the back of a turtle.

and chews it off." Then Martha turned and pushed the screen door open with her elbow and let it slam behind her.

"Come on up here in the shade, Mr. Higgerson!" she called out.

"Yes'm, on my way, Miss Hornbeck," Sod called up to he, as he closed the trunk. "I brung some washing and ironing, if ya have time."

"That'd be just fine," Martha said. Then she turned to her daughter and said, "Lil'bit, run on down and grab Mr. Higgerson's warshin' like a good girl." With that, Martha leaned over and rested her hands along the paint-chipped porch railing and said, "I see JC and the boys coming up the road now. Might as well stay for dinner. We got Brunswick stew[10] with taters and a passel of wild greens. A little late in the season for 'um, but ya cook greens long enough, and they give up their meanness." She smiled and handed Sod a glass of cool tea.

"Them taters come out of Virgil's ear," piped up Adilia as she passed Sod on the porch steps.

"Is that a fact now?" asked Sod jokingly. "Well, seein's I'm so hungry, I could eat a pigtail sandwich," Sod said as he pulled on one of her pigtails. "I reckon I can eat at least a bite of tater."

JC had to force the truck into second gear to pull the small hill, arriving just ahead of his boys who let out in a sprint in order to take a long look at Sod's brand-new black De Soto Businessman coup parked in the shade of the porch.

"Boys!" JC yelled, "don't nar a one of yaw touch that man's new car!"

Monroe immediately jerked his hand back and declared, "I ain't touchin' it."

"Ya waz a-*thankin'* about it!"

---

10. Virginia and Georgia both claim to have originally created the Brunswick stew that was made primarily with squirrel and a few vegetables.

Maybe I waz, maybe I wazn't, Monroe thought, angry that his father worked him and treated him like a rented mule.

Setting his glass of sweet tea on the fruit crate that leaned against the house, Sod navigated down the porch steps to greet JC. Then he glanced at each of the boys and gave them a nod.

"Looks like yaw got enough rocks cleared out to build another wall around China," Sod joked.

"Pert near," replied JC. "Took longer than I reckoned it would. Should have twice as many bolls[11] as we got now. Afraid come winter, still won't have a dang thang in the pan."

"Yaw know I appreciate ya looking out on things the way ya do while I'm away. I'm happy to help in any way I can."

"Well," began JC with measured breath, "that's what neighbors is fer, ain't it?" His eyes panned the front porch, and he noticed his wife pouring his children a glass of sweet tea. He took several measured breaths, then continued: "Best be getting' on up to the house and see what Ma's got for dinner."

"Squirrel stew, I hear tell," Sod announced, and then he smiled.

"Ain't that fond of squirrel myself," replied JC, "but my bread-basket is so dang empty, I could eat the ass out of a rag doll."

By the time Sod and JC reached the screen door they saw the children seated patiently at the table with little Hester sitting in the washtub massaging her gums on a piece of leather from an old belt.

"Go on, take a seat. Ain't nothin' fancy," said Martha as she took a swipe at a house fly with a rolled-up newspaper. "Dang flies. They's better fed than the rest of us."

---

11. Bolls are green pods shaped like tiny footballs that are left behind the blossom. As the boll ripens it turns brown, and the fibers inside continue to expand under the heat of the sun. Unlit, the boll splits apart, and the fluffy cotton bursts.

"Sit next to me, Mr. Higgerson," said Monroe as he extended his hand and patted the back of the newly-mended slotback chair. "I wanna hear again about when ya was a US Marshal in Missouri."

JC quickly rolled snake eyes in Monroe's direction, which Monroe quickly shrugged off. Martha and JC had little doubt that Sod had at least some knowledge about their exploits in Missouri, although he never tipped his hand. Instead, he gently rubbed against them like a cat rubs against an ankle just to make its presence known.

"Hush up an' act like you got some raisin', Roe. Daddy's gonna say the blessin', and then we'z gonna have a nice, quiet dinner."

"That boy collects more stories than a set of *Funk & Wagnalls*,"[12] joked JC. "There ain't one story he can't recollect since the day he was in diapers." Everyone laughed—everyone except Monroe.

"Come on now, JC. Say the blessin' before the food gits cold," instructed Martha.

"And after, I wanna hear how fast you can get your De Soto up to when ya's runnin' flat out," Wyatt said excitedly.

"And I want to hear what's goin' on in Hot Springs. The paper said…" Monroe began.

When JC said the words, "Bow your heads," it sounded like it was a gavel coming down hard on a guilty man, and the room fell quiet with the only sounds coming from the flapping wings of a persistent fly and the gnawing on leather.

"Well, the house seems to be standing all right," said Sod, who had been looking for something cheerful to say as the two men moseyed toward the De Soto after dinner.

---

12. *Funk & Wagnalls* published general reference dictionaries and encyclopedias from 1875 to 1997.

"It woulda come down by now, but it can't figure out which away to fall," JC said, and then he chuckled.

"Maybe ya otta go on up to Conway," Sod suggested as he pulled out his Bull Durham pouch and rolled a cigarette. "They set up a relief station there, and you can load up on food. Why, I hear they got more resources than they got over in Ola."

"I ain't lookin' for no handout," JC insisted.

"Yah, I know, but if Martha gets any skinnier, she's gonna have to stand up twice just to cast a shadow," said Sod in a fatherly manner. "And ain't nobody gonna know you in Conway. Besides, if my eyes don't deceive, I think you got one in the oven again."

"Dang, if she ain't fertile Myrtle," said JC after he turned his head back to make sure Martha was out of earshot. "All I gotta do is look at 'er."

"Well, ya get over to Conway. Need somethin' for gas?"

"Na, I thank we got enough to get there and back. I'll go up in the next few weeks."

"Don't wait too long," instructed Sod. "Ya never know how long these rations will hold, with talk of war and all."

"No, sir, that's a fact."

"I'm headed down to Hot Springs tonight."

"Ya just come back!"

"I know, but my brothers got a situation involving a few fellas that came down from Chicago, and the state's attorney is starting to snoop around. The whole setup might turn into a sidewinder."

"Keep our boots on."

"I *am* the boots," Sod said, and then he laughed as he cursed his cigarette and opened his car door.

"The wife's up visiting her family in Little Rock," Sod said, then paused, wondering if he should fess up and admit his wife had no intention of ever coming back, but then he decided less was best. "So keep an eye on the place. Let me know if you see anyone coming or going. You know how to get ahold of me, right?"

"Sho' do, and don't ya fret none."

JC's eyes tracked Sod's De Soto as it kicked up dust down the hill and along the twisting dirt road until the dust turned to a light haze that was softly carried off by a gentle summer breeze. Then he turned back toward the house where he saw his eldest child, Monroe, leaning over the porch with a piece of straw between his lips, studying and judging him.

"That boy's got a snake in 'im," JC muttered to himself. "And by God, I's just the man to kill it."

⋆

When JC's '29 International was running reasonably well, he could make Conway in about three hours, but if he had to stop to fix a tire, pour water into the leaky radiator, or let the engine cool, it could take most of the day. JC selected Monroe to take along, not just because he was turning into a halfway decent mechanic, but mostly because he wanted to drill some sense into the boy's head, teach him some humility, and there was nothing like standing in line to beg for food from strangers to drive home a life lesson.

While driving eastward, JC rambled on about the value of loyalty and of keeping family secrets. Monroe stared out the window, devising an escape plan, and the fact that he did not have a nickel to his name made no difference. His father's words rang flat.

When they reached Conway, JC pulled into the first filling station he saw and rolled down his window. "Hey there!" he shouted to a young man in greasy coveralls trying to open a can of oil. "Ya know where they's handin' out relief?"

Monroe crouched in the seat and pulled his chin into his chest.

"I reckon they's still got a relief station set up in Lumkin's Store about a quarter mile up First Street. Can't miss it," answered the filling station attendant as his coworker squinted into Monroe's dirty window and asked, "Yaw need sum gas?" to which Monroe pointed his middle finger up to heaven.

And it was true; they could not miss Lumkin's General Store. Over its porch hung an oversized American flag. One of the big glass windows had a long crack running along the bottom where Mr. Lumkin had plastered a piece of tape to help hold the glass in place after a drunk had pushed his head into the window, leaving shards in his head and a trail of blood.

After JC found a place to park, he noticed the relief line stretched two blocks. JC may not have known the people in line by name, but he recognized the hollow-eyed women holding onto hungry, screaming babies and the old ladies wishing they had the strength to run in front of a moving truck. But mostly he recognized the broken-down men whose hopes were once unbreakable but who had become callous and heavy until they could of fallen through a wet paper bag and landed on their own dirty boots like raining dogshit.

"I be waitin' here in the truck," Monroe informed his father.

With temper flaring, JC replied, "No! No ya ain't, boy!" and pulled back on the handbrake. "Ya gonna get your ass outta that dagum seat and get on up those steps if I have to beat you with my belt all the way!"

For Monroe, that was the final straw: he'd had enough of the "spare the rod" bullshit. As soon as he found an opening, he would make a run from his old man.

As JC and Monroe assumed their places at the back of the line, JC took notice of a small group of young men leaning against the doorjamb, blocking the entrance to Lumkin's General Store.

"Do any a-them boys look familiar?" JC asked Monroe.

"Why don't you wear your glasses?" snarled Monroe.

"They's busted," answered JC as he elbowed Monroe.

"No wonder you's such a shitty driver," mumbled Monroe.

"What'd ya say?"

"I said I don't recollect any of 'em," replied Monroe, "except maybe that one with the wonky eye," he added after he finally glanced up out of curiosity.

The line drifted slowly, and as others arrived to take up the last position, JC felt his spirits rise the way you might when you have someone to look down on, if only it is the person standing behind you in the same relief line. For a tiny moment, he falsely felt he was their better.

JC finally said to Monroe, "That's what I was figuring, the fella with the wonky eye…" Then he twisted his chin over his left shoulder and let go of a wad of spit.

"You SOB!" yelled a woman so loud that it drew attention. "That's my young-un ya just spit on!"

"Sorry, ma'am," JC said as he lifted his dirty fedora off his head in a sign of respect.

"Ain't ya got no raisin'?" cried the woman as she quickly took the hem of her skirt and tried to remove the saliva from her small child's head before the child could smear it deep into her scalp.

"And you," continued the woman as she took aim at Monroe, "it ain't no laughin' matter!"

"No, ma'am," answered Monroe as he stared at his feet and tried to stop chuckling.

"Ain't you got no little uns?" she asked JC.

"Yes, ma'am, I do."

"Do you spit on 'em?" the woman demanded.

"Only the boys, ma'am, when they's hair won't calm down," he answered, then he turned to face the front of the line that had started climbing the steps of the general store.

The commotion had raised the interest of two of the young men holding up the store's doorjamb, and they quickly closed ranks and blocked the entrance when it was JC's turn to enter.

"Get outta my way," JC demanded as he tried to push his way past the young men. But the boys were much younger, better fed, and stood much taller than JC's five-foot-four-inch frame.

"You come for relief, old man?" asked the first young man with a low fade haircut.

"I said... get on outta my way!" repeated JC as he tried once again to push past the second young man with the wonky eye who was dressed in a pair of faded blue bib overalls with patched knees. But the young man did not move. Instead, he pulled his hands out of his pockets and took two steps toward JC. Now chest to chest, JC jurked his head back because of the foul stench that spilled out of the young man's mouth like dirty water over a broken dam.

"Get that thang pulled," said JC as he turned his head away from the man's mouth.

"Yaw tank you's man enough to pull it!" the second young man yelled. "Ya know who we'z got here, Grover?" he asked as he rolled his head back toward the first young man.

"No, Fergus, who we got?"

"We got us here a real live commie! Yes, siree, Grover, an honest-to-God, real live commie!"

"Is that a fact!" said a third young man as he stepped closer to JC and Monroe.

Monroe quickly decided he did not have a dog in this fight. *Leave it to the old man to start a ruckus. Just because his initials are JC, he thinks he can act like fuckin' Jesus Christ,* he thought. *Damn him. This time he's on his own.* Then Monroe slowly backed down the steps.

"Indeed, we do. Looky here, folks!" called out Fergus, loud enough for people inside the general store and those standing in line to hear his great revelation. Then pressing his finger on JC's chest, he raised his voice even louder as though he envisioned himself on a pulpit and proclaimed, "This here is Mr. Hornbeck, Mr. JC Hornbeck from over in Ola." And then he lowered his voice and, speaking to Grover said, "And a friend of ol' Sod."

"So, you the crazy-ass religious commie that meets out in the woods?" Grover said with a smirk.

"I ain't no commie. Now let us through."

"Let's see you salute that flag first."

"I ain't gonna do it."

"Well, there ya go, folks!" said Grover loudly as he slowly parted his open palms in front of the growing line of relief hopefuls like he was Moses parting the Red Sea.

The line then became a cluster, pulling tighter together. Murmurs could be heard as feet scuffled along the wooden walkway and people leaned in to get a better look.

"Prove you ain't no commie!" yelled a halfwit old man with an obstinate Red Man[13] stain that ran down his long beard like a waterfall and dripped onto a dirty shirt.

"Why ya takin' food from our babies when our husbands will soon be headed overseas to fight for our freedom?" asked a woman with hollow cheeks. "Ya ain't got no right!"

---

13.   Introduced in 1904, Red Man is a leaf tobacco made by the Pinkerton Tobacco Company of Owensboro, Kentucky.

Now standing on the top step, JC turned to face the swarm that had gathered beneath him and yelled, *"Thou shalt not make thee any graven image nor serve them!"* He then removed his dirty fedora, and his thin strands of hair waved in the light breeze like dead stocks of hay. With self-proclaimed authority and conviction JC shouted again: *"For I, the Lord thy God, am a jealous God."*[14]

Out of fear that the crowd might turn on him, Monroe retraced his steps up the stairs and tried to grab JC by the elbow before the mob attacked him, but the old man planted his feet like a stump on the wooden planks and shrugged his son away.

"Last time I saw a mouth that big, it had a hook in it," Fergus said, and then he laughed.

Pushing himself forward and rolling his fingers into a fist, JC yelled, "If ya don't let me pass I'll jerk a knot in your tail!"

"Wow, slow your roll there!" said a stocky man as he stepped through the shadowy doorway of Lumkin's General Store. "No need to blow your wig! And if there's gonna be any knot tyin', I'll be the one doin' it!"

"Ya just in time, Sheriff," called out the woman with the small child. "We caught ourselves a commie!"

"Is that a fact?"

"Sho' did," answered Fergus as he stepped back to make way for the sheriff. "Mr. Hornbeck refuses to salute the American flag."

"That true?" asked the sheriff.

"Jesus said, *'My kingdom is not of this world,'* John 18:36," recited JC.

---

14. Exodus 20:8-9 (KJV): "Thou shalt not make thee *any* graven image, or any likeness of *anything* that is in heaven above, or that is in the earth beneath, or that is in the waters beneath the earth. Thou shalt not bow down thyself unto them, nor serve them: for I, the Lord thy God, am a jealous God . . ."

"I'll take that as a yes," sighed the sheriff. "Come along with me, Mr. Hornbeck, and we'll let the judge figure it out." And with that, the sheriff took JC by the arm and led him down the steps toward the patrol car.

Turning his head back and searching through the crowd, JC called out to his son, "Get your mamma!" But Monroe could barely hear him over the taunting of the crowd's growing chant, "**Better dead than red! Better dead than red!**"

Quickly finding the key on the floorboard where his father had left it, Monroe sped out of town as fast as the truck would roll.

"Slow down, son," Martha said calmly as Monroe tried to spit out what had happened at Lumkin's General Store in Conway. "Don't get your cows runnin'. Tell it to me in ya own time."

Martha remained seated at the kitchen table and listened patiently. Between getting married to JC at sixteen and birthing six children, she had learned to handle most anything—even the law.

"Well," she said as she slapped her hands on her knees and pushed herself up from her chair, "we gotta get that man home."

"Why?" murmured Monroe.

"You ain't through climbin' fool's hill yet, boy?" Martha asked sternly as she stood and stared down at Monroe. "You think he went up to Conway for himself? That man swallowed his pride for yaw. And I'm here to tell ya, he done did it more than once!"

Martha brushed past her children who stood silently around her, ambled onto the porch, and leaned into one of its supporting posts. The last time they had their backs so tight against the wall was in a little Missouri town just over the border from Arkansas.

That she had not thought about Missouri for a long time surprised her, but then she had spent a great deal of time justifying, reconciling, and repeating, a process that proved self-loathing is often just a fools camouflage. The only times she felt a twinge of discomfort was when Monroe occasionally got on his high horse around Sod. *The little shit,* thought Martha. *How could he possibly remember, as young as he was? He's just pullin' wings off flies.*

★

JC and Martha were on their third child at that time, and the only thing they were able to stockpile was disadvantages and chipped dishes. When the drilling company JC worked for in Oklahoma and northern Texas announced they were pulling out, leaving more than thirty families without jobs, JC became so enraged that he stole one of the company's drilling rigs, stripped it, sold the parts for gas money, and headed to the hills of Tennessee. There on Martha's aunt's front porch, he sat and stitched bits of an old window screen around bent wire and tied colored twine around the edges to make flyswatters. Once a week he took six-year-old Monroe by the hand and headed to Baskins Creek Road. From there, they hitchhiked into Gatlinburg and, in front of the Ogle's company store, Monroe would stand with the bucket of mismatched swatters and shout "Two for a nickel!" while his father sat with a group of men under a yellow birch drinking an amber liquid from a quart jar.

Company and fish smell after three days, and it did not take much longer than that before Martha's family finally had their fill of JC. Kin or no kin, they opened both barrels on him, calling him a "loudmouth, windbag, blowhard, gasbag, and an all-around SOB." Donald, Martha's cousin, punched JC so hard that he went flying off the front porch. To make matters even worse, Donald dug a fifty-cent piece from his jeans pocket and tossed it down to JC, face down in the dirt. "Here," Donald said, "first tank's on me. Now git on outta here!"

JC was too proud to pick up the money, so while he was loading the truck Martha swooped it up and gave her cousin a silent nod of thanks. In under ten minutes, they were on the road back toward Louisiana.

When they crossed into Missouri's Bootheel,[15] they were running on fumes without two buffalo nickels to rub together. The

---

15. The Missouri Bootheel is the southeasternmost part of the state,

night before, JC had pulled the truck over into what looked like a clearing, only to find in the light of day that they had spread their pallets[16] in an old graveyard.

Dawn often brings clarity and hope, but on that morning, it only illuminated their despair. Martha did not need much persuading after JC laid out the new plan he had concocted while leaning over the hood of the truck. After the older kids were loaded onto the truck bed, Martha paused, adjusted the baby in her arms, scanned the dozens of unattended graves, and wished her breast milk had not dried up so quickly.

Monroe and Wyatt, with their backs against the cab, bobbed as their father poorly navigated the potholes. Monroe pretended he did not hear his father tell him to make sure nothing fell off the back of the truck. Lying on his back, he scooted himself toward the back of the truck and, with a swift kick, sent the bucket of mismatched flyswatters tumbling onto the road, causing Wyatt to burst into laughter.

"Son of bitches," Monroe called out as he crawled back to the cab.

"Ya, son of bitches," repeated Wyatt. Then he sat up on his knees, pointed an imaginary gun, and started shooting at the power poles.

They drove about an hour before JC turned to Martha and shouted above the rattle of the engine, "This is as good as any, I reckon." He then piloted the truck to the side of the two-lane blacktop road leading into Cooter. "Now, ain't no reason to get all worked up," he continued. "They's all out lookin' for them other two."

"But what if they done caught 'em by now?"

---

extending south of 36°30′ north latitude. It is so-called because its shape resembles the heel of a boot.

16. Pallets, sometimes called bedrolls, consisted of a blanket or quilt that would soften a hard surface and keep a person dry and warm.

"If they caught up with Bonnie and Clyde, we'd a heard about it, that's one thang for sure!"

How? wondered Martha. *How would we know? The goddamn radio is busted.*

As JC was parking his flatbed truck in a secluded spot, Martha pulled on a set of her husband's work pants and shirt over her dress and slipped an old work hat over her hair. Then she picked up her baby, who was fast asleep, quietly climbed out of the cab, and sneaked toward the back of the truck.

"Roe," Martha whispered. "Roe!" she whispered again.

"Ya?" Monroe grunted back from under an oilcloth he and Wyatt had fallen sleeping on.

"Grab this here baby," Martha said as she pushed the baby into his sleepy arms. "And I don't wanna hear a peep out of yaw until I come for ya," she instructed. "Hear me—not a peep!"

Martha followed JC into the Cooter Bank where she hung back, just as they had planned. Then she extended her arms and placed both hands on the grip of a .38 Smith & Wesson as she watched JC approach the window where the teller had already put his hands in the air and awaited further instructions.

Once back at the truck, Martha grabbed the baby and said, "Not a peep, Moe, not until I come for ya, no matter what." Placing the baby on the seat next to her, she quickly removed JC's clothes and pressed the wrinkles out of her dress with the palms of her sweaty hands. Then she cradled her baby in her arms as JC slowly pulled the truck onto the main road that headed out of town.

After rolling over the service bell of the local Sinclair station, JC asked the attendant to fill the tank, wash the windshield, and check the oil and patch a tire.

"When ya mess with a bull, ya get the horn, JC," Martha said under her breath, but loud enough for him to hear her disapproval.

"They be lookin' for someone who's runnin' all out." And just as he said that, a speeding patrol car squealed to an abrupt stop.

"Hey, Calvin!" the sheriff yelled out his window.

The old man running the filling station pulled his head out from under the hood of JC's truck and shuffled toward the cruiser as he wiped his hands on a dirty oil rag. "Ya, Sheriff?"

"Ya seen two fellas drive past here in the last five, ten minutes?"

"No, sir. These is the only customers I've had in the last thirty minutes."

"Is that a fact...?" the sheriff said as he shifted his cruiser into neutral.

JC glanced at Martha who was holding her baby so tight that she almost popped out of her arms. "Quiet down, girl. I ain't gonna let anythang happen to ya."

The sheriff opened his car door without taking his eyes off JC, and just before he reached the International, JC stuck his head out of the open window and calmly said, "Howdy, Officer."

The sheriff stopped in his tracks, keeping his right hand on the pistol grip in his holster and asked, "Where ya folks comin' from?"

"We'z just comin' from Tennessee. The wife's grandmaw was feelin' poorly."

"Is that a fact?"

"Yes, sir."

"Where ya headin' now?" asked the sheriff as he twisted his head to get a better look at the faded writing on the truck's wooden side panels.

"Like the plates say, Louisiana— Shreveport, to be exact."

"What's your name?"

"Jeb, Jeb Dupree,"[17] JC lied without breaking a sweat. "Any thang wrong?"

"Ya best keep movin'. We don't allow roadside campin' or open fires. Ya get my meanin'?"

"Yes, sir, I surely do."

The sheriff then turned toward an unmarked car that had just rolled up alongside his patrol car.

Resting his elbow on the open window of the unmarked car, the sheriff quietly said, "Hey, Marshal Higgerson."

"Got anything?"

"No, but take these names down: Jeb Dupree and JC Hornbeck. He says his name is Dupree, but he faded lettering on the side of the truck reads 'JC Hornbeck Junk Hauling'."

"All right. What's your gut tell you?"

"Well," began the sheriff, "look at that piece of shit truck. Where in the hell is he getting the money to top the oil off, fix the spare, and fill the tank?"

Marshal Higgerson put some spit on the tip of his stubby graphite pencil and wrote the names and the plate numbers down in the notebook he kept in his breast pocket, then he sat back in his car and watched the filling station attendant patch the tube in JC's spare tire. Higgerson noticed his fingers were thumping the steering wheel in time to a song that was playing in his head. *Or is the tune coming from outside?* he wondered silently as he pushed his ear closer to the open window.

Once the service station attendant tossed the spare into the back of the truck, JC slowly pulled away from the Sinclair station and

---

17. By 1935, only thirty-six states required a driver's license. Proving identity was generally done through witness verification.

purposely drove at a snail's pace past the marshal's car while softly singing these words:

Fare thee well, fare thee well,
Fare thee well, my fairy fay,
For I'm goin' to Louisiana for to see my Susianna,
Sing Polly Wolly Doodle all the day.[18]

In passing, JC and Higgerson's eyes locked for a few seconds, so they doffed their hats to one another.

*

"That's all water under the bridge," Martha whispered to herself. Then she yelled, "Roe, how much gas ya got in that truck?"

Martha quickly scribbled a letter, folded it into a prepaid airmail envelope that she kept for emergencies, and shoved it into Monroe's hand. "Go on down to Hot Springs and see if you can't find Sod. Let him know what happened and see if he can't hep. And drop this here off at the post office as ya go through town. Go on. Ya burnin' daylight, boy."

After he pulled out the choke, Monroe tapped the throttle down with the tip of his toe and turned the engine over. Then he eased the truck back onto the dirt road that ran in front of their property. When he turned onto the blacktop, he pressed the accelerator until it touched the rusted-out floorboard.

For the first mile or so, Monroe drove cautiously, keeping an eye out for patrol cars, careful to avoid suspicion as he was still underage and not eligible for a *bona fide* driver's license. But as the miles stacked up along his two-hour drive, he started to unwind like a snake does on blacktop under a warm sun. He knew he was getting close to Hot Springs by the increase in traffic and that there were fewer trucks and more brand-new sedans, many from Illinois, New York, and Florida—places he had never been. And although he had never been to Hot Springs either,

---

18. *"Polly Wolly Doodle"* was first published in 1880 in *Students' Songs*, compiled and edited by William H. Hills.

Monroe figured the town had to be laid out much like every other town he had seen, so he made for the city center where he found the government buildings. He pulled the truck alongside a man dressed in a gray suit and hat and carrying a brown leather briefcase.

"Say, mister!" Monroe yelled out the open window. "Ya know where's I might find a fella? I thank he's a judge."

"I may. What's his name?"

"Higgerson."

"You a friend of Judge Higgerson?"

"Not in particular. I's actually lookin' fer his brother Sod. He's our neighbor up north a-ways."

"I see," answered the man in a disapproving manner. "Well, you most likely won't find Sod here. But you could try Bathhouse Row or The Ohio Club," he continued, then pointed Monroe in a southerly direction toward Central Avenue.

After thanking him, Monroe popped the clutch, making the truck jerk and stall. Embarrassed but determined, he started the truck up again and slowly pulled back onto the street. As he approached Central Avenue, he spotted a black De Soto coupe parked along a side street and jumped on the brakes. Pleased with his keen eye, he pulled onto the side street and parked next to a "No Parking" sign. After climbing out of the truck, he looked up one side of the street, then down the other. Seeing only one door leading off the street, he headed in that direction.

"Hey, can't you read—no parking!" shouted a barrel-shaped man as he stepped from behind the shadow of several large crates stacked against the building.

"Nar a word!" Monroe laughingly shouted back as he pushed the heavy metal door open.

"Hey, you can't go in there!" the man shouted as he tossed his cigarette into the street and ran toward Monroe.

But Monroe was quick and agile, and once inside the building he found himself in a large room illumined by two incandescent bulbs dangling from electrical cords. The room smelled musty and was filled with wooden kegs and rows of shelving that held hundreds of glass liquor bottles, all neatly aligned like a platoon of soldiers grouped by divisions. Then he heard the outside door open, and slam shut again.

"Hey, you little hood rat!" he heard the man call out in a raspy voice. "You're dead meat!"

On the far end of the room, lying in the shadow of a row of kegs, Monroe could make out a flight of wooden stairs. He shot his way up and turned the knob on the door at the landing before the man in the slick suit had time for his eyes to adjust to the dim light. Once on the other side of the door, he found himself at the end of a long, dimly-lit corridor with a line of closed doors on each side. He paused for a moment, thinking he heard someone, so he quietly put his ear to each of the doors and listened. Behind the third door Monroe heard Sod's muffled voice, then he heard heavy footsteps coming up the wooden stairs. Without knocking, he pushed the door open and quickly shut it behind him.

Monroe stood frozen with his back against the closed door and glared into the back of a naked woman with her legs straddled across a man's thighs. Around her pasty white waist were the large hands of a man who effortlessly lifted her head up and down. Monroe recognized the man without seeing his face by the gold ring with a winged insect insignia—a ring he dismissed as trivial—and when asked about it he simply said, "Ah, ain't nothin'. Just somethin' I picked up."

"Don't you knock, boy?" asked Sod in a tone that was all but welcoming.

When Monroe finally found his voice, he said, "Yes, sir, but there's a big ol' fella chasin' me."

"What for?" Sod asked as he pushed the frizzy-haired woman's face off of him and through his bare legs over the side of the bed where he had tossed his clothes.

"Ya ain't gettin' no refund!" snapped the woman as she slipped her naked body into a blue silk kimono.

"Best tell me what's going on then, as you seem to have ruined Miss Ellie's day," laughed Sod as he stepped into his pants.

Monroe glanced at Ellie and offered his apologies.

"Don't worry, kid. He already got his money's worth!" she replied as she lit a cigarette and gave him a wink. Monroe's face turned bright red. "Well, ain't you just a jem, one eye the color of a blue sapphire and another sparklin' like an emerald."

Ellie moved her legs slightly, wrapping the opening of her kimono over one of her knees, exposing a small puff of soft, auburn hair.

"Kitty got your tongue?" laughed Sod.

Pivoting toward Sod, Monroe said, "No, sir. They got my daddy."

"Who's 'they'?"

"The sheriff over in Conway. They sayin' he's a commie." Monroe unwound the whole story, including a detailed description of the instigators, Grover and Fergus.

"I get the picture, Roe. I reckon we need to get this taken care of once and for all," said Sod as he stepped toward the door. Then he turned back toward Ellie. "See ya next week, sugar."

Just as they stepped into the corridor, they heard huffing and puffing coming from the barrel-chested man who had been hunting for Monroe behind each closed door.

"There you are, you little shit!" he yelled as he caught sight of Monroe.

"He's with me, Freddy," Sod said as he threw up his palm to stop him.

"Why didn't he just say so!" yelled Freddy. "Next time I'll fit him for a Chicago overcoat."

"It won't happen again, Freddy."

"Today of all days. We got 'deliveries,' if you get my drift," Freddy complained as the three headed toward the back of the corridor and down the wooden stairs. "Everything was goin' smooth until this little shit gummed up the works."

When the three reached the bottom of the stairs, they heard a loud commotion coming from the side street. The two men quickly exchanged glances. Sod motioned for Monroe to stay quiet and to crouch behind the wooden barrels as he and Freddy each drew their handguns from their shoulder harnesses.

"Can ya make out what's goin' on?" asked Freddy, who was hanging back.

"Sounds like someone just got pinched," replied Sod.

"Who?" asked Freddy.

"Who do ya think?" answered Sod sarcastically. "Your special delivery, I'm presuming." Freddy shook his head. "Well, they don't call him 'Lucky' Luciano for nothin'."

"You shred it, wheat," laughed Freddy as they both put their guns back into their holsters.

Sod shook his head at Freddy, then motioned for Monroe to come out from behind the barrels and walked him out the back door, giving the handcuffed "Lucky" a nod.

Guiding Monroe by the nape of the neck with a firm hand, Sod managed to keep him from gawking, and moved him past both their vehicles. "Nice parking job, city slicker," Sod whispered.

"I was…" but Sod tightened his grip and cut Monroe off before he could defend himself.

Once they rounded the corner to the front of the building, Monroe read the name of the establishment aloud: "Ozark Bathhouse." Then he gawked in utter amazement at the beauty of the buidling.

Sod instructed Monroe to stay put and, after looking up and down at his patched jeans and dirty jacket, he added, "And do not draw attention to yourself."

Monroe shoved his hands deep into his coat pocket to fish for his harmonica as he strolled along the sidewalk, a little hurt that Sod had not invited him into the bathhouse, but the hurt soon passed as he reflected on what he had just seen—a naked woman with small, firm breasts and perfectly round, pink nipples, a woman who was not afraid to let the small patch that covered her sweet spot peek through a silk kimono.

After a few starry-eyed moments, he realized that one of his hands was gripping a piece of paper inside his pocket, and then he remembered his mother's envelope. Panicked, he stared up and down the street, spotted a mailbox on the corner, and without reading the address on the envelope, he dropped it through the slot.

It wasn't long before Sod returned from making two telephone calls, the first to his brother, a sitting judge to give him a heads up on "Lucky," and the second to the sheriff in Conway.

"Everything is going to be just fine, Roe," Sod promised as he rested his hand on Monroe's shoulder and walked him back to the now empty street where they had parked their vehicles.

"Ya need to get on back to Conway and pick up your daddy. I covered his bail, so he's ready to go. Let him and your mamma know that I got him a good lawyer. Ain't nothin' to worry about."

"Except for…" began Monroe.

"Here ya go," said Sod as he handed Monroe a five-dollar bill. "After you get the truck gassed up, get yourself a pop and a slice of pie. Your daddy can sit a spell. You've had a man-makin' day." Then he gave Monroe a wink and firm slap on the shoulder.

Back on the road with a belly full of Royal Crown Cola, Monroe pondered Sod's words: *"a man-makin' day."* And each pothole on the way home seemed like a nail that set his manhood more firmly into place. He decided this would be his defining moment, the day he really did become a man. And as he reflected on his father he said aloud, "Oh, how the mighty have fallen." It was then he resolved to never again surrender to the rod of his father.

With one hand on the steering wheel, he reached into his coat pocket and pulled out the Horner Marin Band harmonica he had purchased at the music store next to the café. *Who needs a fat slice of buttermilk pie?* he thought. With one hand he flipped the case open and delicately removed it, letting the smooth metal cool his hand. "Church in a case," he said aloud. Then he stomped on the throttle and ran the truck full out as he played like he was auditioning for Gwen Foster, [19] and spit out *"The Bully of the Town".*[20]

*

The judge set the trial date. The letter Martha had written to JC's younger sister did not disappoint. Noreen, her four children, and Mother Jane rode into Ola like the Crescent City was again under siege by the British. When they arrived, they found JC had already had his hearing and that he had been released on $300 bond that Sod had put up. JC's spiritual needs were being met by Brother Isham Toomey, who had assembled his small flock to offer daily prayers and words from the scriptures. After all, JC was now a highly-elevated martyr who had earned the

---

19. Gwin Stanley Foster, also known as Gwen or Gwyn, was an old-time country harmonica and guitar player known for work in The Carolina Tar Heels and the Blue Ridge Mountain Entertainers.

20. *"The Bully of the Town"* was written in the mid-1800s and first recorded in 1926 by The Skillet Lickers.

direct attention of the Watch Tower Bible and Tract Society Incorporated.

"What did the jailer feed ya, Uncle JC?" asked Clyde, Noreen's oldest boy who was just coming up on twelve.

"Cornbread and beans."

"Shucks, that ain't bad. Bet I could do time," Clyde bragged.

Shaking his head, JC thought, *I bet you will at that.*

There was not much room in the house for JC's children, let alone the newly-arriving relatives, so when it came time to bed down, Martha handed the older children two tattered quilts and told them to make their pallets on the back of the truck.

"Momma," whispered Adilia, "can't I sleep in the house?"

"No, Lil'bit. Your grandmaw's taken our bed, and your daddy and I will be needin' your spot."

"But Clyde gives me the heebie-jeebies," Adilia begged. Her mother just shook her head.

That night, siblings and cousins—seven altogether—laid out their quilts over the wooden planks of the flatbed truck. They told stories until the younger ones, dirty-faced with even dirtier feet and still wearing the clothes they had worn all day, drifted to sleep under the moonless sky. Without an adult nearby to tell them to "hush up," Monroe and Wyatt pulled out their mouth harps and played a melancholy tune, *"The Cowboy's Lament,"*[21] and those who felt like singing did so:

Oh, beat the drum slowly and play the fife lowly,
And play the dead march as you carry me along;

---

21. *"The Cowboy's Lament"* is a famous American cowboy ballad in which a dying cowboy tells his story. Derived from the English folk song *"The Unfortunate Lad"* or *"Unfortunate Rake,"* it has been performed, recorded, and adapted numerous times with many variations.

Take me to the green valley, there lay the sod o'er me,
For I'm a young cowboy, and I know I've done wrong.

Get six jolly cowboys to carry my coffin,
Get six pretty maidens to bear up my pall.
Put bunches of roses all over my coffin,
Roses to deaden the clods as they fall.

Then swing your rope slowly and rattle your spurs lowly,
And give a wild whoop as you carry me along;
And in the grave throw me and roll the sod o'er me,
For I'm a young cowboy, and I know I've done wrong.

Adilia began to feel her abdominal muscles settle onto her spine and her shoulders fall flat onto the wooden planks beneath her as her mind traced the words to the song. At ten, the only thing she seemed to have mastered was fear, exhaustion, and a washboard. But that night, as Monroe or Wyatt played music, she felt a cool breeze wash over her, making her feel clean, as though she had stepped out of a warm bath and slipped into a sun-bleached white dress and floated weightlessly on a cloud in a linen shroud.

Slowly, she began to descend and crash into her own body. It was then she realized something was pushing its way under her dress and picking at the edges of her cotton panties. She was startled and pushed herself into a sitting position, kicking and pushing a hand away. Through the darkness she could see the outline of her brother Virgil as he reached over and jerked Clyde up by his hair.

"I thank you'd best be sleepin' on the ground tonight," Virgil said as he rolled Clyde, who was older and twice his size, over the side of the truck.

"At least throw me down a cover," called out Clyde from the rocky ground.

"No," said Virgil. "Sleep like the dog ya is!"

Martha always fed the children first: jokingly, she said it was to get them out of the way for civilized folk, but it really was to make sure the children had food. When Virgil came to the house the following morning, he found the kitchen full of kin already seated around the table.

"Come on over here, honey," invited his Aunt Noreen as she squeezed a fruit crate between two chairs. "Sit right next to your cousin Clyde."

After Virgil plopped his body down on the crate, he turned and gave Clyde the stink eye.

Noreen tossed her fingers through Virgil's hair. "I found Clyde sleepin' on the ground this mornin'. Said ya pushed him off the truck."

"I thank he rolled off in his sleep," replied Virgil.

"Well, whatever the case, yaw's family, and we'z all gotta get along," Noreen said as she bent over and gave her son a kiss on top of his head.

Clyde gave Virgil a sinister look that sent a message that shot up Virgil's spine like a hot poker.

Chapter 3

Walking the Cow

Arkansas, 1936

A VISIT FROM KIN can be both a blessing and a curse. There were more mouths to feed, and the close quarters had a propensity to rub up against already fragile nerves. And with the trial still several weeks off, hard decisions had to be made.

"Virgil!" JC yelled...

When Virgil heard his father's call, he swaggered down the porch steps, chomping on a squirrel bone he had found on someone's abandoned dinner plate.

"Ya wantin' me, Daddy?"

"Virgil, in the morning I'm a-gonna need you and Orson to walk on over to Queen City."

"Where's that?"

"Just up the road a piece," JC lied.

"How long it gonna take?"

"Well," JC hesitated, "well, let's just say it's gonna take a fair amount a time."

"How much time?"

"If truth be told, I don't rightly know. I reckon it depends."

"On what?"

"Well, there's a fella who's gonna meet you along the road, so it could be a day, or maybe two, depending on how fast you both is movin'."

"How come I gotta go?"

"I need the bigger boys here to get this cotton up."

The truth was JC desperately needed money, and he did not trust his two older boys. They were at ages where they would just keep walking and never look back. He knew that by tethering Virgil to his younger brother Orson and a cow with her calf, his chances were good that he'd get them all back, plus some.

Early the next morning, just before sunup, JC heard Martha scurrying around the kerosene-lit kitchen, stuffing a small bar of homemade lye soap, a change of clothes, a few biscuits wrapped in newspaper, four hard-boiled eggs, and a small metal bucket into an old cloth flour sack.

"Ya about done in here?" whispered JC as he walked through the front door, careful not to let the screen door slam and wake everyone up.

"Wish I could pack them somethang more," answered Martha, "but this here is all we got."

"We sendin' the cow with 'em and a bucket, so they's got milk, more than we all got here," JC reassured her.

Holding the hemp rope that bound the cow and calf together, JC led the two boys to the main dirt road with Martha lagging behind, shouting various precautions that the boys would forget before the day was out. With their flour sack slung over the cow's back, JC pointed the two boys down the dark dirt road.

"Stay on this here road until yaw get to the crossroad, then ya take the left road all the ways into Queen City," instructed JC.

Then he handed Virgil the lead and brushed his hand through the child's hair.

JC and Martha stood in the middle of the dirt road and watched their two bare-footed sons walk until they turned into specks. Then JC reached out and tried to squeeze Martha's hand, but she briskly returned to the house.

Virgil did not trust himself to turn around and wave at his parents. It didn't matter that he was six years old and put in charge of his four-year-old brother and two cows. There were two things both his parents would not abide: whining and bellyaching.

The going was slow, and it didn't take long for Orson to become cranky, so he plopped himself on the ground and refused to go any further. Virgil first tried to distract him the same way he had recalled his father distracting the older boys when they became restless on long road trips.

"The road is *soooo* flat," Virgil told Orson.

"How flat is it, Virgil?"

"Flat enough to watch your dowg run away from home for three whole days," answered Virgil.

Then Orson would laugh and ask, "That's a Texas road, ain't it?"

And Virgil would answer, "Yip."

Then Orson would beg for Virgil to say it all again.

The trip they had set out on would have been about a fifty-hour walk for a grown man, but they were young boys, one barely out of diapers. The first day's journey filled Virgil with apprehension, and he eventually found his spirit faltering. At one point he stopped to let the docile cow Dahlia and her calf Minnie graze longer than he thought they needed, hoping to give his parents time to catch up. But when there was no sign of either of his folks, he pressed on. When night fell, he let out the lead a little more for the cow and her calf to graze, then gathered up soft needles to form a bed like he had seen his father and mother do when they were traveling back and forth to Shreveport.

After the first day turned into the second and then slid into the third, Virgil developed more confidence and determination to drive this journey to its end, so to himself he said, "I don't know where the heck I's goin', but I'm walkin' a cow." Then he started singing a ditty as he meandered down the pockmarked road.

Soon, he accepted his role as the trail master and pushed on. He had no idea where they were, how many miles they had walked, how far they had to go—or even where they were going—but he figured they must be more than halfway to Whereeversville, and he was in charge.

"Orson, today ya gonna ride on top," Virgil informed his little brother as he hoisted him up on Dahlia's back. "We need to put down some miles."

"I need a pillow," complained Orson. "These bones hurt my butt."

"Hush up! If ya wasn't lollygagging around so dang much we'd be there by now," Virgil lied.

"Where's 'there?'"

"If I told ya, ya still wouldn't know a dang thang."

With the lead in hand, Virgil moved his small caravan west, this time rarely looking back in the hope of liberation. It was about midmorning when he thought he heard something—maybe a car, he wished—which would be a rare sight on this washed-out road that could only kick up the kind of dust that choked dreams. When he finally turned to investigate, he saw Orson standing upright, balancing himself on Dahlia's hip bones and pissing over her back end. Dahlia, incensed, frantically swished her tail so that a good portion of Orson's piss landed back on him like a lawn sprinkler.

"What in tarnation is ya doin'!" yelled Virgil so loud that he startled Orson, almost causing him to lose his balance. "If you don't sit your scrawny butt down, I'll put a knot on your head so big that calf can suck on it!"

"I'm plumb warn out!" whined Orson.

"Well, ain't that just too dang bad. We'z *all* warn out."

"But now I got piss all over me!"

The sun was losing its heat when the boys encountered an old truck with a tall drop-down tailgate zig-zagging in a futile effort to avoid the ruts. Along the wooden siderails someone had painted "Bonebreak Farms" in bright red letters. The name meant nothing to Virgil. He was not good with letters, and his parents had put stock in the predictions of his lazy-eyed first-grade teacher who explained that Virgil would never learn to read or write, and on that news, he never returned to school.

Virgil moved his small caravan to the far side of the road to avoid getting hit by the erratic truck. Once it cleared them, the truck made a U-turn and came to a stop just ahead of Virgil. A middle-aged man dressed in matching khaki shirt and pants jumped out of the cab and headed back toward the back of the truck.

"Here, let me help yaw load 'em," said the man as he unhooked the chains that let the tailgate drop onto the road.

"No, sir, I can't allow ya ta do that," said Virgil in a low but determined voice.

"Come on, now, I want to get off this blasted road before it gets dark," the man said as he motioned Virgil over.

"No, sir, I can't allow ya ta do that," repeated Virgil as he led his cows further off the road.

"Yaw get on over here. Your daddy and me made a deal, and I wanna get home before dark," insisted the man.

Virgil stood his ground, trying to search his memory for what his daddy had said. Then the man in khaki spoke words of magic.

"I figured yaw would be hungry."

"What you brung—fried racoon?" asked Virgil, hoping that good luck would conquer tragedy.

The man shook his head and thought, *Who in Sam hill would have a preference for a greasy coon?* "Well, fact of the matter is, I brung yaw a few soft bread mayonnaise sandwiches that ya can eat on the way back to Queen City."

With Dahlia and Minnie loaded, the truck bounced along the dirt road, tossing Virgil and Orson around the cab like a carnival fun ride. Gripping his sandwich, Virgil asked what they would be doing when they got to Queen City.

"Didn't your daddy tell ya? With everybody runnin' off to the big cities to find better work or ordered to show up at a checkpoint, we'z short on help. Yaw gonna be pluckin' cotton."

They rode along in silence until the man in khaki crinkled his nose and glanced at the two boys seated next to him. "I smell piss," he said.

Chapter 4

Caravan of Blues

Arkansas, 1936

CONTRARY TO SOME local assumptions, Sod was not a *bona fide* attorney. He was what was known as a "backwoods" lawyer, someone who knew about the law and could sometimes get others to bend it. Mostly, he knew how to skirt the law. But in JC's case, he realized that an accusation of being a communist deep within the Ozarks would take some legal artistry to wriggle out of, so he called in a sizable favor from Mr. Arthur (Art) Haack.

Most of Art's recent cases had involved some interaction with the newly-formed Alcohol Tax Unit, a department that sat within the Bureau of Internal Revenue, a group of career fast-trackers eager to contribute to the coffers of the politically inept in Washington, DC. The repeal contributed $258 million in alcohol taxes in the first year alone, nearly 9% of the government's tax revenue, which helped finance Roosevelt's New Deal programs.[22] Art served as legal counsel for Eastern bootleggers on probation after they were caught trying to offload their overstock in Hot Springs, and although he had a full caseload, he agreed to take on JC's case.

Once Art committed to the case, he and Sod immediately pulled a few strings, the most important being getting the trial moved

22. Christopher Klein, "The Night Prohibition Ended, 80 Years Ago," *History Channel*, December 5, 2013.

near Ola. As there was no official government building in Ola, the presiding judge agreed to allow the trial to take place in a nearby one-room schoolhouse. It was not surprising that the prosecutor did not object. Selecting a jury from that part of the Ozarks ensured a short trial and a quick victory. So, with the jury selected, the trial began at 9 a.m. on Monday, June 22, 1936.

Adilia herded the entire Hornbeck clan onto the flatbed truck like a gaggle of geese the morning of the trial. Upon their arrival at the schoolhouse, they found the door still locked, so they stretched their legs under a large white oak until the clerk arrived with the key.

"It's such a somber, sad day," Noreen said to no one in particular. "I mean, with Martha due in a few months, what...?"

"Oh, hush, Noreen!" shouted Jane, then turned towards her grandchildren before she continued: "Makes no dang sense to ring the bell before school starts."

Jane softened her tone, then spoke directly to the children. "Now, which one of you got a fiddle in your pocket?" She looked at each child. "None of ya?"

They all giggled and shook their heads.

"Reckon we'll have to settle for a harp then. Which of y'all got one of 'em?"

Within seconds, three appeared. "All righty, then," she said as she took the harmonica from Monroe and played a few notes. "And I do believe y'all knows this'n. Adilia, you tell the story, cuz you got such a purdy voice, and I'll back ya up."

Jane kicked *"Arkansas Traveler"*[23] off with a short intro, and Adilia stood and flattened her dress with her hands and straightened

---

23. The song was printed in New York circa 1850. It was later reprinted in *The Arkansas Traveler's Songster* (1864) with credit given to Mose Case as author and composer. In 1896, *Century Magazine* credited the music to Jose Tasso, a famous fiddler of the time.

her braids before she began to recite the words as though she was Cordelia reading from King Lear.

The county clerk arrived midway through Jane and Adilia's performance, and upon seeing the ragtag clan, he wondered why anyone in their right mind would arrive early to what would unquestionably be their own hanging. *And good riddance to the lot of them!* he said to himself, but aloud he yelled, "Yaw might as well come on in!"

"This here is the first time I seen any of my young'uns run into a classroom," laughed Noreen.

"Ain't that just the truth," Martha said as she smiled and shook her head before calling out to every child within hearing distance. "Now act like yaw got some rearin' and glue those behinds to a seat and stay there."

"Listen to your mamma," chimed in JC. "If I hears any ruckus, I'll beat the tarnation out of yaw." Then looking directly at Clyde, he continued: "And I don't care who your daddy is. Got that?"

The children quietly selected a desk and let their bottoms drop hard onto the chairs to make their protests known.

"Ain't it just like school?" whispered Wyatt under his breath.

"Yip, just why I quit after the sixth grade," agreed Monroe.

The clerk motioned for JC to sit in the front row on the right side of the classroom. Then he handed him a folded daily newspaper and said, "Here's some *light* reading material," emphasizing the word "light."

JC set his hat on the table in front of him and unfolded the week-old newspaper. The front-page headline read, "FRANCE GIVES UP PARIS TO NAZIS". He then gently laid the paper down and felt for his rabbit's foot that had been processed by a cross-eyed man and, as hard as he tried to think otherwise, he still could not help thinking that if it weren't for bad luck, he'd have no luck at all.

Slowly, people began funneling into the small schoolhouse. Many belonged to Brother Toomey's congregation. They had resigned from their daily toil to offer prayer over the proceedings and lend spiritual support to their courageous brother. And mixed between the assorted curiosity seekers and communist haters was a small group of about nine men, mostly under the age of twenty-five, who took their places along the outer left wall, leaning in as though they were a vital and significant structural brace. Another group found twelve seats reserved specifically for them toward the front of the classroom. With hats in hand, they avoided eye contact with JC for fear of prematurely revealing their already affirmed verdict.

Without looking to his right, JC knew the members of the jury had seated themselves, but he would not permit himself to acknowledge their presence. They were not his peers, after all; they were unbelievers whose bones he would bury after Armageddon's wrath.

Staring straight ahead at the slate blackboard, JC did not need to look behind him to know the schoolhouse was filling up. He could feel the change in the room's temperature that, only a half hour earlier, had been cool and fresh. Now it was warm and stale with a light scent of farm animals that permeated off the clothing of men and women coming in from morning chores.

The acoustics also had changed. Where he once heard the familiar and reassuring voices of his mother, sister, and wife, he only heard a low hum as though he was looking down on a swarm of hornets feeding upon a carcass, and it frightened him. The palms of his hands began to sweat, and his faith began to show hairline cracks. He squeezed his eyes shut and prayed to God to give him the faith of Habakkuk.[24]

---

24. The prophet Habakkuk was perplexed. He could not understand how a righteous God could use barbarians to execute judgment upon a people more righteous than they.

JC's concentration on his prayer was so intense that he did not hear Monroe urgently hissing to get his father's attention once he recognized Grover and Fergus, two of the young men they had encountered on the steps of Lumkin's General Store. But it was JC's mother, Jane, who relied more on her instincts than God's protection, and quickly sensed a darkness enter the room as though someone had thrown a wet horse-blanket over the entire schoolhouse, and she put her finger to her lips and shushed Monroe.

Having seen her share, Jane could smell trouble and saltpeter from a hundred yards. Without making eye contact, she quickly tallied at least eleven guns along the left wall. A couple of the men didn't even bother to hide their revolvers. They shoved a pistol behind their belt buckles while others tried to be more discreet by attempting to hide their weapons under ill-fitted jackets or by shoving a Banker's Special[25] deep into stretched coat pockets.

"Best be gettin' these babies outta here," Jane whispered to Martha, who was holding a wooden spoon up to Hester's gums.

"What's ya thankin'?" Martha asked.

"Too much iron for a schoolhouse," Jane quietly said. "And I only got one," she added as she patted her hand on her pocketbook.

"Where's Sod?" worried Martha as she turned in her chair and stared toward the door. "More men are coming through," she whispered as she counted about ten enter single file and line up along the right side of the room. Then her voice began to quiver: "Dang, Mamma, ain't sure we gonna get outta here!"

"Of course we is. This ain't how we all gonna die," Jane said as she smiled softly and patted Martha comfortingly on the arm. She then wrapped the handle of her pocketbook around her

---

25. Colt introduced the Banker's Special revolver with two-inch barrel (snub-nosed) in 1928. It was advertised "for easy carrying and quick access—especially adapted for use by bank employees."

arthritic wrist and slowly rose to her feet. Turning to the back of the room, she called out to her grandchildren: "Yaw give them there seats up to the grownups. Go on now."

The older children pulled themselves out of their seats, grabbed the hands of the younger ones, and made their way to the door.

"And go on up to the house; we'z be along directly."

Adilia grabbed Hester from her mother and followed the rest of the children. Then she stopped at the door and waited for Monroe, who had paused to deliver a silent message to Grover: *"This ain't over yet."*

As Adilia and Monroe walked down the schoolhouse steps, they saw Sod clearing the way for JC's attorney through the growing crowd of locals who had come to see a communist put on trial.

"Somethang is goin' on in there," Monroe whispered to Sod.

"Don't ya fret. I got this one covered," replied Sod. "Yaw run along before I get hungry and need to grab me a pig's tail." Then he reached out and gave Adilia's hair a light tug, which made her giggle and blush. It was their thing. Having Sod, a pillar of the community, tease her made her feel less invisible, less of an appendage of her mother.

As he paused at the threshold, Sod blocked the sunlight streaming through the schoolhouse doorway, creating a halo effect around his muscular frame and causing those seated in the gallery and those who had already taken their positions as jurors to turn in his direction to see what had eclipsed the light. Stepping boldly into the room, he let his leather-soled boots fall flat on the wooden floorboards. Intentional, solid, and in control, he moved forward along the right wall where the second group of men pinched together to give him room to stand alongside them.

Quickly sizing up the room, Jane placed her feet squarely on the floor and took deep, measured breaths, slowing her heartbeat until her seventy-two-year-old body felt as though she were a delicate blue moth balancing on an angel's whisper. "This ain't our circus, ain't our monkeys, unless they make it so," Jane concluded. Without looking at her knotted fingers, she unclasped the latch on her pocketbook with her left hand, reached in with her right, and let it gently rest on the butt of her "Rainmaker."[26]

Jane was right. This trial was not about being a communist. It was about two headstrong families picking at each other's scabs. Sod had picked his side long ago, making JC an enemy by association. Without looking at anyone in particular, the circuit court judge could feel the silent innuendos passing between the outer walls of the gallery. He patted the outside of his robe for the cold steel he carried under it, determined not to have a repeat of Carroll County.[27]

The judge ordered the clerk to read the charges aloud:

The judicial court of Arkansas, of which Searcy County is a part, in the name and authority of the State of Arkansas, on oath, accuses the defendant, JC Hornbeck, to have willfully and publicly exhibited contempt for the United States' flag against the peace and dignity of the United States.

After the prosecutor, Len Jones, and JC's attorney, Arthur Haack, delivered their opening remarks, the judge kept them moving at a rapid pace.

Judge: Call your first witness, Mr. Haack.

Haack: Thank you, Your Honor. I would like to call Grover Murdock.

Grover dragged his boots across the wooden floor and swaggered to the front of the room where the clerk asked him to take

---

26. "Rainmaker" was a name for the Colt M1877, a double-action revolver. It also was known as the "Lightning" or the "Thunder."
27. In 1912 five people, including the circuit judge, were killed and seven people were wounded in the Carroll County Courthouse in Hillsville, Virginia, by an influential family clan.

the oath and state his name, after which he took a wooden chair positioned between the judge and the jury.

Q. What is your occupation, Mr. Murdock?

A. I work in various family businesses.

Q. That would be the businesses owned by your daddy, who is also the county assessor, is that correct?

A. Yes, sir, that would be my daddy.

Q. What were you doing at Lumkin's General Store that day?

A. My daddy owns that store, and I always help when the commodities are being handed out.

Q. What are your duties?

A. At that time I talked to all who came in and questioned their cases.

Q. That was part of your duties?

A. Yes, sir, because I handled every order as it come up.

Q. What do you mean by "questioning their cases"?

A. Just as I said, if a rumor was brought to us, certain things were not right; it was my duty to ask about those things.

Q. Are you under federal law to ascertain this information?

A. No, not directly.

Q. Did you have any instruction from any federal agency not to let Jehovah's Witnesses have any commodities unless they salute the flag?

A. No cult was named. They were sworn by affidavits that they wouldn't receive anything unless they were a loyal American citizen.

Q. Then you asked him to salute the flag as a test?

A. I said, "To quiet the rumor, there is the flag, let's see ya salute it."

Q. Did you say anything more on that occasion?

A. No, because I told him to hush and get off the steps.

Q. Where did you hear these rumors?

Rumors have a way of roaming. They become unraveled and get distorted. Orators who spread rumors have already bought into them before they utter the first syllable, and when the rumor becomes disentangled, the orators' vanity obligates them to brace it up on partial facts that often reveal their true intent. And so, the jurors had no option but to acquit on the charge of being an enemy of America but guilty for inciting a riot at Lumkin's General Store, and so the jury foreman handed the clerk the findings:

We, the jury, find the defendant, Jedediah Chester Hornbeck, guilty as charged in the information and fix his punishment at a fine of $50 and imprisonment in the county jail for twenty-four hours.

J. T. Baker, Foreman

The sheriff led JC by the elbow to his cruiser and whisked him back to serve his twenty-four hours at the county jail. Key court officials quickly followed suit in fear that the disappointed public would form a mob because they were denied the opportunity to see capital punishment carried out.

"Yaw get on now," Jane told Martha and Noreen. "Get that truck started if ya can. I'll be along shortly. Gotta just let this sank in a bit." Then she leaned back and said, "And Martha, today you are going to learn to drive that damn tuck like a Hornbeck!"

Martha closed her eyes and prostrated herself over the steering wheel in prayer. After giving thanks, she strengthened her aching back. She didn't know why, but she felt more powerful, more in charge, than she had ever felt before. She turned the engine over and laid on the horn. "Come on, Noreen!" she yelled out the window. "Let's get them young-uns fed!"

"We'z gotta wait for Mamma," Noreen said as she scanned the crowd mingling outside the schoolhouse for any sign of her mother. "There she is," she finally said. "We'z over here, Mamma!" Then she waved and repeated, "Over here!"

Art Haack leaned inside the passenger window when he heard Martha call to him over the roar of the engine.

"You done a fine job, Mr. Haack, a fine job. I don't know what we'd done without ya! How can we ever repay ya?"

"It was my..." Art Haack began to say as he was removing his hat.

"Yes, sir, Mr. Haack, most appreciative," said Jane as she elbowed him aside to open the door of the truck. "Jump in, Noreen. We have to get on outta here. I'll ride shotgun."

Noreen slid into the middle of the bench seat, and Jane jumped in after her, almost slamming the door on Mr. Haack's fingers.

"Mr. Haack," continued Jane, "ya better get on outta here faster than a monkey on moonshine. They's about ready to tear into each other in there."

Mr. Haack followed Jane's line of sight and put his hat back on. "Yes, ma'am, much obliged." Then he turned on his heels and rushed to his car.

"Step on it, girl," Jane commanded.

Martha jammed the truck into first, kicking up some dust, then double-clutched it into third before she sharply turned onto the blacktop, causing the back end to fishtail. She turned into the slide and quickly regained control just as they heard gunshots coming from the direction of the schoolhouse.

Martha gripped the steering wheel and pushed the throttle to the floor while Jane and Noreen stared out the back window.

"Woo-wee! If that weren't a close one!" Noreen yelled as she turned herself around. "I thank we all deserve a cold beer!"

"I thank you's right, sugar," agreed Jane, "and I'm a-buyin'."

With that, Martha pulled into the next wide place along the road where sat a small general store. A long wooden bench ran the length of the front windows. Martha and Noreen sat on the bench while Jane went inside. When she returned, she had three cold cans of beer. She handed one to Martha and another to Noreen.

"Thank God this ain't a dry county," said Noreen. "Let me see ya 'church key', Mamma."

Jane fished through her pocketbook and pulled out a can opener and, after puncturing two holes in her can of beer, she passed it on. The three sat quietly, slouched on the wood bench with their eyes in a resting position, each digging deep into their personal piles of hope like they were hunting through a basket of dirty laundry for diaper pins, only to come up with a handful of shit.

"Hey!" The women heard a man's loud voice yelling to them. "Heard yur old man got off easy!"

Martha opened her eyes to see a fat-bellied old man in a wrinkled summer suit looking down on her.

"Go to hell!" she shot back. "Ain't nothin' come easy fer none of us!" Then she chugged the rest of her beer and tossed the empty onto the dirt.

Before the fat man had time to respond, Jane jumped to her feet. Staring into his red-pocked face she spat out, "Don't let me start the headlights on t hearse!"

Noreen and Jane chugged what they had left of their beers and tossed the cans onto the ground next to Martha's and ambled back to the truck.

As they sped away, they could hear the fat man yell, "Trash! Yaw nothin' but ugly trash!"

"Another man's trash..." Martha started to say, then she began to laugh until all three melted into the truck seat and laughed until their sides ached.

"I thank I leaked!" snickered Noreen.

"Ya always was a bedwetter!" joked Jane.

★

With his back leaning against the siderails and the heel of his boot propped up on the running board of JC's truck, Sod finished rolling his cigarette and broke the awkward silence between him and JC.

"Wish you'd reconsider," Sod said as he struck a match with his thumbnail. "It's only been a month since the trial. Things'll cool off and get back to normal."

"I done looked at it ever which-a-way," said JC, who was still looking down on the cotton field below, one that had not produced anything but near starvation. "What's with Noreen's husband gittin' hit by lightning while down 'spectin' a boiler? Of all the dirty rotten luck."

"That's why those boiler operators[28] make the big dough. Wouldn't catch me down there."

"Now they's as destitute as the rest of us."

---

28. In an oil refinery, boiler operators routinely clean and check the system's health, which requires them to drop into giant drums used to store oil in its various processing stages.

Distracted by all the kids running and screaming like a house full of demons, Sod looked up at the old shack and saw Noreen leaning over the porch, staring off into nothingness, her eyes almost swollen shut from endless crying over the uncertainty. *She clearly is not from the same stock as Martha or Jane*, he thought.

"I get that you're broke, but you can always fix broke."

"Broke?" spat JC. "Hell, I'm as broke as the Ten Commandments, and ya can't fix that kinda broke."

"Well, I can't stop ya, so I won't even try."

"Ya know the Hornbecks will never forget what ya's done fer us."

"I know. And I won't ever forget yaw neither," said Sod as the two men shook hands, squeezed each other's upper shoulders, and patted the other's back in what is the three-stage, wordless farewell ceremony men go through to express deep emotional sorrow and comfort. But whenever JC hit the wall, he hit the highway. It's what families like his did for generations. It's how they kept hope alive.

JC turned back toward the house and yelled, "Come on! Let's get this caravan of blues back on the road!"

Stepping out of the doorway, Martha called down, "We gotta fetch Virgil and Orson on the way."

JC spat on the dusty ground. Then, with the toe of his boot, he smeared his saliva into the shape of a cross. "Might need Virgil at that. He got the best eye for them coons."

Chapter 5

Reflection on Self

Texas, 1940

THE HORNBECKS WERE NOT readers, aside from religious pamphlets and the Bible, an outdated newspaper, or an old *McCall's* magazine fished out of a trash can. Martha was the only one to have gone all the way through high school. The rest had not gone beyond the sixth grade. But their lack of extended secular schooling in no way implied they were unaware of the current events that affected their lives. While they did not indulge themselves in dime store romance novels or detective stories, they did their best to keep up with the local and regional dailies that published articles and photos pulled from the Associated Press. At the Grange halls, seed and feed stores, and over the hoods of rusted old trucks they exchanged opinions with those who, like them, were bent and broke. And nearly all agreed on one defining fact—that not all Southern migrants were "Okies." After that, men the world over could generally be divided into four principal groups.

First, there were the self-proclaimed "deciders" who could be spotted easily in their freshly pressed suits and shirts, starched by the hands of a skilled colored woman, but never by their fragile wives or debutante daughters. They conducted business sitting in barber chairs while their hair was sprinkled with sweet-smelling tonics or in exclusive and segregated men's clubs. Those men did not obey the law; they influenced it—if they didn't write it themselves. When other classes challenged their greed, they repeated the mantra, "With hard work, you can accomplish anything," giving the impression that it was through their own diligence, and not on the broken backs of others, that they had amassed their power.

The second group, the "believers," were those who tottered between poverty and destitution. They took the proclamations of goodwill from the mouths of the deciders as though they had come directly from the Gospel itself. They also held a strong belief that barber chairs and secret handshakes were awaiting them if they would simply support the ambitions of the deciders. And so they defended the false claims and promises, because failure to do so would seal their fate, destroy their hope, and abolish their will to live. Only prudent believers would dare look beyond their blinders to the cold, hard truth and realize that, without hesitation, their hands would be swiftly chopped off should they attempt to climb the ladder beyond their station.

Then, of course, there were the "pitiful," the beaten-down, the left-behind, the forgotten; those who had nothing to start with and would die with even less. They were the lepers, the unclean, bottom feeders, the ones to avoid eye contact with for fear of becoming one of them. They were the ones whose names even God would have a hard time recalling once they were on their death pallets. Their meager luck left them hunting for morsels that could barely sustain their own breath, let alone those they fathered or birthed. While sheepish in the light of day, they gathered in a kind of tribe under the light of the moon's glow where their spirit mist was reborn into brave and noble heroes who fought battles where there were no winners.

And then there was the fourth group, the group the Hornbecks pledged their allegiance to, the "disparagers." While being God-fearing in spirit, they were shy of being godly in all their manner and deeds. Although they loved their country, it had left them black and blue. When the government asked for men, they offered their bravest, and when armies needed food, they slaughtered their last hog. They had helped carve out the freedom road since the early 1600s, but after three hundred years, they had cashed out. They were in the red, and had decided to go it alone. They had lost respect for authority and laws, believing they had become nothing more than wretched refuse. So, they had chosen a side... their own.

The deciders in the South feverishly disowned John Steinbeck's novel, taking it as a personal smear, and they resented outsiders who meddled in their affairs, considering those addressing contemporary problems as subversive renegades, anarchists, and agitators. They claimed Steinbeck's book was bombastic, blasphemous, and communist propaganda, so they warned readers with these words:

"Any reader who has his roots planted in the red soil will boil with indignation over the bedraggled, bestial characters that will give the ignorant East convincing confirmation of their ideas of the people of the Southwest... If you have children, I'd advise against leaving the book around the home. It has *Tobacco Road* looking as pure as Charlotte Bronte when it comes to obscene, vulgar, lewd, stable language."[29]

JC and Martha, with their sons Monroe and Wyatt in tow, were among the first in line to see *The Grapes of Wrath*. After the 129-minute film was over, they exited into an exceptionally warm night with faces pointed straight ahead as they trudged silently toward their truck, not bothering to dodge the soft chewing gum dotting their path. As they forced one foot in front of the other, they could not help but overhear the surrounding conversations.

Men dressed in starched shirts and pressed slacks walked arm in arm with women wearing store-bought dresses. One overstuffed woman who had never missed a weekly beauty parlor appointment could be heard haughtily saying, "So California wants nothing but cream!" While a fella who looked as though he had come straight from a bank vault barked out, "Enough to justify a civil war!" Others could be heard calling out explosive words like "vulgar, immoral, dirty, lying, and filthy," yet those who were disgusted managed to sit through the entire

---

29. Mr. W. M. Harrison, editor of the *Oklahoma City Times*, devoted his column, "The Tiny Times," to a review of *The Grapes of Wrath* on May 8, 1939.

film, glued to the screen, sometimes letting out audible sounds of disapproval. The only moviegoers not chattering were those in bib overalls and hand-sewn dresses made from flour sacks who moved lightly along the concrete sidewalk with eyes cast straight ahead and lips tightly pinched so as to betray neither their heart nor their pride.

"This here is why I ain't packed us all up," JC told his wife and boys as he pulled out the choke on the International and pumped the gas pedal with the toe of his work boot. "They ain't got it no better out there than we'z all got it here."

"But they got water," Monroe said.

"Ain't gonna do a dang bit of good if you ain't gotta patch ta work, boy," argued JC.

"Spec' not, I reckon," Monroe mumbled. Then he reached into his shirt pocket, pulled out his Hohner, and lightly blew a few notes from *"Blue Moon of Kentucky"*.

"Put that dad-blasted thang away!" snapped JC.

"Oh, leave him be," demanded Martha.

Monroe lowered his shoulders and dropped his hands and harmonica onto his lap like a mound of wet clay.

As JC slowly drove away from the Wichita Theater, past the shuttered windows of the small merchants along Indiana Avenue, he felt the tension in his two boys who were sitting beside him. He glanced at Martha, trying to get a read on his wife, but she turned her face away and gazed out a half rolled-down window as the streetlamps slowly disappeared. JC suddenly regretted forking over the eighty cents for the movie tickets. Now there was no way to dim the light that so brightly illuminated their economic plight.

The old International lumbered along the dark and narrow two-lane blacktop that led out of town like a tired and lathered horse heading back to the barn. The only thing that could be heard was the sound of a weary engine humming in high gear and the rattling of the loose wooden planks that covered its flatbed as the truck bounced in and out of potholes. The boys leaned their heads against the back of the seat and pulled in the warm night air from their mother's open window.

It is peculiar how the brain clinches to a memory the heart wishes to repel—or is it the other way around? Whichever the case, memories seem to have a will of their own, collecting, connecting, and clumping similar experiences together in a tiny corner, then growing until they overtake the cerebrum. Untangling that mess requires addressing one memory at a time.

The movie had stirred up dozens of emotions in Wyatt that pinged around inside his head until he felt dizzy. He closed his eyes and tried to suppress the bitterness of shame that is poverty's constant companion. He felt his stomach push into his throat and wished he had sat in the back of the truck. One by one, he sifted through his thoughts as though he were sorting nuts and bolts into old coffee tins. Yet just as he placed one in the tin, one or two would jump out again. One such unsettled memory was of the Hagenbeck-Wallace derailment.[30]

The thought of the wreck would not stay put, and the more he thought about it, the more it clung to the sides of his brain with such a grip that he could not claw himself away. He felt the same hopelessness and humiliation that he had felt in Miss Mumford's class. He sucked air through the gap in his front teeth and ignored Monroe's elbow digging into his ribs.

*

Most of the children in Miss Mumford's class were among the poorest in the county, children of farmers, millers, packers, pickers, seed sellers, gas station attendants, general merchants, and more than a few drunks. Many came to school barefooted, if they came at all. When they did show up, they often arrived

---

30. The Hagenbeck-Wallace train wreck (aka Hammond Circus Train wreck) occurred on June 22, 1918, near Hammond, Indiana. It is considered one of the worst train disasters in US history.

late with boisterous stomachs that sounded like a thunderous and tragic crescendo in a Puccini opera.

With all the challenges her students faced, Miss Mumford felt it was important to provide her charges with opportunities to connect with the country and the world at large, to give them hope and a place to expand and grow. That's why she gave her class a weekly current events assignment. Each student was required to turn in a written report, and one or two students would be selected to read theirs aloud.

"If you do not have access to a newspaper or a radio," Miss Mumford instructed, knowing many lived without electrical power and that even finding a newspaper could be a hardship, "borrow one from a neighbor or run by the barbershop on your way home."

By the time Wyatt got around to remembering his assignment, his mother had already used the newspaper to light the fire in the smokehouse after killing their fall hog.

"Why ya lookin' like the last pea at pea-time?" Martha asked Wyatt.

When he told her about his assignment, she suggested he ask his daddy: "He done read the paper this week over at the seed and feed."

JC could not recall a story worth sharing with a fourth-grade class. So, after pondering a while, he told Wyatt the most riveting newspaper story he had ever read, one that had left a lasting impression on him as a young man of eighteen. Wyatt was so enthralled by the story he forgot all about writing it down. The following day, although Miss Mumford said he would be docked ten points for not turning in a written report, he could deliver an oral one.

Standing before his class in patched overalls, Wyatt began the gruesome tale of how an engineer driving an empty troop train weighing 150 tons had fallen asleep at the throttle and barreled into the back of a stopped circus train, killing several trapeze artists and bareback riders along with a lion tamer, strongman, and a clown's entire family, among dozens of others. Wyatt had his classmates mesmerized; not even a growling stomach could be heard. No one dared drop a pencil. The only movement Wyatt saw came from the outer wall where he noticed Miss Mumford moving toward him. Thinking she might cut him off, he leaned into his story and delivered his epitaph.

"Eighty-six of 'em died," he quickly told his wide-mouthed classmates. "Some of 'em was burnt so bad they couldn't tell who they was, so they buried 'em all in the same grave."

"Thank you, Wyatt. You can take your seat now," said Miss Mumford as she placed her hand gently on his shoulder and guided him toward his seat.

As Wyatt returned to his chair, the older boys gave him their approval with a short nod. Although the story was gruesome and sorrowful, to most of the children it was a welcome interruption to the constant focus on Germany's invasion of Poland.

Wyatt sat proudly in his seat, his back straight, his chin high. Even Pearl, a popular, yellow-haired girl, was staring at him as if seeing him for the first time.

"Yes, Thomas," asked Miss Mumford. "What's your question?"

"Miss Mumford, what do you think will happen to all them circus animals now that the train crashed?"

"I don't think we need to worry about the animals. They survived, and this event happened over twenty years ago."

"So, it ain't current?"

"No, Thomas, it is not."

The class broke out in hysteria and ridicule, saying Wyatt's family was so poor they couldn't even afford a current newspaper, and that his daddy was such a slow reader that he hadn't finished reading the papers from 1918.

*

It was a gut-wrenching feeling of despair and panic. Usually, Wyatt came away from the picture show feeling rejuvenated, but tonight, at fifteen, his pride fell below his knees, and he sensed that he was slowly sinking into muddy waters.

Almost an hour had passed before JC turned onto a narrow, pot-holed dirt road that jostled the International so violently that it caused the headlights to dance like fireflies in the pitch darkness. Martha removed her mauve cloche hat, rolled her window all the way down, and pushed her arm out, letting the soft breeze lift her palm up and down as if it were a kite. She could feel her body relax into the springs of the seat when, suddenly, her head crashed into the roof of the cab as JC hit a huge pothole.

"I think ya missed one, daddy," Wyatt laughed as he rubbed the top of his head and glanced at his mother sitting next to him. Then he extended his hand and rubbed her head too. "Ya all right, Mamma?"

"Sure am, and we'z all gonna be just fine!" Martha said with a proud and strong voice that sabotaged any chance the boys may have had of returning to the darkness of their own self-pity.

Martha had been replaying a letter from a reader she had seen in a month-old newspaper opinion column that read like this:

"To many of us, John Steinbeck's novel, *The Grapes of Wrath*, has sounded the keynote of our domestic depression and put the situation before us in an appealing way. When the small farmers and homeowners—the great masses upon which our national stability depends—were being deprived of their homes and sent roaming about the country knocking from pillar to post, when banks were bursting with idle money and insurance companies were taking on more holdings and money than they knew what to do with, Steinbeck attempted a sympathetic exposition of this status."[31]

---

31. Miss Mary E. Lemon, *Oklahoma City Times*, Dec. 22, 1939.

"I thank we all can find some measure of comfort," Martha continued. "God the Father has declared Five Woes[32] and has proclaimed, 'Thou hast consulted shame to thy house by cutting off many people and hast sinned against thy soul.'"[33]

With a tightened jaw, Martha slapped her hand down on her faded cotton floral dress and closed her eyes. She began humming a soft tune that dripped from her lips like sweet syrup from a Northern maple. Then, as though the rattling and clanking of the truck beckoned her, she began to sing *"Victory Ahead"*[34] aloud, and as she reached the chorus crescendos, the family joined in.

"Can I get a little hep with a Hallelujah?" called Martha.

"Hallelujah, Hallelujah!"

---

32. The Five Woes (theft and lust for control, greed and unjust economics, slave labor, irresponsible leaders, and idolatry) are the cause and effect that cannot be violated because it's a law of the universe as illustrated by the example of Babylon (Habakkuak 2:1-20).

33. Habakkuak 2:10, King James Version.

34. *"Victory Ahead"* was composed by the Reverend William Grum in 1905 and was set to the tune of *"When the Hosts of Israel, Led by God."* Grum's song has appeared in over forty hymnals.

Part 2

"The first step towards getting somewhere is to decide you're not going to stay where you are.

J.P. Morgan

Chapter 6

Boys Runnin'

Texas, Oklahoma, New Mexico, 1946

MONROE AND WYATT ran off in the small hours of the morning after a fight with their daddy came to blows. Breaking ranks was not a new idea. It was as though the notion had been prophesied at their birth and was finally being manifested in the flesh.

Monroe had been putting an escape plan together as far back as Arkansas. He would have taken off then, but just as he was ready to launch his plan, one thing or another popped up, compelling him to stay, despite his better judgment. First, it was JC's trial. Then there was the loss of two babies—Hester, who died of a diarrheal disease[35] behind the cookstove before she was two, and baby Ebba, who had come into the world no bigger than a newborn kitten. Martha lined a roasting pan with a quilt and laid Ebba on the open door of the oven. The boys kept the wood stocked to a low, even temperature to help keep her warm, but even the all-night vigils couldn't save her. Ebba died within a few days.

Monroe and Wyatt spent months weighing the pros and cons of leaving North Texas, devising ways in which they might even persuade their father to load up the old International flatbed

---

35. Diarrheal diseases are a collection of diseases caused by multiple viral, bacterial, and parasitic organisms that share the common symptom of diarrhea.

and carry them all to Bakersfield, California. They did their best to convince him there was no future in working dead patches of ground that the bank would sell out from under them to rich oil speculators on a whim. But their father was a tenacious man. Each time a link broke in the family's prosperity chain, he clung all the harder to what little ground he had salvaged. And having returned to Texas, no one could pry Martha loose from her mother's bosom. Besides, JC knew Mazie, Martha's mother, could possibly be the key to their future prosperity.

With their pallets tucked under their arms and boots in hand, Monroe and Wyatt quietly stepped between the sleeping bodies that dotted the plank floor like landmines. Through the light of the moon limping through dusty windows flanked by tattered curtains made from old flour sacks, Monroe thought he saw Virgil's blue eyes peering back at him as he snatched a guitar that did not belong to him.

When Wyatt reached the back door, he paused for a moment to take one last look at the room and fill his nostrils with the scent of sweat, the sweet smell that is unique to sleeping children. And as he made his way through the door, he rubbed his hand over the newspaper his mother had plastered to the wall using homemade flour paste to help insulate against the blowing dust. He smiled as he remembered helping her cut pictures from discarded magazines that she used to decorate around the door jambs and window frames, providing each opening with a unique edging. Around the door frame she had pasted a collection of colorful pictures of what she called "Godly thangs" found in the natural world: animals, flowers, and winding green rivers. Around the kitchen window hung a collection of fruit and vegetables, along with beautiful baked goods and lovely canning jars filled with bright green pole beans and yellow kernels of corn. A small patch on the lower right corner of the kitchen window trim once displayed a bright picture of freshly-picked peaches that had been scratched away by little fingers searching for a taste—if only for pretend.

Sitting quietly on the back stoop, Monroe and Wyatt pulled on their boots next to the galvanized washtub and a barrel of dirty diapers that were patiently waiting on tomorrow. Wyatt whispered, "We got to do right by them."

"We gonna. Mamma deserves a heap better. The old man, an ass whoopin'!" replied Monroe as he jumped up in renewed anger and headed toward the tack shed, careful not to trip over the screen door that still lay halfway between the back porch and the outhouse after it had been ripped from its hinges months earlier by the unyielding wind. It was not that they were too lazy to rehang it; rather, they reasoned, it was a waste of time, as there was not much left in the kitchen for the flies to be curious about.

They gently saddled two old bay mares and quietly strapped on the meager provisions they had collected the night before, and led the horses to the dirt road that ran alongside their property line. Then they mounted up. They suspected their daddy was awake and that his pride would keep him from getting out of bed and trying to make amends, and they were right.

In his heart of hearts, JC had little doubt that his two older boys were correct. One day he might come to forgive them for abandoning the family in its time of need, although he could not recall a time when they were *not* in need. But at that moment he had dug deeper into the discomfort brought on by disappointment and betrayal, the unremitting pain that felt more like comfort than agony. He lay on his bed, exposing his chest as if it had been sliced open, and his boys had reached in and pulled his heart out. Instinctively, his hand felt for blood, the same hand he earlier had twisted into a fist and used to punch his sons. He saw himself growing old and weak and becoming one of the pitiful. His stomach started to twist so tight that he dropped his arm to the side of his bed to feel for the chamber pot. He wanted to jump up and punch something or someone. But at the same time, he wanted to die a quick death.

It wasn't that JC was unsympathetic to his boys. There was a time when he considered going out West himself and remembered the first handbill he had read, just after the bank sold the mineral rights on his last farm to oil speculators, a farm that had brought them just above even on a good year and just below on a bad one:

MEN WANTED

GOOD WAGES

PLUS

SLEEPING QUARTERS

WORK IN CALIFORNIA

STRONG MEN NEEDED

TO PICK FRUIT

ABLE WOMEN & CHILDREN ALSO NEEDED

Unlike his younger sister Ona and brother Jessie, who had taken the handbill up on its offer, JC was quick to wad it up and toss it into the gutter outside Wright's Discount Store on Main Street in Shreveport. He reasoned that even if he could rustle up enough money for gas and tires, his old International had, as far as he could tell, over 300,000 miles on it from ten years of driving back and forth between Oklahoma, Tennessee, Arkansas, Louisiana, and Texas. He felt his odds were better working the patch of ground provided by the Wichita Gardens Subsistence Homesteads Division,[36] but then he was a man who chewed his own tobacco.

According to Monroe and Wyatt's calculations, they could make between fifteen and twenty miles a day on horseback if they followed Route 66. Food, feed, and shoes for the horses could be a challenge, but they had taken that into account when formulating their plan. And they were right to be confident: townspeople often sought their skills as knuckle draggers,[37] and they had

---

36. Part of the US Department of the Interior's New Deal, The Subsistence Homesteads for Industrial and Rural Workers was enacted at the end of 1934. The program "hoped to demonstrate the value and feasibility, for wage earners, of the combination of part-time industrial employment with home gardening on a scale large enough to furnish a considerable proportion of the family food supply." *Monthly Labor Review, Vol. 40, No. 1 (January 1935), pp. 19-37.*

37. "Knuckle dragger" is slang for a mechanic who is either

done their share of work as juice jerkers.[38] And it went without saying that they could fluff a bag better than most.[39] Whatever it took, they were hell-bent to make it to California, even if they had to walk in barefooted.

They rode in silence for about an hour, when Wyatt came to stop at the entrance of a narrow dirt lane, "ya thankn' what I'm thankn'?" he asked.

"It'd serve the son of a bitch right fer what he done to Adilia," Monroe answered.

After tying the horses, Monroe and Wyatt snuck down the lane leading to their Aunt Noreen's house and quietly snuck into the closed-in back porch were their Cousin Clyde slept and stole his rifle and his only pair of boots.

For a good part of the first three days, the brothers rode along dusty and rutty dirt roads and a few pothole-infested paved ones where the county had run out of funds for maintenance. They then cut over to a dirt trail running along the Red River that they hoped would eventually lead them to Route 66—if they timed it right, they would hit blacktop by the time their father and the law had given up their search for the stolen horses.

The river trail meandered through the herbal pine fragrance of silver-leafed Texas rangers[40] that, eventually, met up with miles of river birch that set their roots close to the banks of stream beds lined with clumps of sumacs dripping with berries too green to harvest.

---

professionally trained or has a deeper interest in learning how and why machines work, i.e., a step up from a "wrench turner" or a "grease monkey."

38. "Juice jerkers" refers to milking cows.

39. Fluffing cotton was a trick field hands used to make a cotton sack look fuller than it was.

40. Texas ranger, also known as Texas sage (*leucophyllum frutescens*), is an evergreen shrub in the figwort family *scrophulariaceae*. It is native to the Southwestern United States and the states of Coahuila, Nuevo León, and Tamaulipas in northern Mexico.

On the fourth day, the Red River narrowed around the eastern Prairie Dog Town Fork, and it was there that Monroe first noticed a lone rider on the opposite bank who was matching their pace.

"How long you figure that colored cowboy been ridin' alongside us?" Monroe asked.

"First time I seen 'im," answered Wyatt.

"Ain't a thang out here. Had ta come from somewheres," said Monroe.

"I reckon he did," replied Wyatt.

"I find it kinda unnervin'."

"Ain't nothin' to fret over," Wyatt said matter-of-factly. "He got himself a better horse and, by looks of it, he's better outfitted than we'z is, so if anybody be on the lookout, it otta be him."

"He probably stole that there horse."

"If he did, he'd be ridin' a lot faster than he is, and when ya get on down to it, we ain't exactly asked for permission for the ones we'z on. Besides, ain't that Virgil's guitar you got strapped to your saddle?" Wyatt joked.

They continued to ride until dusk. Then they stopped along the riverbank where the horses could drink and feed on new shoots of grass. After the horses were unpacked and curried with a branch Monroe ripped off a cottonwood tree, he cobbled them and let them roam.

Wyatt rustled up some dry underbrush to start a small fire, which he thought was futile, since they had already been on the trail for four days and there was nothing much left to eat but a few pecans and a couple of pieces of dried meat. Sitting on their pallets, not ready to sleep, Monroe picked up Virgil's guitar and started strumming—no song in particular, just waiting for something to come into his head. Then he heard a deep, rich tone of another guitar coming from across the river where the black cowboy had camped.

As though his fingers were marionettes connected to strings he did not control, Monroe and Wyatt began to play the chords, and the cowboy began to sing the words in a baritone voice, strong and full, nothing held back. The rich sound drifted across the river as though on the wings of moths that darted from one campfire to another, guided by a magnetic celestial power. The cowboy sang *"The Red River Valley"*[41] as though it was his own story of a life he was leaving behind, never to return.

They played that song repeatedly as though they were trying to prove who had lost the most. One by one, the players stopped playing until the only sound heard was the vibration from the strings of the cowboy's guitar across the river.

Monroe and Wyatt saddled up the next morning just as dawn was spitting itself over the horizon like a fast-approaching prairie fire. Gazing across the river, Wyatt tipped his hat at the saddled cowboy.

When that day ran headlong into another night, Monroe and Wyatt fed and watered their horses. Hungry enough to eat the leather off Clyde's boots, Wyatt set out to see if he could snare a rabbit, and Monroe pulled out an old tobacco tin in which he had neatly rolled about twenty-five feet of line attached to a couple of lead weights and a hook. After turning over a few river rocks, he found a small worm and placed it on the end of his hook. He then attached his line to a three-foot branch he cut from a cottonwood with his Bowie knife. With his boots lying on the river's edge and his pant legs rolled up, Monroe dropped his line into the water.

---

41. *"The Red River Valley"* is an American folk song dating back to the 1870s. It was first recorded as *"Cowboy Love Song"* in 1925 by Carl T. Sprague, one of the first cowboy singers from Texas. The biggest hit of the cowboy version came in 1927 by Hugh Cross and Riley Puckett. In both recordings, the lyrical associations are about the Red River Valley that marks the border between Arkansas and Texas.

As the sun descended, Wyatt returned empty-handed, and Monroe had nothing on his line. They were too tired to start a fire, and there was nothing to cook anyway, so they sat in the dark.

"Sho' could use some help with these here pork and beans!" they heard a voice from across the river shout at them.

Without hesitation or a word, Monroe grabbed his guitar, Wyatt shoved spoons into his pocket, and they waded through the cool water and sat next to the cowboy's fire.

Over a can of pork and beans, warmed alongside the fire's soothing blaze, the brothers learned that the cowboy had crossed the Oklahoma Plains and had passed through Monroe's birthplace, Earlsboro,[42] a town named for James Earls, a local African American barber and suspected bootlegger who had been an orderly for the Confederate Commander Joseph "Fighting Joe" Wheeler. Now the cowboy was headed to Grand Junction, Colorado.

"The War Department is openin' up a refinery fer somethang they call vanadium,[43]" the cowboy explained. "They say all them mines is openin' up."

"What's vanadium?" asked Wyatt.

"And what's the War Department gotta do with it?" asked Monroe suspiciously.

"Fer as I can tell, it's some kinda mineral they pull up outta the ground. All I knows is that they's payin' good money, so ya gotta pack up, no matter what."

"I reckon that is purt near the case for everybody," said Monroe solemnly. "Our old man," he went on to say, "has a high opinion

---

42. Earlsboro was infamous for being the hideout for Pretty Boy Floyd who shared his bank robbery loot with the locals for their hospitality.
43. In 1943 the US War Department acquired fifty-four acres at Grand Junction as a refinery for the Manhattan Project (atomic bomb). Because of wartime secrecy, the Manhattan Project would publicly admit only to purchasing the vanadium, and did not pay the miners for the uranium content.

of himself and his abilities. Can't seem to stay in one place long enough to let paint dry."

"Move around a bit then?"

"Yip, if it weren't the drills, it was the dusk or a half-witted attempt to grow cotton on a pile of rocks. Ya might say we wore the white line right off the blacktop," laughed Monroe.

"We moved around some ourselves," said the cowboy. "My daddy was a buffalo soldier, so we never unpacked." His father had served under Captains Charles T. Boyd and Lewis S. Morey on a search for Pancho Villa, and he was one of the twenty-three buffalo soldiers to have been taken prisoner in Carrizal, Chihuahua, Mexico.

"Almost didn't make it back," the cowboy said somberly, and he touched his old bolo tie with a piece of cyan-green turquoise carved into the shape of a moth. "This here is the only thang I got left of 'em," he said, and then he tossed on another piece of wood.

"How'd he get back?" asked Wyatt, eager for a new story.

"Seems like the Mexican Colonel Rivas decided to execute them, but then the guide talked 'im out of it. Say if he done it, there'd be no way he'd ever get any of their Mexican prisoners back alive, so upon deep reflection, the colonel decided he weren't gonna execute nobody. So, they ended up bringin' 'em all up to Juarez, and then they walked straight over the bridge into El Paso."

The cowboy glanced around and saw that the brothers were inside their heads trying to swim through history they could not change. Concerned that the mood might turn melancholy, he reached over, picked up his guitar, and asked, "Yaw know this'n?" Then he picked a few chords of *"Make Me a Pallet on Your Floor."*[44]

---

44. *"Make Me a Pallet on Your Floor"* (also *"Make Me a Pallet on the Floor,"* *"Make Me a Pallet,"* or *"Pallet on the Floor"*) is a blues/jazz/folk song

"Ya kick it off and we'll fallow ya," said Wyatt as he reached into his shirt pocket and pulled out his mouth harp and followed as though they had been playing together since childhood.

He's a country man, done just moved to town.
He's done sold his cotton, and he's just a walkin' 'round.
Make him down a pallet on your floor.
Make him down a pallet on your floor.
Just make him down a pallet on your floor.
And send him back to the field so he can raise some more.

That night, Wyatt and Monroe slept well and awoke at dawn refreshed. Monroe pulled on his boots and walked the horses down to the water for one last drink before they hit the trail again. Looking across the river he expected to see the cowboy, but to his surprise, his camp was empty. All that was left was an unopened can of pork and beans sitting on a rock.

Dang it, Monroe said to himself, and for a moment he felt shame. *I never did ask his name.* His shame was justified. He had never thought that asking a black man his name was important, and he had servilely ridiculed his younger brother Virgil for his generosity when giving away fresh carp and catfish to the people living in the black section.

"Bet that colored fella is an outlaw," Monroe surmised.

"Na, he's more like a mother-fuckin' gunslinger," Wyatt said. "His hands were steady, and nar a sign of fear."

Once they hit blacktop again, they found themselves on Route 66 where the road wound by abandoned cars picked over by wingless birds of prey in hopes that one man's loss was another man's gain.

---

now considered a standard. The song's origins are somewhat hazy but can be traced to the nineteenth century. The lyrics presented here are from a version by Sam Chatmon.

They overtook a small family making their way to McLean on foot after two of their inner tubes had blown beyond repair.

"If I can round up a couple of tubes, I'll come back and fetch the car," said the gangly man as he set two tattered suitcases down.

"Looks like folks is thankin' thangs left alongside the road is free pickin's," cautioned Wyatt.

"Might not be much of the car left when yaw get back neither," added Monroe. "Might want to think 'bout findin' yourself another plan."

"Already done that," the man said. "I reckon the wife and babies will have to squat somewheres around McLean. I'll catch a westbound and send for 'em after I find work."

Monroe glanced at the man's frail, hollow-eyed wife with a baby on her hip and another child clutching her hand while sucking on the end of an old rag. *Looks like the car ran over her and backed up for good measure,* he thought.

"Wish we could leave yaw somethang," said Wyatt, "but we ain't got a pot to piss in or a winder to toss it outta."

"Don't ya boys fret none," said the man. "We gonna be all right. Good luck to yaw."

As Monroe and Wyatt continued westward, the number of abandoned automobiles grew. Cars bearing plates from Alabama, Tennessee, Georgia, and Mississippi seemed to fail most often, perhaps because they had the furthest to travel, and they had already been on their last legs at the starting gate. Monroe and Wyatt picked over the roadside carnage for food or bits and pieces that could be of use to them in the miles yet to go. Occasionally they would stand at the side of the road in silence, stare across barren fields where once feed crops grew, and wonder about the state of the country and whether there ever would be a return to the general prosperity and abundance their parents recalled. They, having been born during the Depression, only knew a life of loss—loss of food, loss of land, loss of opportunity, loss of dignity and—most of all—loss of trust in authority, as there seemed to be no shortage of men like J. Paul Getty, J. D. Rockefeller, and John Jacob Astor who used human plight to their advantage. If wages were to be had, men like Getty offered them at a depressed rate, pushing the wage disparity ever wider.

There was far less commerce along the highway and more competition for work than they had expected. But the slower pace of riding on the back of a horse gave them a unique perspective. Around Shamrock they spotted an old church-going cotton farmer stuck in a black gumbo trap.[45] They earned one and a half dollars after they pulled his truck free and mucked out a cowshed. The farmer and his wife took pity on the boys and fed them a hot meal of pinto beans and ham hocks, wild spring mustard greens, and warm cornbread with a cold glass of buttermilk. The farmer let them bed down in his barn for a couple of nights after making it clear he did not have enough food or money to keep them on.

Once they had collected a few nights of good sleep on a soft bed of hay, Monroe and Wyatt rose early one morning with a little money in their pockets. Feeling like J. D. Rockefeller, they rode into the nearby town of Shamrock to buy a few canned goods. And as they rode down the main street they read the large billboard announcing they were approaching the only café within a hundred miles. They hitched their horses to a pole outside the U-Drop Inn and headed inside for a 15-cent cup of coffee.

"Now this here's the life," Wyatt said as he leaned back on the tan Naugahyde swivel chair and sipped hot coffee at the counter. "It sho' 'nuff is."

"I do appreciate the fan," said Monroe, "but can't say I see what all the fuss is. Coffee ain't as good as Mamma's."

"I bet there ain't a chipped cup in the whole dang place," said Wyatt as he checked out the café. "Besides, ya ain't gotta strain the grounds through yur teeth."

---

45. "Black gumbo" is a dark soil that is sticky and moldable when wet.

"Is that what ya always pullin' through?"

"And I ain't had nobody so dang purdy pour me a cup," Wyatt said as he eyed the perky young bottle-blonde waitress in her crisp white uniform and starched yellow apron. "Would ya look at Miss Lora Lee!" he continued after reading her plastic name tag pinned just below a small handkerchief that had been folded like a daisy.

The waitress caught him staring at her, so she slowly made her way down the counter, carrying a carafe of coffee and offering free refills.

"Can I top yaw off?" she asked Wyatt as she stopped, shifted her weight to one leg, and flashed a shy smile.

"Why, yes, Miss Lora Lee, you surely can top me off, if ya don't mind," Wyatt said as he locked his blue eyes with hers. "Say," he continued, "how would ya like to come on out to California with me?"

"I just might," Lora Lee whispered as she shot a quick glance around to see who might be within hearing range. "What yaw drivin'?"

Lora Lee might have been young, but she was not blind. She often told people that all her mother's stupid children had died. She knew the town was hemorrhaging and would never bounce back. Working at the U-Drop Inn, she saw all sorts of fool-hearted people heading down the long white line. She also had met many on their way back who were worse off than when they had left.

"He ain't drivin'!" piped up Monroe. "He's ridin' an old nag named Nancy, and she threw a shoe about a mile back."

Lora Lee lifted her chin and leaned forward to get a better view through one of the café's large front windows, and to her surprise, she saw two horses tied to a pole. "Figures!" she mumbled to herself. "All the pips drive junked-up tin cans, and all the greaseballs drive new ones. These two ain't even got a decent saddle."

"What do you take me for, a twit?" she snapped. "I wouldn't go to a dogfight with yaw. And if yaw know what's good for ya, you'd start driftin' *now*!"

For fear of having a pot of hot coffee dumped on them, Monroe and Wyatt leaped from their chairs, downed the last drops of their coffee, and tossed thirty-five cents onto the Formica countertop. "Keep the change, hun," Monroe said as he grabbed his hat and headed toward the front door, wearing a wide grin.

"Ya don't know what ya be missin'!" Wyatt yelled back to Lora Lee as he let the café's screen door slam behind him.

"Kiss my go-to-hell!" yelled Lora Lee as she stood holding the coffee carafe in one hand and the thirty-five cents in the other. But to herself she said, "But Lord Jesus, they were a couple of aces!"

There were nights when Monroe and Wyatt would bed down near abandoned, windburned-out prairie farmhouses whose broke-back farmers had packed up what they could carry and headed west years earlier after their patch of ground slid back to the bank. When the boys happened upon such a homestead, they often pulled water from hand-dug wells and, if lucky, they managed to scrape together a little grain that had been overlooked by hungry field mice in the dilapidated barns and outbuildings.

On nights when the sky was clear, they laid back on their saddles near a warm fire and watched their cobbled horses graze in overgrown kitchen gardens that once had been caringly nurtured by a God-fearing woman who prayed nightly for a better life for her children. Under the constellations, with all the confidence of youth, they surmised how they would not have made the same mistakes as those now so forlorn. It was all conjecture, for they had yet to be tested.

Pulling off their boots, they ate from a can of beans and a box of soda crackers or made sandwiches of soft bread and sliced baloney bought at the meat counter of a family-run market, pitching the peeled casings to the side.

"If anybody wanted to find us, all they'd have to do is follow the trail of baloney skins," Monroe joked as he tossed another casing into a scrub.

"How much further do ya thank we gotta go yet till we hit Bakersfield?" asked Wyatt.

"I don't rightly know, but I reckon a fer piece yet. I figure we might wanna give these here horses a rest—maybe trade for a truck."

Bakersfield had been on their minds since their daddy's sister Ona started sending letters pleading for him to pack up and come out there. Monroe and Wyatt recalled sitting around the kerosene lantern as their mother read letters from aunts and uncles saying that, although the employers were taking advantage of workers' impoverished situations by paying deflationary wages, they had pretty much all landed jobs and were scraping by. The letters painted a picture, not so much of satisfaction or hope, but of survival. Their bellies may not have been full, but they did not seem to be in dire need.

So as not to appear braggadocious, they carefully crafted words that described moments of joy—such as Sunday swims in the Kern River after a late Saturday night in honky-tonks discovering what would become known as the Bakersfield Sound.[46]

---

46. The Bakersfield Sound is said to have started in 1949-50 by simple-living people who had to leave their farms to go West.
While Buck Owens and Merle Haggard are often the first artists that come to mind regarding the Bakersfield Sound, it was musicians and songwriters like Oscar Whittington, Eugene Moles, Jelly Sanders, Johnny Cuevelo, and a host of others who created the rawer, twangier, and rockier country sound in the smoke-filled honky-tonks of Bakersfield.

Just on the outskirts of Albuquerque, they came into a thriving agricultural area and easily found the local seed and feed. It was surrounded by an assortment of trucks parked haphazardly as though someone had tossed them like dice in a bunco game. They tied the horses to a wooden banister, brushed the dust off their hats, and marched into the feed store with the confidence and swagger of a teenager who had just gotten laid. The four men in striped bib overalls standing around the counter stopped talking and turned toward the entry when they heard the cowbell on the door sound off.

"Hey, fellas, anybody here wanna trade a truck or car, goin' or not, for two horses?" asked Monroe.

"They still got wear on the hoof," added Wyatt.

The men in overalls glanced at each other before breaking into belly laughs that made the metal hooks on their overalls jingle like sleigh bells. One of the fellas finally spoke up after the laughter died down and said he had a '36 Ford truck, and he was ready to swap.

"It doesn't run, mind you," said the farmer. "The engine froze up going on three, maybe four years back."

"Mister, you got yourself a deal!" said Wyatt, and then he laughed as he shook hands to make the deal binding.

The farmer, Douglas Moneymaker, had no need for horses: he had a new International Harvester and two dozen field hands at the ready, and when he needed it, he could round up a hundred cotton pickers before noon. Nor did he need a gift for his horse-crazy granddaughter, upon whom he doted. She rode a thoroughbred, sitting high on a custom saddle that was elaborately carved with a thousand taps made by a tiny wooden hammer in a little shop in the small town of Magdalena, Sonora, Mexico. What he lacked and was searching for was a link to his youth, but not to the firm triceps and abs on the lean and powerful body that he once had, but to the hunger for purpose that fueled gumption, the power he had felt when he was a young boy who had become a man on the battlefields of World War I.

Without asking, Moneymaker knew he had more than his Southern roots in common with Monroe and Wyatt, for he too had broken his daddy's heart when he failed to return to the family home along the Cumberland River near Nashville, Tennessee, to take up a job at Old Hickory[47] after the war. As a layer[48] in the artillery, he set his sights on more than the enemy across no-man's-land.[49] He learned to stand back and put himself in his own crosshairs, and nothing shows a man's true worth more than the life he lives after being mustered out, and these boys reminded him of that fact.

Mr. Moneymaker lent Monroe and Wyatt a box of tools and gave them a place to bed down in one of his barns next to giant sacks of cotton seed gleaned from his cotton processing plant to feed his small but growing dairy operation.

"Those bales will give you some insulation. Don't let the sunshine fool ya; it gets pretty cold at night," said Moneymaker.

"Yes, sir, we done found that out already," Wyatt replied.

"Well, better let you boys get at it. You still have over 800 miles to go, and some of 'em is hard miles," said Moneymaker as he ambled over to give instructions to his foreman.

It only took a few days for the boys to get the engine unlocked, and they fused together a rope they found in the barn to create a makeshift fan belt. The rods were knocking a bit, and there was a small oil leak, but they figured it would hold out until they could buy a two-gallon can of PurAvis motor oil, and before long they were driving flat out down Route 66, heading straight into Albuquerque and feeling like they were highwaymen on the run.

---

47. Old Hickory was a gunpowder plant the federal government authorized DuPont to build in 1918. It was a massive undertaking resulting in the migration of thousands. The plant went into production in July 1918 and, within a few months, was producing 700,000 pounds of smokeless powder per day.

48. A layer is responsible for the gun's alignment and elevation.

49. "No-man's-land" is a term used by soldiers to describe the ground between two opposing trenches.

Chapter 7

Up the Road Apiece

New Mexico, Arizona, 1947

BY THE TIME MONROE and Wyatt hit Albuquerque's city limits, the sun was falling behind the Sandia Mountains.

"Would ya looky there!" said Monroe as he pushed hard on the brakes, killing the engine in the middle of the road.

"Sho's purdy," agreed Wyatt, "but we might not get this dang truck started again."

"Ain't that a fact now!" Monroe snickered, but he made no move to turn the engine over. It did not take long for several cars to pile up behind them. Some slowly passed while a few stopped to ask if they could be of help.

"No, sir, we'z just gettin' acquainted with that there mountain over yonder," Monroe replied. The incensed drivers would shake their heads and yell, "Goddamn Okies!"

Just inside the city limits, Monroe spotted a large, newly-paved parking lot in front of the Hicks and Olson Tires store with a "Closed" sign hanging from its door. Monroe suggested they settle in for the night among the parked cars and trucks that customers had dropped off.

"We might even work off a set of tires," Wyatt said hopefully after Monroe jumped the curb and landed their truck between a Hudson and a Pontiac.

"We'll be purdy much hidden here," Monroe said as he looked from one side to the other. "Ain't nobody gonna be lookin' at the ugly girl." Then he cut the engine.

They sat back on the cab's bench seat, tightening their denim jackets around them to ward off the evening chill. Monroe grew sleepy and flipped down the sun visor to block the light from the big, flashing General Tire neon sign that hung from the inside of Hicks and Olson Tires' full plate-glass window.

"Well, that son of a gun!" called out Monroe in surprise as he picked up the crisp five-dollar[50] bill that had been folded like some kind of butterfly that had fallen on to his lap.

"If that don't beat all," whispered Wyatt. "That there's seed money. And right now, I'm nearly starved. Let's fill up the bread-basket."

Around the corner from the tire store, they found a hash joint. And after they settled into a couple of wobbly chairs, they waved over a middle-aged waitress who looked like she walked on stumps.

With one hand on her hip, she looked Monroe and Wyatt over and, in the voice of a fisherman's wife, she barked, "You boys have any money?"

Insulted, Monroe answered, "Hold your hat on, Jenny!" then fished through his jean pockets until he found the folded bill. "Now what ya got to say for yourself!" he continued, and he waved it in her face.

Incensed, she threw two greasy, plastic menus down so hard that they almost slid off the table. And as she turned to leave, she shouted, "And my name is *not* Jenny!"

"Hee-haw!" brayed Wyatt.

---

50. Five dollars in 1947 was equivalent in buying power to about $61.34 in 2021.

With only bones remaining from the fried chicken and only backwash in their beer bottles, Wyatt sat back, sucked air through his front teeth, laughed, and said, "Dang, if we ain't et enough chicken to be fartin' feathers all night."

Just before dawn cracked the following morning, Monroe and Wyatt crept into the bathroom at the Texaco station next door to the tire shop for a wash-up and rinse-out. With their hair still wet and slicked back, they opened the heavy double glass doors, each one painted with the initials "H and O" in a heavy black New Detroit font.

Mr. Hicks explained to the brothers that a jack had given way, and his business partner, Mr. Olson, was laid up and could wind up losing his leg. He shook his head and said how the timing could not have been worse as they had just invested in a new buffing machine, hoping to make a killing on retreads.

Monroe shoved his hands deep into his back pockets and shifted his weight from one leg to another. As he stared at his feet, he said with empathy, "Dadgum it, and all them there cars stackin' up."

After a few moments of silence, Mr. Hicks rose and made them an offer. "Tell ya what, boys. I'll try ya out for a day. If you're as good as you say, I can give you work until Mr. Olson gets back on his feet."

"Well, let's get ta doin' it then," said Wyatt as he and Monroe started to roll up their sleeves.

"Slow your roll there, fellas," said Mr. Hicks as he flashed a "Whoa, mule!" flat palm in the air. "You have to put on coveralls."

The boys raised their eyebrows as they followed Mr. Hicks to what looked to be a catch-all room. Against one wall stood a mop bucket next to a utility sink. Along another wall stood four full-length lockers.

"Here you go, Wyatt," said Mr. Hicks as he tossed a pair of dark blue six-pocket coveralls with the letters H&O embroidered over the left breast pocket. "And here's one for you, Monroe."

"You can call me Roe."

"All right then, Roe, and you can call me Bernie," replied Mr. Hicks, then he continued to give them their instructions. "This is an uptown, modern establishment that caters to respectful families and businesspeople. We must always be clean and polite. We are a 'yes' business, so the customer is always right. We have a reputation for providing great customer service that we protect at all costs."

"Well, ya can count on us!" Monore called out after Bernie had already started out of the utility room. Bernie was thinking the boy's daddy must be cutting the herd, but what he needed was more brawn than brain, and the boys looked healthy enough.

"That's right, Bernie," chimed in Wyatt. "We'z polite when it comes to housewives."

"Dang it, Wyatt," snickered Monroe, "ya gonna get us fired before we get hired!"

Bernard Hicks ticked all the too-familiar boxes of an up-and-comer in a small town. He had been the favored pitcher at the local high school with many of his fans placing bets that he would be picked up by a major league team. But he stumbled and fell, had no one to blame but himself, and wound up married one week after graduation. His new father-in-law put up the down payment for the tire shop, and thirty-six years later, his wife Lydia still would not let him forget it.

Lydia had threatened to walk out on him the night before when he tried to cut her off after her fourth sidecar,[51] and she was hell-bent on taking the business with her as it was her daddy's money that got it started.

---

51. A sidecar is a cocktail that is a mix of brandy, lemon juice, and orange liqueur.

Bernard considered his top two options. They were more like dreams—fantasies really—that would not let go, clinging to him like the bulbous toes of a persistent gecko. He could walk away with the clothes on his back a free man, maybe travel to a sunny beach in Southern California or catch up with the Union Pacific and ride to Cheyenne Wyoming and wander the plains with the wild buffalo. Then he took a step back and stared at the bald fifty-four-year-old with a flat ass gawking back at him through his mirrored closet doors and concluded his third option was the most logical. He would stay with Lydia and stop insisting she cut down on her drinking. After all, if he wasn't buying, she would just find someone else who would, perhaps even one of his Rotary Club brothers. And from that moment on, he reasoned, it would be best to consider her just another misguided wife from the Inner Wheel.[52] He could live with that; he'd have to.

By 3 p.m. the H&O parking lot was empty, and customers were dropping off cars, trucks, and light farm equipment to be serviced the following day. That night, after proving themselves, Monroe and Wyatt negotiated a wage of thirty cents per hour, plus a bonus for upselling customers that would be paid in thirty days in the form of a set of retreads. Pleased with the deal, Bernard picked up the tab for a steak dinner and got the boys settled into a twelve-dollar-a week flophouse on the south side.

It was not long before customers, kittenish housewives in particular, were calling H&O requesting service for low air and flats in the early afternoons after putting their children down for a nap.

Bernard had seen his share of femme-fatales, and he was almost certain his wife was one, but he himself was a businessman who still felt he had to prove himself to his eighty-seven-year-old father-in-law, and two dollars tax free spend like three. He had seen the flirtatious exchanges the boys made with the female customers who picked up their husbands' cars, and he was sure

---

52. Inner Wheel is an organization for the wives and daughters of Rotarians who generally prohibited women from becoming members.

the boys would get on board; besides, he knew they were itching to get back on the road, and a little under-the-table money would be welcomed. So it did not take long before business was booming and more popular than S&H Green Stamps.[53]

"Susanne Casters got another nail," Bernard yelled into the shop, "and she needs one of you to go out and fix her tire so she can pick up her husband from work by 4:30!"

Monroe ambled over to the curing machine Wyatt was working and killed the switch.

"Did ya hear Bernard?" asked Monroe.

"No, what's goin' on?"

Monroe told him about Susanne.

"I went last time," Wyatt said.

"Let's draw straws," suggested Monroe.

"Nope, I done it last time," Wyatt insisted, and he flipped the curing machine back on.

"She likes you a bunch," Monroe barked over the piercing noise.

Wyatt shook his head while Monroe kicked the curing machine and stomped away.

Monroe casually climbed into the H&O truck and slowly headed north toward the outskirts of town. Then he drove onto a dirt road that led into a small canyon until he came to a stop in front of a small, weather-beaten house with a rusted tin roof that nestled between a small grove of cottonwoods. Susanne kept the windows of her small house darkened with heavy

---

53. S&H Green Stamps were a line of trading stamps popular in the United States from the 1930s until the late 1980s. They were distributed as part of a rewards program operated by the Sperry & Hutchinson company (S&H) founded in 1896 by Thomas Sperry and Shelley Byron Hutchinson.

drapes, and the front flowerbeds had long been forgotten, making the house look lifeless.

Monroe killed the engine and sat behind the wheel as he gazed at the wash flapping on the clothesline, thinking it looked like the same wash that was hanging the last time he was there. Then he saw Susanne leaning against the dilapidated porch post, watching for the dust rising from a fast-moving truck. No matter what time of day or what day of the week, Susanne always wore the same outfit. Her hair was the color of black licorice and pulled back into a ponytail. She wore her husband's white shirt fastened by a loose knot, exposing her belly, gripping her breasts and nipples that were hard from the cold wind that blew up the canyon.

Monroe shook his head, reached for the door handle, and thought, "Dang, that girl's pants are so tight I can see her religion."

Monroe relished the attention women showered on him. He could tell when they powdered and perfumed themselves and slipped into something soft and silky in anticipation of his arrival. They reminded him of Miss Ellie, and he fancied himself a strong and fit US marshal.

But Susanne was different. She made him feel ugly and dirty. Where other women let him lead, Susanne was strong and unapologetic. She squeezed his balls, sunk her teeth into his nipples, and made him feel as though he had no control. Her conduct conjured up a specific memory that sickened him, and there was no place in his memory he could hide from that time when, on a whim, he and two older boys had sneaked into the murky cellar of a men's club operated by a secret society. After their eyes adjusted to the dark, they found about a dozen of the society members seated on church-like pews in their long white robes, some peering through holes in their hoods while others were brave enough to let their faces show. The men were gawking at an old, silent black-and-white film they projected onto a white wall.

Luckily for the three boys, the men were fiercely focused on the film and would not have heard a cyclone coming. The boys crouched behind two large wooden crates to wait it out. After regaining their bravado, they peered over the crates, and although the film was grainy and jumped around, Monroe could make out a man in pinstriped pajamas carrying a naked woman across the room and placing her on a metal-framed bed, letting her legs dangle over a mattress covered in soiled ticking. The thought of lying on the filthy mattress made him feel queasy and nasty, so he quickly looked away, letting his eyes bounce around the room. And there, in the last row, he saw two men gently reach under the other's white robes, then let their bodies slip further down on the bench like jelly falling from the edge of a table until their eyes fluttered and closed. Monroe's eyes shot back to the screen again just as the man separated the woman's legs and slowly inserted himself. Monroe's legs began to shake, and his knees began to collapse. He turned away from the screen and, with his back to the wooden crates, he let his body quietly slide down until he was sitting flat on the cement floor.

"Well, looky there. Roe went all gaga!"[54] whispered one of the older boys as he pointed out the wet spot on Monroe's jeans. He would have jumped up and killed the kid, but they were hiding in a room full of Klansmen.

"Took you long enough," Susanne said as she crushed her lipstick-stained cigarette with the toe of her worn-out loafers and tapped on the window, startling Monroe.

He reluctantly jumped out of the truck and walked around her dark gray Buick Special Coup. "Where's the flat?" he asked after seeing all the tires were full of air.

"Could have been something I imagined, or it could just be a slow leak. I was hearing hissing this morning," Susanne answered. "Anyway, the husband said to have it looked into."

I just bet he did! thought Monroe, but aloud he said, "I'm gonna have to charge ya no matter," and he walked around all four

---

54. Slang for sexually aroused from the 1930s.

again and gave them each a solid kick. And for a fleeting moment he questioned how he could have so quickly created a life in the presence of both the Devil and the Lord.

"Well, I guess you had better come on up to the house then, Roe," said Susanne as she sashayed through the darkened door.

Monroe trudged onto the creaking porch, pushing aside a gray cat that was rubbing against his pant leg.

"I still haven't gotten a new broom since the last time you were here," Monroe heard Susanne say from somewhere deep within the dark house.

"You don't need a broom," Monroe mumbled under his breath. "What you need is a shovel." He then made his way into the house, cautiously treading over piles of newspapers, soiled clothes, and dirty dinner plates until his eyes adjusted.

"Missed you, baby," Susanne said in a voice that was more maniacal than sultry. She dropped the needle onto an LP and let Sammy Kaye's smoky voice whisper *"That's My Desire."*[55] Susanne slowly rocked her hips and shuffled toward Monroe until she was close enough to cup her hands around his ass and pull him tight against her.

Monroe crinkled his nose. "You're hitting the bottle pretty hard," he said as he pulled his face back.

"What do you care?" she said, and she reached up with her long, red lacquered nails and grabbed a handful of his thick, wavy black hair. "You're getting paid." Then she covered his mouth with her lips and burrowed a hole into which she slipped her tongue. With the power of an ancient serpent, she wrapped an arm around his waist, pulled him closer, and pushed her pelvis into his groin.

---

55. *"That's My Desire"* was recorded in 1947 by Sammy Kaye with vocals from Don Cornell & The Kaydets. Music was by Helmy Kresa and lyrics by Carroll Loveday.

Without saying a word, Monroe laid two dollars down on the H&O counter in front of Bernard and headed back to the shop.

"You look a little worn out there, Roe," Bernard said without looking up from his paperwork. "Susanne has a special way of wearing even a young man out."

"She French-kisses like a washing machine. I need ta get some Lavoris," answered Monroe without stopping.

"I need you well-rested tonight," called Bernard. "I have a special job for you and Wyatt tomorrow."

Monroe stopped and turned toward Bernard. "Tomorrow's Sunday. We're closed."

"I know, Roe, but for this job to be effective, it has to be done on a Sunday, and this Sunday to be exact." Bernard filled him in on the job, then he sweetened the deal. "If you get it done, you get your tires early." Bernard had weighed his special offer before he extended it. There was the risk the boys would take off once they got what they needed. But he was still hoping they might stick around a while longer, collecting on their side jobs, or at least until Olson was back on his feet.

That night, at an out-of-the-way joint called the Alabi, the boys met up with Lenard from the neighboring Texaco station. He was an overweight, baby-faced fella who, according to Wyatt, "put the *ick* in *slick*." Over a few beers and dried out meatloaf they finalized the details on Bernard's plan.

Once satisfied, Lenard took off with the drunk girl who had been sitting at the bar. Peeking over an umbrella drink, she made goo-goo eyes at him all night. "It's a sure bet that if you pick an ugly one, you'll never go home empty-handed," he laughed on his way out. Monroe and Wyatt rolled their eyes and yelled out as Lenard helped the drunk girl put on her coat. Then they took off for their flophouse to make their other plans.

At seven on Sunday morning, Leonard picked up Monroe and Wyatt in his tow truck and drove to the Immaculate Conception where they took cover in the alley behind the church. It was Easter Sunday, and the church parking lot was filling up fast with church regulars and bi-annual worshippers.

"Why the hell *this* Sunday?" whispered Lenard.

"Because he's goin' for impact," answered Monroe as he jumped out of the cab and walked slowly around the church to size up the situation.

"Good news," he said, and he smiled as he jumped back into the cab. "Service starts at eight, and they blocked the car off with cones so he can get out front ways or back ways—makes no never mind. We got a clear shot."

After allowing the latecomers to clear the parking lot, Monroe and Wyatt grabbed tire irons and calmly marched toward a shiny burgundy Cadillac with a set of new whitewalls and quickly popped off the hubcaps and loosened the lug nuts. Lenard backed up the tow truck and lowered the hook so Wyatt could hoist the front end of the car while Monroe placed a scissor jack under the rear end. Once the front end was in the air a few inches, Monroe and Wyatt pulled off the tires and threw them into the back of the tow truck. Lenard lowered the front while Monroe lifted the scissor jack just enough for him and Wyatt to remove the back tires and roll them to the truck. Then they jumped into the cab.

Just as Lenard was pulling away, Monroe slammed his hand on the dashboard and yelled, "Hold up! Hold up! Forgot one thang!" Then he grabbed something from under the seat and ran back to the Cadillac.

When they pulled out, Father Theophilus Martin's Cadillac was sitting on metal, and taped to his windshield was a note written on a roll of butcher paper, large enough for the flock to read from ten feet away:

"Pay to all what is owed to them." – Romans 13:7

In a week's time, the boys had a newer set of tires mounted on their old truck rims, and they had replaced the rope with a *bona fide* fan belt.

"Wish you boys would reconsider," said Bernard as he draped a Minnequa[56] canvas automobile water bag[57] across their truck's radiator cap. "Well, anyway, here's a little something to remember us by."

"Ain't that somethin'," Wyatt said as he patted the two-gallon water bag and read the slogan aloud: "'Road Runner Land of Enchantment,' and enchantin' it sho' 'nuff is."

"Well," continued Bernard, "just make sure you take your time. You rebuilt the engine, but it still has a lot of wear on it. And for the love of Pete, slow down. There's a curve up around Mesita they call 'Dead Man's Curve,' and they ain't lying neither. Lydia lost her sister and brother-in-law on that curve, and she ain't been right since." Bernard took a long pause, placed his hands on his hips, and looked up and down the street before he continued. "And honk if you can't see over the hill or around a corner. That thing has a horn, right?"

Monroe and Wyatt nodded and held their tongues, letting Bernard come to his words naturally. They owed him that much.

"I know you both to be tenderhearted, but don't be taken in by do-gooders who weave a good story. You got to do what you got to do, and I know that," Bernard continued, "but just know it ain't what you might expect out there. You most likely will not find that land of milk and honey." Then he paused again before

---

56. Minnequa is a Native American word that means "to drink." It often appeared on flex canvas water bags in the Southwest with an image of a native chief.

57. Flex canvas water bags were often used to help cool an engine. The strap was hung from the radiator cap, and the canvas bag holding the water would be placed in front of the radiator itself. As the wind blew the water off the bag and onto the radiator, it would give it a slight cooling effect.

he added, "I found that out the hard way, but if you find yourself needing to come back, remember, you need not go back all the way. New Mexico has its finer points."

"Yes, sir," said Monroe after he was sure Bernard was finished with his dos and don'ts. Then the boys shook hands with him before leaping into the cab of their thirty-six flathead Ford. Monroe gave the gas pedal a few hits to pump the gas into the fuel line and then cranked it up. They weren't more than a block before they started feeling their adrenalin kick in, the adrenalin that makes the heartbeat faster when faced with the unknown, the anticipation of an adventure that could lead to possible death. Their minds kept wanting to poke holes in the veil that hid what was ahead for them, yet their fear forbade it, lest they turn back to where they had come.

The highway followed the Rio San Jose and touched the base of Mt. Taylor, the tallest mountain the brothers had ever seen. As the road dipped and rose again, they would lay on the horn and jokingly yell, "This one's fer you, Bernie!"

Filled with bravado and buffoonery, they bounced up and down on the springs of the truck's battered bench seat, imagining they were their childhood heroes, Black Jack Ketchum, Charlie Bowdre, and Billy the Kid, outlaws hiding among the Indians in the high cliff dwellings carved into the landscape. They were so tightly swaddled in their capricious tales that they missed the yellow road sign that warned, "Hairpin Curve Ahead."

Monroe's knuckles squeezed the large steering wheel, and his right foot let up on the gas and gave the brake pedal a few taps, resisting the temptation to push it all the way to the floor knowing it could cause the truck to spin out.

"The horn!" yelled Wyatt. "Hit the horn!"

Monroe downshifted, causing the truck to jerk backward before it slowed down, but they were still moving too fast for the curve. With both hands back on the wheel, Monroe tapped the brakes again until he felt he had regained control of the truck, then he peeled one hand off and laid on the horn as he tried to stay in the far-right lane. As he guided the nose of the truck into the hairpin, he could see a black truck piled with wooden crates filled with live chickens coming toward him. He edged the Ford closer to the shoulder, which caused the right tires to act like shooters, knuckling down and kicking up rocks like nibs in a game of marbles that pinged the undercarriage. The black truck hugged the ridge, lifting its right tires, which caused the wooden crates to lean and send the birds into a panic with feathers flying. Monroe focused on the loose gravel on his right. The tires had been upgraded, but they were retreads.

Wyatt leaned out the passenger window as he yelled, "Cuttin' it a little close, Roe!" Monroe pulled their truck closer to the center of the road just as the cab of the chicken truck was even with theirs. He stared into the other driver's face, and they locked eyes for a split second. The other driver was an old man wearing a Panama hat, and he gave Monroe a nod. Then they heard the scraping of metal on metal. Pumped full of adrenalin, Monroe pressed the throttle to the floorboard and gunned it out of the curve.

"Only lost the side mirror. Well, what's behind us ain't important," screeched Wyatt like a hyaena as he jumped up and down in his seat.

Banging on the wheel, Monroe shouted, "We'z ridin' on Lady Luck all the ways ta Cal-i-forn-i-a, that's fer damn sure!"

Chapter 8
Jim Charlie
New Mexico, Arizona, 1946

MONROE HAD BEEN running flat out until about five miles west of Chambers when the engine began to knock louder than usual, forcing him to pull to the side of the road and popped the hood.

With his shirt sleeves rolled up, he stood on the front bumper, leaned in over the engine block and announced, "She's spewin' all right."

"What ya reckon we should do?" inquired Wyatt.

"Run 'er till she blows, I guess."

Monroe drained the last drop of their reserve oil into the engine like a drunk upending a bottle before tossing it into a ditch. With both hands, he began to guide the rusted hood back down when he heard a stranger's deep voice behind him.

"You need oil."

Startled, Monroe let his hands slip, and the hood fell with such a crash that Wyatt, who was taking a leak, quickly zipped up and ran to the front of the truck.

Spinning around, Monroe saw a tall, lean man towering over him. Pinned between the truck and the man, Monroe demanded, "Ya better step on back, mister!" as he dropped his hand into his front pocket to fish for his pocketknife. "Where in the Sam hill did ya come from?"

As Monroe kept his eyes focused on the stranger, Wyatt scanned the landscape of softly-rolling mounds of sand, cactus, and gullies carved by spring rains that meandered their way toward Mexico. But there was not a single sign of human life, let alone a vehicle.

With his back still pressed tightly against the hood, Monroe tried to read the strange man only two feet in front of him. The stranger stood tall with a backbone that mimicked the pride of an old growth tree. He had planted his well-worn boots squarely on the ground and showed no signs of aggression or retreat. The bright sunlight rolled over his smooth chestnut-colored skin, cascading over the deep valleys on his face and across a nose that was as sharp and powerful as an eagle's beak. His long black hair was as dark as his eyes and shone like polished obsidian. Although hidden beneath the long sleeves of his dark shirt, Monroe could tell the man's arms were as strong as petrified wood.

"You need oil!" repeated the man.

"Don't look like *you's* carryin' any," Monroe replied sharply as he slid himself along the edge of the hood, getting himself caught on the Road Runner water bag.

"'Where'd ya come from?" asked Wyatt. "Ain't a dadgum thang out here."

"I been away. Now I walk home."

Looking the stranger up and down, Wyatt said, "Well, ain't sure how far we gonna get, but we can carry ya as far westward as we can."

The three piled back into the cab, leaving the empty can of oil along the roadside.

Other than exchanging names, they rode in silence. And although the sun shone brightly upon the sage-speckled desert, the cold winter chill was not yet willing to let go of its grip on a spring day, and the stranger, Jim Charlie, leaned his elbow out the open window, staring at the road ahead while Monroe and Wyatt pulled up their collars and said nothing until they rolled into the outskirts of Holbrook.

Pulling into Whiting Brothers service station bell, Monroe said he was going to see if they had any used oil, and he made a point of taking the key.

"And I'm a gonna unfold my kneecaps and talk to a man about a horse," announced Wyatt as he glanced at Jim Charlie, thinking he was going to do the same. But Jim Charlie made no move to open his door. Instead, he pulled his elbow in and rolled up the dirty window.

You might have thought Monroe and Wyatt would have had a stash of cash from working a steady job in New Mexico. But a fool and his money are soon parted, and nothing spends sweeter than new money in poor young hands. When the world still lies at your feet, your body is bursting with prevailing power, and your faith is unshakeable, you trust that your "bowl of flour shall not be exhausted, nor shall the jar of oil be empty."[58] So when the boys left Albuquerque, they rode out in new hats, silver belt buckles, and custom boots.

From the inside of the cab, Jim Charlie watched Monroe push his palms down into his back pockets as he shifted his weight from one foot to the other. He did not need to hear the conversation to know what the gas attendant said. *It's always the same with them,* he thought.

Opening the driver's door, Monroe poked his head into the cab. "Looks like we ain't gettin' any oil, so I'll be damned if I spend money on gas here."

"I get the next tank," said Jim Charlie. "Let's go."

---

58. 1 Kings 17:14 New American Standard Bible.

"Come on!" Monroe yelled to Wyatt just as he was leaving the restroom and rubbing his fingers through his wet hair. "Let's blow this dump."

Wyatt slid into the middle seat from the driver's side and glanced at Jim Charlie, then back at Monroe, and whispered, "Reckon that'd be why they call 'em 'wooden.'"

"Hush up. He's gittin' the next tank," Monroe whispered out of the side of his mouth.

Monroe peeled out of the Whiting Brothers service station, spitting gravel until it pinged off the gas pumps, then slammed his left palm down on the steering wheel. "Sons of bitches!" he yelled. After a minute or two he turned and asked, "Where we headed, Jim Charlie?"

Jim Charlie directed Monroe down a residential side street, then told him to stop the truck. The boys watched Jim Charlie amble up to the side of a house, pull a knife, and cut a three-foot chunk off a green garden hose before serenely heading back to the truck with the confidence of a man who knew he was invisible.

"Must be kin," snickered Wyatt.

Monroe had turned back onto a main street when Wyatt spotted a post office. "Pull over, Monroe. I wanna run in and get a postcard off ta Mamma."

Monroe yanked the wheel and pulled along the curb.

"Give me 2 cents, and I run in. You take too long," insisted Jim Charlie as he stuck his hand in front of Wyatt's face.

Pulling his head away from Jim Charlie's hand, Wyatt said, "Where you been? They's 3 cents now." And he chuckled.

Wyatt dug into his pocket, pulled out a dime, and said, "And ya better bring back the change."

As Jim Charlie walked toward the post office, Monroe whispered, "Notice that he's got on two pairs of pants?"

Leaning his head back against the seat, Wyatt rested his eyes and said, "Yip, and those there black-and-white striped ones ain't long underwears, neither."

Once inside the post office Jim Charlie took his place behind three women, all wearing hats, who were waiting in line. Their powdered faces, painted lips, and swishing hemlines did nothing to veil their indignation. Upon seeing him come through the doorway, the women bunched together, leaving a large gap between them and Jim Charlie as though his heathen soul would leave an imprint on their blackened hearts. The blonde-haired woman with the pug nose and eyes the color of squid ink pinched her face up like a clothespin and looked him over from his head to his boots. Then she nudged the other two women who, in turn, stared at the cuff of his pants and began to whisper. But when Jim Charlie met their gaze, they became skittish, retracting their tongues of self-righteousness and turning their backs to him, which pleased him very much as it gave him a chance to scan the unfamiliar room at his own pace. And to his shock, there on the bulletin board of the United States Post Office, next to an advertisement for a new postage stamp commemorating the one hundredth anniversary of the United States, was a black-and-white poster of a much younger man he barely recognized.

Monroe elbowed Wyatt. "Look alive, here comes Jim Charlie, and he looks like he's in a hurry to get on out of here." Monroe then started up the truck.

Wyatt sat up in the seat and watched Jim Charlie crush a sheet of paper in his large, callused hands and push it into his pants pocket as he hurried toward the truck.

"You write your mother another day," Jim Charlie said harshly as he slammed the dime down on the metal dashboard.

Monroe quickly pulled away from the curb and said to Jim Charlie, "Alrighty then, where's to?"

With the gas tank full, all they needed was oil, and Jim Charlie had a plan that would give them enough to take them all the way to California. All it required was a little side trip.

Once they turned onto a rough road, Jim Charlie took the wheel and guided the truck down a washed-out, red-parched riverbed that patiently awaited June's flash flood waters that would turn the desert's speckled mounds into sprays of wildflowers, gravel ghost, desert marigolds, hall's sun cups, Indian paintbrush, and dozens more. All stood at the ready, just like their ancestors had, in that exact spot, a million years ago.

Veering off the riverbed, Jim Charlie made his own road on windblown sand, traversing shrubs and trees and circling towering sandstone buttes. Monroe and Wyatt forgot about the oil and fell with ease into the unfamiliar landscape.

There was a time when Jim Charlie knew every coyote by name and every raptor by sight. But he had been gone over twenty years, and he had no expectation that he would be remembered. His only hope was to see his young son, now a grown man, so he could enter the underworld through a sacred hole in the canyon where he would meet the One-Horned God who would look into his heart and know that his intentions were honorable. Then he would be allowed to follow the Sun Trail to the village of the Cloud People.

Jim Charlie let his outstretched arm catch the wind from the open window and slowly, unconsciously, his body began to settle into the seat like a feather slowing falling from a bird in flight—tipping one way, then the other, turning somersaults in a free fall, until he sucked in a deep breath from the desert floor, then slothfully exhaled, knowing the Chihuahuan raven had flown ahead to announce his homecoming.

He knew his people would exonerate him for his transgressions, but glancing at Monroe and Wyatt's bobbing heads, he knew he would never be forgiven for leading two white men into a sacred place, especially the one whose eye colors did not match—a ghost man, a man who could see in two worlds.

The late afternoon sun began to dip behind a large plateau that hurled its large black velvety shadow over the ground, and the temperature began to sink like a heavy weight. Jim Charlie's heart began to pound under his breast bones, and he could feel how close he was. He could smell javelina[59] cooking on a low fire. Jumping on the brake, he brought the truck to an abrupt stop, throwing Monroe and Wyatt forward.

For the first time, Monroe remembered the oil. "Where in tarnation is you fixin' to find oil around here?" he demanded.

"It's close. You wait here," Jim Charlie answered as he grabbed the door handle. "Don't leave. There are many dangerous and hungry animals here," he explained. "I will be back." And before Monroe or Wyatt could protest, Jim Charlie was out of sight.

Monroe could not tell how long Jim Charlie had been gone since neither he nor Wyatt owned a wristwatch. But it was growing darker and colder, and Monroe was impatiently pacing around the truck. "Don't waste all the ammo!" he yelled to Wyatt, who had pulled Clyde's rifle from under the seat and was shooting holes in a cactus.

Heading back toward the truck, Wyatt waved his hand high. "Here comes old Jim Charlie," he announced.

Jim Charlie carried tea in an earthen jug, and food and in a woven blanket which he laid on the tailgate.

"My brother has gone to get oil for you, but it will take a few hours. I bring you food and drink," Jim Charlie explained. "The tea is bitter, but it will warm you. Build a small fire with ground brush to help keep you safe." And with those few words, he disappeared again.

Monroe and Wyatt knew the drill and quickly pulled out the truck's bench seat and started a small fire. They ate delicious ja-

---

59.   A medium-sized, pig-like, hoofed mammal of the family Tayassuidae found throughout Central and South America and in the Southwestern area of North America.

velina wrapped around flatbread, letting the fat drip down their chins.

Monroe and Wyatt reasoned that Jim Charlie would not leave them stranded. What little they knew about him, they considered insurance. Besides, Jim Charlie had brought them provisions. They leaned back on the bench seat, settled in, and drank bitter tea and took in the vast open desert.

Wyatt glanced at the cactus he had shot only an hour or two earlier, and to his amazement he saw the bullet holes were glowing and pumping out blue and white neon sparklers that shot hundreds of feet above him before exploding into a million pieces. He hopped like a jack rabbit, falling and picking himself back up repeatedly in a futile attempt to catch the pieces before they melted like snow on hot sticky blacktop. Finally, he caught one and clutched it tightly. He could feel it wiggling and tickling the palm of his hand, and he became giddy as a goat. And when he could hold back no longer, he slowly opened his hand and was overtaken by the strong smell of licorice. Then he brought his lips to his palm and sucked in the bright blue spark.

Monroe leaned his head over the seat just as his stomach turned upside down. Wiping his mouth on his sleeve, he slouched back into a sitting position and stared into the small fire. The loud snap and crack of the burning sage alarmed him, causing him to scoot so far back that the bench seat tipped onto its back, dropping him onto the ground. Peering over the turned-up seat, he watched the flames change colors—Han blues and purples with edges dripping in vermillion and golden ochre. The flames began to leap up and down with such force that they vibrated the ground beneath him. The flames then took on the form of elongated soldiers performing drills. Monroe then heard a drum beating, and the soldiers made way, leaving a gap large enough for a boy about the age of his brother Virgil to appear. The drummer was dressed in a man-sized Union blue jacket embellished with rows of glowing brass buttons, and on the drummer's bare feet were white spats.

Wyatt felt the blue spark fly into his mouth, then flop around inside his belly, causing him to bounce around the ground as though he was on a Tilt-A-Whirl.[60] And just as he was entering a state of jubilation, as though someone had killed the switch, he stopped, stood, and stared up at a twenty-foot tall green neon light that flickered on top of the cactus and read, "ALLEY – OOP." Above the name was a large red olive pierced with a white toothpick that leaned on the side of a blue martini glass.

"If that don't beat all!" yelled Wyatt. "Roe, ya gotta see this! They's got a dadgum honky-tonk out here, and they's pourin' blue-and-white confetti from the sky. It's a sight! Ya gotta come see!"

"I can't," whispered Monroe. "We'z been called to go forward. Fetch me that there rifle."

Wyatt ignored Monroe's request and started jumping around like a boxer in a ring trying to catch a handful of blue-and-white confetti as it floated down around the cactus.

Monroe heard the drummer change his tune, now calling for a lie down.

Without lifting his eyes off the drummer boy, Monroe eventually managed to flip the bench seat into its upright position. Then he cautiously stretched himself out and gripped a phantom rifle.

Wyatt snickered uncontrollably as he clenched his fist tightly. Holding onto what he thought was glowing confetti dropped from the heavens, he walked toward the fire, trying to get Monroe's attention, when he passed the truck's only remaining side mirror and shrieked.

The drummer boy's beat grew louder and faster, and his electric blue eyes flashed back and forth as though they were pocket watches swinging from a long chain to hypnotize an onlooker.

---

60. The Tilt-A-Whirl is a flat moving ride, first built in the late 1920s. It could be found at amusement parks, fairs, and carnivals.

At the ready, afraid to blink, Monroe stared deep into the boy's eyes and waited for the preparative command.[61]

Forsaking the confetti he clutched, Wyatt grabbed the side mirror and spat on the glass. Then with the hem of his T-shirt he wiped it clean, and the more he polished the glass, the larger the mirror appeared until the frame itself melted away. The mirror reflected the fire burning behind Wyatt, and walking through the fire was Jim Charlie, dressed in a long white robe belted at the waste with a gold cord, and around his head was a crown of thorns. In each of his hands he caried two large plastic containers, and Wyatt whispered in awe, "Jesus Christ Almighty."

Still leering at the drummer boy, Monroe's eyes became dry and filled with smoke from the fire, but he stayed steadfast. The drummer boy's iris began to quiver faster and faster after taking the shape of wings, and the eyes lifted themselves from the drummer boy's sockets and, after a few flutters around the fire, they took off to explore the meteorite shower, Draconids, which pelted the earth with thousands of meteors per hour.[62]

The sun was approaching mid-sky when Monroe and Wyatt started to stir. They had no idea how long they had been out, but feeling no worse for wear, they broke camp and headed west.

---

61. The preparation, or preparative, was a signal to make ready to fire.
62. The 1946 Draconids had Zenithal Hourly Rates of thousands of meteors visible per hour, among the most impressive meteor storms of the twentieth century.

Chapter 9:

Truth Be Known

California, 1947

THERE WAS A WHITEOUT around Flagstaff, and Wyatt had to walk in front of the truck to make sure they stayed on the road. In some spots, the snow came down so hard that the one halfway decent windshield wiper could not keep up and just gave out altogether. They slept in the back of the truck, unless it was snowing or raining, in which case they would sleep under it. When they got to Barstow, they headed north on Highway 466[63] across the Mojave Desert where they had no less than three vapor locks[64] during the day when record temperatures reached over 100 degrees Fahrenheit and dropped below 40 at night.

"This dang weather just can't make up its mind. If it ain't pourin' down bullfrogs, it's hotter than the Devil's armpit," Wyatt said as he pulled at the blanket he stole from their Albuquerque motel room.

"Ain't that the truth," replied Monroe as he pulled the brim of his hat down around his ears.

---

63. Highway 466 was renamed Highway 58 after 1964.

64. Older carburetors often had vapor lock issues, which cause a vehicle to stop running when the fuel in the system overheats. It mostly happens when driving on hot days and in stop-and-go traffic. Constant acceleration and deceleration will make the engine work harder, causing it to run hotter. Excess heat causes the fuel to vaporize, which keeps the fuel from reaching the engine.

They would have rather driven through the frigid nights, but the truck threw back so much cold air that even wearing socks as gloves, their fingers turned numb, and they could hardly hold onto the steering wheel.

As they turned onto State Route 223, they began to recognize the names on the road signs, names their mother had read to them by the light of a kerosene lamp, names relatives mentioned in their letters, names like Hooverville[65] and Weedpatch. Their chests began to pound faster, and their breath accelerated until their heads felt like helium balloons wrenching at their strings in an effort to break free.

Countless months and over 3,000 hard miles provide ample time for a dream to convert itself into a well-formulated plan or an unachievable hallucination. When the expedition reaches its end, the student must become the master, the rubber must hit the road, and the confidence and arrogance of youth must manifest its own truth.

The final miles would have been delighted to announce themselves on the odometer, but it was broken. The boys fought against the flashback blues that befell adventurers with a 'no return' policy. They surreptitiously thwarted relentless regrets by pelting them with boastfulness. They slew them with arrows built of dreams carved on the strength of young wood that had yet to be tested. This was not a journey measured only in miles. Their intellect, morals, and faith also were measured. This journey was where they laid the foundation of what kind of men they would become; this was their rite of passage. And the fact they had made it to California, they reasoned, already made them greater men than their father.

---

65. "Hooverville" was the name given to any migrant camp that emerged near a work area. A typical Hooverville was close to water and homes were tents, weed-thatched enclosures, or even paper. They were called Hooverville because President Hoover was widely blamed for the Great Depression, which caused many families to become destitute.

But the way they achieved their aspirations had raised self-doubt about their character and pricked their honor. They had committed illegal and immoral transgressions that no mother should ever discover, actions that could only be reverberated in the soundproof chambers of their hearts and dark corners of their minds. Inwardly, they vowed they would not allow their infractions to define them, and like the side mirror they had lost in the near fatal crash with that poultry truck west of Albuquerque, they concluded that what was behind them was not important.

Peering through a bug-splattered windscreen, they gazed down miles of navel orange trees, thousands of trunks standing like wooden soldiers, tall and in perfect formation. Despite the smell of an engine running hot, the sweet scent of oranges blossoms filled the truck's cab. They rolled down their windows and saw young boys no older than thirteen yanking smudge pots[66] off a trailer that was being pulled by a tractor and placing them evenly between the rows of trees, while older men followed in trucks loaded with several fifty-gallon metal oil drums. Just the thought of another cold night made Monroe shiver.

"They don't seem so happy to be seein' us," said Wyatt after the fieldhands failed to reciprocate his waves.

"Well, they can piss up a rope!" snarled Monroe. "We ain't turnin' back."

"Seein' we'z ridin' in on fumes and ain't nowheres else to go!" Wyatt said as he let out a belly laugh.

Gas was running about eleven cents a gallon, but they hardly had a dime between them. To find kin before nightfall they

---

66. Smudge pots, aka choofas or orchard heaters, are oil-burning devices with a large round base and a long flue up the center. Pots are placed among fruit trees to provide heat when lit, but more importantly they create smoke that blocks infrared light, thus preventing radiative cooling that creates crop-damaging frost.

would need a strategy, and they thought about Jim Charlie, but he had freed himself hundreds of miles back. Yet, if there was one thing Hornbecks excelled in, it was tracking relatives. No matter how cold the scent, there was no hiding place, no matter how determined they were to remain concealed.

Shortly after leaving the small town of Arvin on their way to Weedpatch, they came upon a scattering of people clustered around two derelict buildings that had a newly-painted wood sign fastened to the fascia boards by two chains. The sign read, "Arvin Federal Emergency School".[67]

"What the heck is goin' on here, I wonder?" said Monroe as he slowed the truck down.

"Must be sumpin' important; everybody and they's dogs done showed up," Wyatt said as he rose in his seat and stretched his neck to get a better view.

"Since everybody's been invited, we'z might as well pull in," said Monroe, and he guided the truck onto the soft dirt next to the other trucks that looked like they had traveled more than their share of two-rut roads.

"Wouldn't want to disappoint," Wyatt said as he pushed air between his teeth to dislodge any leftover food particles and then ran his fingers through his hair like a comb.

Monroe wiped the tips of his boots on the back of his jeans and caught up to Wyatt who was making his way toward a crowd of about forty people.

---

67. Leo Hart, superintendent of Kern County Schools, convinced the school board to set up the Arvin Federal Emergency School after seeing the general plight of migrants and the bullying they received from residents. He leased ten acres between Arin and Weedpatch next to migrant camps. Classes were held in two converted derelict buildings and in the belly of a decommissioned airplane. Lessons were designed to help students civilize migrant camp life and learn shoe cobbling, sewing, and how to make toothpaste and shampoo. Vocational classes in raising livestock, agriculture, carpentry, masonry, airplane mechanics, and more were soon added.

"What's goin' on?" Monroe asked a woman who was wearing her husband's worn-out work shirt as an apron.

"Well, the school district done donated this here old auditorium," she started to explain, "so we'z sawed it off their school and hauled it down here for our younguns."

"Well, ain't that there sumpin'!" answered Monroe. "Come on, Wyatt, let's git in there and help these boys."

Monroe eyed the situation and found an unmanned jack while Wyatt rushed to grab the end of a tow chain. When given the orders to pull and hoist, the boys put their backs into it.

Once the heavy work was done and the cool air started settling onto the valley floor, the boys turned on their charm as though someone had dropped a nickel into the jukebox and, without hesitation, they took their spot in line at the potluck table where they fed on red beans and rice, bologna casserole, collard greens, hot water cornbread, and soft bread sprinkled with sugar. With their plates loaded they took their place next to men seated on a lumber pile and watched the cremation of old tires as they surrendered themselves in an endless stream of black smoke on an open fire.

After the bent tin plates and chipped dishes were rounded up, several people walked back to their trucks and returned with guitars or fiddles; others whipped out mouth harps from their bib overalls. There was never a discussion as to what tune to play. Someone would just kick off with a few chords, and the others would follow. When Monroe and Wyatt got back from their truck with their guitar and harmonica, the group was just breaking out *"T for Texas."*[68]

---

68. *"Blue Yodel #1" ("T for Texas")* was written by Jimmie Rodgers who recorded it on November 30, 1927, in the Trinity Baptist Church in Camden, New Jersey. It was released on February 3, 1928. Rodgers developed a unique musical hybridization that drew from both Black and White traditions, as exemplified by the blue yodel songs.

After the last verse, a jug started making the rounds. Monroe declined, but Wyatt said, "Well, I reckon I be takin' your sip then, Roe," then he opened his throat and let the warm hooch fall down like high water over a low levee.

After playing a few more tunes, Monroe and Wyatt weaved through the assemblage of familiar Southern accets, many of them a patchwork similar to their own, a result of living pillar to post just to stay alive. They introduced themselves and made inquiries as to the whereabouts of their kin. It did not take long before the boys had a bead on their daddy's sister and a gallon of gas to get them to her front door.

You might think the refugees provided is aid out of the kindness of their hearts, but that would be only partially true. Sure, it was in their born nature to be kind and generous, especially to one of their own, but those were unusual times. It was all they could do to keep their kids from eating gravel, so the best they could do was keep these boys moving up the road.

"Well, it's too dark to plow, so yaw might as well bed down over by us in the ditch bank[69] over yonder, and we'll get ya some gas in the mornin'," said a hollow-cheeked man wearing patched overalls and a shirt with frayed cuffs.

"Much obliged," answered Monroe.

"Ain't no bother," the man said. "Your Uncle Earl and Aunt Ona is good people. He got my son-in-law hired on when he landed an oil job, so we'z much indebted."

---

69. Many set up what was called "ditch bank" camps along irrigation canals in farmers' fields, which often created poor sanitary conditions and developed into a public health problem.

Chapter 10
Truth Be Told
California, 1948

BY MID MORNING, seated around a wooden kitchen table, Monroe and Wyatt were feasting on fresh farm eggs, grits, bacon, soft bread stacked on a chipped floral saucer, and cowboy coffee, the likes of which they had never tasted.

Ona, their father's youngest sister, was built close to the ground—squatty, some would say. JC often joked that if cooking were a way to a man's heart, Ona would marry a king, and she would wear her floured coated butterfly apron as her crown. No one would look at Ona and think she had ever been a looker, but her smile would have made even Clark Gable burrow himself into her ample breast.

She wore her hair cropped at the neck, and she trimmed it herself to save the cost of the beauty parlor. Earl, her husband, regularly left a few dollars on the kitchen table before he left for work, and he made sure to say, "This ain't house money. It's for you." But she would just pick it up and stuff it into the old sock she kept in her bureau drawer. And every Saturday night, like clockwork, she set her hair in pin curls and carefully tied a nylon kerchief around her head to hold the bobby pins in place until she readied herself for church the next morning. Yes, she was a frugal woman, the kind who easily became invisible at a certain age, the kind that was always seen in sensible shoes, and her home reflected all that. The doilies were strategically positioned over the threadbare arms of her click sofa[70] and the back of an upholstered chair that had been stained with the hair oil of inconsiderate men. Ona's walls were decorated with calendar pictures she had accumulated from local businesses, such as the ones from the drugstore and the butcher.

When drinking coffee, everyone avoided the fragile handles of her eclectic dishware, fearing the watered-down glue would give way.

The boys gave their aunt the edited and rehearsed version of their adventuresome journey, and she told them it was only by the love of God she and her family were still alive.

"We was a-hopin' to get a little chunk of land when we got out here," smiled Ona as she gently rubbed her finger along the edges of the French travel decal she had pasted to the corner of the wobbly kitchen table, "but that ain't never gonna happen. The wages are so dang depressed, can't put enough together to get a postage stamp, and the farmers cuttin' off any chance of organizin'."

"But yaw stayed," piped up Monroe as he flipped his fork over and stirred the sugar in his coffee with the handle.

"Sho' 'nuff," Ona sighed. "Where ya gonna go? We'z plum wore out."

"But yaw ain't whooped," said Wyatt as he looked around the small house. "You can see that for sho'."

"We'z ain't livin' high on the hog. Every thang ya see here pert near come from the country dump, and sure, we'z worn out, but you's right—we ain't licked yet, honey." Ona closed her eyes, spread her arms, and gently patted the back of her nephew's hands with her calloused palms and let out what sounded like notes to an old hymn.

---

70. A click sofa has metal hinges, like a car seat, which allows the back to drop and form a cot. It made a clicking sound when it was converted into a bed.

"The Lord blessed us all," she began again. "He opened the door to an oil job, and this here abode, albeit's got a leaky roof, it's a sight better than Hooverville."

That night, after their Uncle Earl and Cousin Brady returned from work in the oil fields, Ona dragged in a wooden orange crate from the back porch so all five could sit down to a supper that was fit for kings. She spared nothing. She served fried pork chops, sweet rice, fried okra, wild greens cooked in salt pork, and endless glasses of cornbread drenched in ice cold buttermilk.

"Earl, hun, would you say grace?" asked Ona.

Earl put his large hands together, interlocking his tree-trunk-like fingers, and bowed his head. He was a large man on all accounts, around six-foot-four, and he was built like a diesel locomotive. When idle, he was a quiet and gentle man, hard to get riled up, but when he got a notion, his broad shoulders and strong legs gave the impression that he could pull a 300,000-pound payload uphill without breaking a sweat. His hair was thick and dark like mahogany, almost black, and matched his almond-shaped eyes. Some suggested he was part Apache because of his square chin, raised cheekbones, and lack of body hair, but he never said.

His dress was peculiar in that he always wore his pant legs tucked into high brown leather lace-up boots to which he carefully applied Goddard's Saddlers Wax every Sunday like they were going to church. He occasionally indulged himself in a rough-cut tobacco, neatly packed into the bowl of a Kaywoodie pipe, gifted to him by a cousin in Atlanta who had worked as a traveling salesman for the Kaufman Brothers and Bondy Company before the crash. Sometimes in the evening, sitting on the front porch by himself, Earl would laugh and say, "They ain't got nothin' on me," as he pictured the lawyers and congressmen pulling smoke from their Kaywoodies.

Monroe and Wyatt fired out one question after another as they drank their after-supper coffee in the intimate living room. The boys learned that the stories they had heard from their father were not so far-fetched. And after seeing the faces of Ona, Earl, and Grady, the situation may well have been underreported.

Earl explained how the California Citizens Association was hell-bent on creating itself in the image, sophistication, and enlightenment found in the major cities of Europe. If laws would not relieve them of the poor, then they would run them out with the threat of starvation and police harassment.

"We done seen some ungodly thangs," Earl told them as he reached out to take hold of Ona's hand as she sat quietly at his side on the click sofa. "When them fields was overflowin' with tomatoes and corn, they went in and burnt what they couldn't sell, just to begrudge hungry people.

"A Southern man," Earl continued as he glanced at Ona—"or woman for that matter—well, every time we go into town they's callin' us 'Okies' and spittin' in our direction like we wasn't the ones who built this country and then died for it."

"We ain't even from Oklahoma," chimed in Grady.

Ona gave him a wink.

"Except ol' Roe here!" said Wyatt as he laughed and gave Monroe a sucker punch to his shoulder.

"Don't matter much. We all the same to them anyhow," said Earl, and then he added, "and ain't a doggone thang wrong with Oklahoma, neither."

"I already got arrested three or four times," began Grady as he leaned forward over two long, thin legs stuffed into a well-worn pair of heavyweight Red Wings. He was in his early twenties and soft-spoken like his father, nice enough, but no one would say he could set the world on fire. The only thing one really noticed about him was that he used an overabundance of Vaseline Hair Tonic. People would often joke that he brought his own oil to the drilling sites. He had an older brother who died years before they left Shreveport, Louisiana, from injuries sustained when he fell off the back of a farm truck. Now it was just Grady and his older sister Beth, who was married and living north around Marysville with her husband's people in hopes of a better situation.

Peeking up at her husband, Ona said, "But I thank it's gittin' better."

"How do ya mean 'gittin' better'?" asked Monroe. "Don't sound much like it to me."

"It's been purt near two weeks since I been pulled over by a crumb[71]," laughed Grady.

"How come you gittin' pulled over so many times?" asked Wyatt.

"There's this one crumb," explained Grady, "who can't stop flippin' his buzzer. He's always sittin' at the turnoff and is crazier than a dog in a hubcap factory. He'll pull ya over and holds ya up just long enough to make ya late fer work. If ya ain't got papers, he's a-runnin' ya in."

"That there's a fact," said Ona. "He ran Grady in, says he done stole his own dang truck."

"I told him that if I was a-gonna steal somethang, it'd be a brand new Ford," laughed Grady. "Then he tells me, 'Well then, you must be some kinda commie spy,' so he runs me in anyways, and I lost that there job."

"We had a commie situation ourselves," Monroe chimed in.

Everyone rocked their heads just thinking about JC and his trial.

Ona then turned to her son and said, "That's all right, honey, but ya ended up gittin' a better job anyways." Then she turned to look at her nephews and continued: "And that cop otta know we ain't no commies. We'z Christian people, for cryin' out loud. We go to the same church."

---

71. A 1940'term for a police officer.

They all sat in quiet reflection for a few moments, then Ona jumped up from the sofa and said, "I'm gonna bawl ya up some water for a bath, son."

"Thank ya, Mamma," said Grady as he watched his mother push herself up on the sofa and head out to the back porch to grab a bucket. "But it ain't all bad. They's enough of us with our heels dug in and lookin' after each other when the push comes to shove. But hey, enough of the sour talk. I can't wait to take yaw in ta Bakersfield to a couple o' spots with some great music—and they got four movie houses—four!"

"We gotta get some work first," said Wyatt.

"Don't ya worry none about that," said Earl with authority. "It might not be great startin' off, but it'll get ya goin'. I'll call in a few IOUs tomorra."

That night, Monroe and Wyatt slept on the click sofa, happy not to be sleeping rough, thankful for the meal, and grateful for the family. But it was more than the shifting between the broken metal springs that poked through the upholstery that kept Monroe from falling into a deep and restful sleep.

They had taken a great risk to body and soul, and the pure fact that they had reached their promised land, the land flowing with milk and honey, proved they had gumption. But the land turned out to be scorched, void of sustenance and decency. Worse than the lack of moral fiber was that his father may have been right all along. There they were, spiting the noses right off their faces, landing right in the middle of what you might consider another civil war where California farmers chose to burn their fields rather than feed starving children.

Was it not a Biblical command? thought Monroe as he silently reflected on the Bible verse his Aunt Ona had quoted earlier that night:

"And when ye reap the harvest of your land, thou shalt not make clean riddance of the corners of thy field when thou reapest, neither shalt thou gather any gleaning of thy harvest: thou shalt leave them unto

the poor, and to the stranger: I am the LORD your God." – Leviticus 23:22 (KJV)

The smell of pork sizzling in a skillet woke the boys.

"Mornin', boys," Ona called from behind the stove. "Come on, the coffee done been saucered and blowed,[72] and I got grits and more pork chops in the skillet. I declare, you boys need to get some meat on them bones. Yaw so skinny you'd have to run around in the shower just to get wet!"

"Everybody gone off ta work?" asked Monroe as he and Wyatt started folding up their pallets and clicking the sofa back into a sitting position.

"Yap, it's just us. I thought since yaw have a truck we'd ride down to the Woolworths later today," Ona went on, without stopping to pick up air. "We need ta pick up a 'Greetings from Bakersfield' postcard and send on to your folks ta let 'em know yaw arrived in one piece. Your mamma's bound to be sick with worry."

"That'd be good, Aunt Ona," Monroe said.

"Might wanna uhddress it to 'General Delivery,'" piped in Wyatt. "They mighta gone back to Shreveport. Thangs still ain't lookin' too good in Wichita."

"If we could just get your Grandmaw Mazie to leave Earlsboro, then I'm sure your momma and daddy would be more likely to come out," said Ona as she wiped her hands on the blue moth apron she reserved for company. "I do worry about 'em."

"She ain't like Grandmaw Jane," said Monroe. "Us goin' off to Tennessee and then Arkansas about killed 'er, but we still can't

---

72. "Saucered and blowed" originated in the country method of cooling coffee. Step 1: Pour some hot coffee into your saucer and blow it until it's cool enough to drink. Step 2: Either pour the coffee back into the cup and drink it or drink it straight from the saucer.

drag 'er from Earlsboro no which-a-way—at least not while Miss Birdwell's still alive. They's connected at the hips."

★

Mazie was nothing like Jane, that much was true. She had her fill of moving from pillar to post. Finding herself in Earlsboro, a red dirt town with low expectations, suited her just fine. She came from an old well-appointed Georgia family, born two years into the Civil War and nursed on the breast of a black woman. The only thing she inherited was a grudge fueled by her mother and a key to a box of yellowed paper that held her father's unrealized dreams.

Secrets and disappointments are sisters, so they often build an inseparable bond. Mazie and Miss Birdwell, both widows, met at a land auction for a local family who had been dusted out. Neither of the ladies came to buy; they were there to support the family whose farm was being repossessed by the Earlsboro Bank.

"They need ta get what's comin' to 'em!" Mazie said under her breath as she watched the well-dressed man from the bank try to push up the price of a combine.

"That you can be assured of," Mazie heard a voice next to her say.

"I pray ya's right, Miss..." Mazie replied to a tall slender woman with a long beak nose and hair piled high.

"Sarah Frances Birdwell," replied the woman, "but you can call me Frannie." Then she extended her arm and shook Mazie's hand.

And true to Frannie's predictions, the Earlsboro Bank was robbed[73] of $3,000[74] on March 9, 1931.

"Nobody can say your grandmaw ain't loyal. But why in God's good name do she have ta stay in a town that whiskey built and oil broke?" Ona asked with more than a hint of sarcasm.

"I reckon it's the only place safe enough for that there trunk of hers," Monroe joked.

"Which one?" asked Ona.

"The locked one she keeps beside her bed, the one she sets her kerosene lamp and Bible on," replied Monroe.

"The one that fits that sacred key she wears about her neck like it was a piece of wood from the cross the Lord Jesus himself died on?" asked Ona.

"That'd be the one," said Wyatt. "Last time we'z was up there, Grandmaw showed us what was in..."

"She done *what?*" interrupted Ona as she plopped into a kitchen chair in surprise. "What was in it? Ya mamma said that all whiles growin' up she never let nobody within ten feet of that dang thang. Yaw's daddy and I would tease ya mamma, sayin' all 'er family's skeletons was in there."

They all leaned on the back legs of the kitchen chairs and let out a good laugh, thinking about all the bones rattling around in that old trunk, until Wyatt revealed the trunk's secrets.

"Dang if it ain't fulla money and paper!" shouted Wyatt. "I tell ya true!"

"He's right. I seen it with my own eyes," confirmed Monroe.

---

73. Sarah Frances Birdwell, George's first recorded robbery was on March 9, 1931, when he and Floyd (Pretty Boy Floyd) joined William "Billy the Killer" Miller in robbing a bank in Earlsboro, Oklahoma.
74. Equivalent in buying power to about $49,560 in 2018.

"Well, I'll be doggone! If that don't beat all," said Ona, still looking puzzled.

"Thang is," continued Monroe, "she said all them is Graybacks,[75] a bunch of 'em with Lucy Holcombe Pickens'[76] picture and a bunch more with Stonewalls[77] on 'em. Said her daddy left 'em for her for safe keepin', just in case their value come back."

Ona shook her head and said, "Well, that ain't likely gonna happen. They ain't never gonna be worth a dagum thang. Was that all the papers she had?"

"Not all. Seems that they's some stocks from the Choctaw & Memphis Railroad Company,[78] and some of 'em was land deeds," Monroe explained. "Grandmaw said they all had money way back when. But then the war came, then the crash, then the water dryin' up, then the dust. Well, thangs changed, I reckon. But she said she was gonna still hold on to 'em in case thangs changed back again, cuz she'd given her word to her daddy and all."

"Times done changed all right, honey, they surely did," said Ona.

The room then fell quiet, like someone had asked for a moment of silence to reflect on the life that was, the life that is, and the life that might yet be.

---

75. Graybacks referred to here are the Confederate States of America (CSA) bank notes first issued in April 1861.

76. Described as the "Queen of the Confederacy," Lucy Holcombe Pickens was the only woman to be depicted on Confederate currency, three issues of the $100 CSA Wyatt and one issue of the $1 CSA Wyatt.

77. Thomas Jonathan "Stonewall" Wyatt served as a confederate general during the Civil War.

78. Choctaw & Memphis Railroad Company Common Stock certificates were issued in the 1890s. The Choctaw & Memphis Railroad Company was originally chartered on September 15, 1898, to acquire the property of the Little Rock and Memphis Railroad Company (which it did on October 25, 1898), and to construct a railroad line between the City of Little Rock and the Arkansas-Indian Territory line.

Finally, Ona softly continued: "Well, it looks like Grandmaw and Miss Birdwell keeps each other's company quite well!" She then let out a belly laugh and hit the wooden kitchen tabletop with her palm so hard that coffee splashed over the brim of her cup.

"Both of 'em sittin' in a dyin' town waitin' for the payroll train that ain't never gonna pull into the station," joked Wyatt. "Especially since Miss Birdwell's son got himself killed."

"Ya ain't far from wrong," said Ona as she got up to fetch a dishrag to wipe up the coffee spill.

"Speakin' of payin', we gotta get to work as quick as we can, Aunt Ona. We gotta send money back," Monroe said.

"Oh, honey, don't you worry none. Your Uncle Earl and Cousin Grady is gonna fix yaw up."

Earl and Grady were true to their word. The boys got their feet wet by picking oranges in some of the same fields they first saw when they rolled in on fumes. But it did not take them long until they were working in the Mountain View oil fields between Arvin and Bakersfield, sometimes as roustabouts[79] when they could land it, but most often as derrick hands.[80] Within a few months, even with the wages depressed, they were making more money per month than their father had seen all year working a patch of ground. After sending money back home and contributing to their room and board, what loose change they had rattling around in their jeans was spent on flashy pearl button shirts, haircuts, and shiny boots.

On Friday nights they strutted into the Alley Cat, Blackboard, or Trout's like they were the cocks of the henhouse. Wyatt pur-

---

79. Roustabouts are general oil field laborers whose general responsibility is to guide the operators and attach slings to lift the loads. They also mix drilling mud used to lubricate the drill bit that bores into the ground.

80. Derrick hands monitor the drilling fluid, maintain the pumps, guide the drill pipe, remove jams, and perform various lifting, pulling, pushing, and other pump-related activities.

sued as many girls as he could by whirling them around the dance floor to the music of house bands like Bill Woods[81] and the Orange Playboys who would often present new arrivals to the San Joaquin Valley. Monroe, on the other hand, took a more subtle approach, perfecting his art of persuasion through a display of perceived interest, erroneous flattery, and prying open insecurities by way of clever manipulation. And it was in this practice that he first noticed Shelda standing against the wall in the shadows, a tall girl with large, fleshy mounds covered in a tight red satin blouse with a low, heart-shaped neckline. He stood along the fringe and watched her breasts rise and fall with each breath *like Moses in the reeds*, Monroe thought.

Shelda was an independent girl in her early twenties, the middle child between two older and two younger girls. Her mother had died of tuberculosis just about the time the family arrived in the San Joaquin Valley from Tennessee. Her father, a roustabout, traveled the oil fields up and down the valley, leaving the five girls to bring themselves up. The girls thought the loss of their mother was too much for their father to bear and forgave him for his absence, but Shelda once confided in Monroe that she had it on good authority that her father had taken up with a woman whose husband was stationed at Castle Air Force Base near Merced. She said that's when she realized that she would live life on her own terms, dance more than her mother had, wear more lipstick than her mother would have dared, and love freer than her mother had the chance to. She modeled herself according to the pages of Hollywood magazines like *Photoplay* and *Modern Screen* that she stole from beauty parlors and cheesecake magazines like *Flirt* and *Titter*, "America's Merriest Maga-

---

81. Bill Woods, originally from Denison, Texas, came to the San Joaquin Valley at the age of sixteen. By twenty-six, Woods was the bandleader at the Blackboard Café. His big break came in the late 1940s when he was hired by former Bob Wills vocalist Tommy Duncan to play piano and fiddle. Tommy Hays, a guitarist and bandleader who still plays in Bakersfield, once said that Bill Woods could darn near play anything, including keyboards, guitar, and fiddle. Woods was a key factor in many performers' careers including Buck Owens, Ferlin Husky, and Cousin Herb Henson.

zine," which she found on the bottom shelf of the barbershop where she waited for Monroe to get his ears lowered.

She took to wearing her shoulder-length, dark, wavy hair parted on the side in a peek-a-boo style that imitated Veronica Lake. Her lips were always painted a glossy red to match the enamel on her nails. Her eyes were flanked by two thick, black pencil lines that were capped with full, dark brows. Behind her back, people would say that Shelda was never seen in town without her trottin' harness on. Some may have been envious that she appeared to have enough disposable cash to pay for such frivolities, while others had witnessed her antics, and those of her sisters, at the Woolworth's makeup counter firsthand. But Monroe would fight tigers in the dark with a switch for her and would not pay heed to disparaging gossip.

Shelda worked in the ticket booth at the Kern Theater, and once the movie started, she would make her way to the rear fire escape and open the door for Monroe. If he had seen the movie, the two would snuggle in the back corner under the balcony where they would quickly find their hands inside each other's underpants, plowing through grass, hoping to find the sacred keys to the kingdom before the intermission lights came up.

She done put an apple in his eye and a pea in his brain, thought Ona. Yet, she let well enough alone, just as she did when Martha's letter arrived announcing that JC had moved the family to the Northwest and pleaded with Monroe and Wyatt to join them.

Part 3

"There will come a time when you believe
everything is finished; that will be the beginning."

Louis L'Amour

Chapter 11

Oregon or Bust

Texas, Oregon, 1950

AT THE END OF THE ROAD there is always a mirror. JC and Martha's two eldest sons did not return with their tails between their legs. The next two boys, Virgil and Orson, were openly making plans to cut a trail. And Wichita Falls turned out to be yet another in a long line of dead-ends leaving JC still with nothing in the pan. His last hope died along with Martha's mother Mazie, who left nothing but a trunk filled with worthless paper. And now Martha, suffering from the baby blues,[82] could not roll herself out of bed. So he relented, tucked his pride into the heel of his boots, loaded everyone up, and headed to the Northwest woods to work alongside his step-brother Floyd.

As Wichita Falls faded in the rearview mirror, JC and Martha could not help feeling betrayed, first by the landscape, then by the corrupt and self-serving politicians. They themselves had been raised on the three Bs—BBQ, broke, and the Bible. They adhered to the divine agreement and loyalty promise that if they got behind the mule every day, anything was possible. It was that vow of obedience JC's early ancestor Davy agreed to when he signed The Oath of a Freeman[83] shortly after arriving in the

---

82. "Baby blues" was an earlier term used to describe postpartum depression.

83. First written in 1631 and revised in 1634, The Oath of a Freeman was a vow taken by the freemen of the Plymouth Colony in the Commonwealth of Massachusetts to defend the Commonwealth and not to conspire to overthrow the government.

Commonwealth of Massachusetts in 1631. And Martha's family had been equally committed to America when they arrived in New Amsterdam on *De Bonte Koe*[84] in 1663. This commitment was passed from one generation to the next to remind them of their duty. It was announced from the pulpits and shouted by baby-kissing politicians with ten-gallon mouths at county fairs. And their ancestors had answered every call of duty that left them with nothing but enough widows' pensions to wallpaper city hall while unscrupulous traders squeezed the commodity market, and crooked bankers sold the mineral rights to greedy oil speculators who poisoned the soil until the mule that drove hope for many finally died.

JC was doubtful they would make it past the smoldering embers of the Bum Blockades[85] with his International loaded down by an ever-growing number of children and whatever meager belongings he could salvage. There were still numerous vigilante groups, many within law enforcement, who were hell-bent on keeping Okies out of the Golden State. That is why he chose a route that bypassed California altogether, opting for a longer and more perilous route through the mountains of Colorado, Utah, and Idaho, then across eastern Oregon until they reached a small Pacific Northwest lumber camp near Vernonia, where they met up with Floyd.

Floyd was born in Alabama and grew into a large man, about six-foot-five, and although his large frame was often hard to fit, he had a taste for fine clothes and leather. He was always a gentleman around women, but when he was drunk his temperament was unpredictable, just like his father, Mr. Dunks. He inherited a personality that his father's people in Alabama said

---

84. *De Bonte Koe* (*The Spotted Cow*) was a Dutch ship used to ferry immigrants from the Nederlands/Holland to the Nieuw Nederlands, what we now call New York. *De Bonte Koe* sailed from Amsterdam on April 16, 1663, and arrived in Nieuw Amsterdam, Nieuw Nederlands between May 11, 1663, and August 17, 1663.

85. Various police departments set up a border patrol, dubbed the "Bum Blockade," at major road and rail crossings to turn back would-be visitors who lacked obvious means of support.

reminded them of the legendary Dallas Stoudenmire[86] who was short-tempered and, when riled, could chew up nails and spit out a barbed wire fence. Unlike JC, Floyd lacked the patience for farming, and while he worked a few short stints as a hand for wildcatters[87] around Louisiana and Texas, it was the resin in the southern long leaf pine that leached into his veins, and he would forever remain a woodsman, logger, lumberjack, or woodcutter, but no one would call him a shanty boy.[88] So rather than heading for the agricultural fields of California like many Southerners, he drove his wife Nadene and family directly to the Pacific Northwest woods and worked his way up from skid road[89] to a donkey puncher[90], and fashioned himself into the quintessential image of the Northwest logger.

Unlike mill workers who toiled for larger sawmills and often had the luxury of settling into small, wood-framed cabins built especially for them, many loggers lived rough, especially the new arrivals. Loggers moved quickly from one ridge top to another or along lower creek beds and across canyons. If it made strategic sense, some logging outfits would construct doghouses[91] that did nothing more than meet basic shelter requirements for a dozen or so single men. Loggers with families found accommodations in nearby towns, but the Western Pacific Railroad was laying new tracks to support the timber industry, which led

---

86. Although Dallas Stoudenmire was a lesser-known lawman/gunfighter who was born in Alabama in 1845, his "four dead in five seconds" hit the national newspapers from New York to San Francisco.

87. A wildcatter drills exploration oil wells in areas not known to be oil fields.

88. A shanty boy is a young boy just breaking into the trade, a "greenhorn."

89. Due to the unreliability of employment in the timber trade, loggers hung around on the skid roads (later "roads" became "row"), hoping for work. A skid is a track made of greased timber in which logs are moved along until they reach their transport by truck, rail, or river.

90. A donkey puncher is the operator of a small steam donkey, a machine used in logging in the nineteenth and twentieth centuries.

91. A doghouse was a smaller and more primitive structure intended for short-term use for loggers who slept on the hill.

to housing shortages that sometimes fueled fights and late-night brawls, so many lumbermen set up family camps on the hill.

The first winter was hard on newcomers living on the hill, especially those who had come from warmer and drier climates. The dampness of the Northwest was relentless. Rising before sunrise, JC would sometimes lean over, kiss Martha, and light-heartedly say, "Honey, can ya scrape the moss off my back so as I can get my shirt on?"

While JC, Floyd, and their older boys headed off to the woods in the early morning on a belly of leftover biscuits that had been soaked in a skillet of salt pork fat, those who stayed in camp picked weevils out of beans, rice, and flour bags, diapered babies, and nursed children who were sick with asthma, bronchitis, or pneumonia. They hauled water from nearby streams, and if they could get it, they would take in laundry from the loggers bunking in a doghouse further up the ridge. Each morning, mothers rose from their damp pallets with an ache in their bones and told their children and each other how thankful they were for their abundance, but when alone with the deepest and dankest parts of their hearts, they begged God for their deliverance in the form of a good death.

That winter, Floyd and JC each lost a baby to pneumonia and secretly buried the two cousins side by side beneath a young Douglas fir sapling, praying they'd all grow old together.

There were times in the evenings after the kids were in bed when JC and Martha sat by their small open fire and drank watered-down coffee as they watched Adilia sneak off to visit a man living in a doghouse.

"This coffee is so dang weak I can read a newspaper through it," JC joked.

"Oh, when was the last time you had time to read a newspaper?" Martha said, and then she laughed.

Sometimes the wind carried Irish or Scottish tunes favored by the few old-timers who still wore tin pants,[92] men who were once strong but who had nowhere else to go, or men who had simply lost track of time and had never found their way back to Ontario, Canada, many of them with noses that had grown beards, and men who had formed whisky bellies. When the old loggers pulled out their well-worn fiddles or guitars from beneath their bedrolls, they often played melancholy tunes and allowed their minds to drift across the gulch of their remembrances and let the notes drip from their horsehair bows like tears.

The night air picked up the notes from the sad songs and carried them five hundred yards or more. Martha and JC knew those tunes—or at least the sadness they invoked. On such nights, after JC pulled off his corks,[93] Martha would extend her small hand, place it over her husband's callouses, and softly sing along with the fiddler's song:

I wish I had someone to love me
Someone to call me his own
Someone to sleep with me nightly
I'm weary of sleeping alone.

Tonight is our last night together
The nearest and dearest must part
The love that once bound us together
Has cruelly been torn apart.

　　　　- Chorus -

Meet me tonight in the moonlight
Meet me in somewhere alone
I have a sad story to tell you

---

92. Tin pants are a reference to loggers' heavy, waterproof canvas pants.
93. Corks, aka, caulk boots, are spike-soled boots worn by loggers, tree planters, and other forestry laborers. They are particularly associated with the Pacific Northwest and Canada.

That I'll tell by the light of the moon.
- Chorus -

I wish I had ships on the ocean
I'd line them with silver and gold
I'd fly to the arms of my true love
A young lad of nineteen years old.

- Chorus -

If I had the wings of a swallow
I'd fly far over the sea
I'd follow the ship that he sails in
And bring him home safely to me.

- Chorus - [94]

Sleeping in the woods, up on the hills, allowed Floyd to save enough money to buy ten acres in West Union. He bought an old chicken house from a neighbor who had decided to get out of the poultry business. He, JC, and their boys hauled the forty-two-foot coop on the back of a log truck and set it in place. Then they removed the roosting bars and nesting bins and gave it a general cleaning before using a post hole digger to put in a seventy-five-foot deep well behind it. Finally, they moved their families in, along with a small pack of hound dogs, much to the chagrin of their neighbors.

That move sparked a virus of independence in Floyd and JC, a renewed drive to show the world they were young and fearless men who lived by the logger's motto:

> *"I can walk the log,*
> *I can fuck the dog,* [95]
> *I can drink muddy water*
> *Out of a greasy hard hat."*

---

94. *"I Wish I Had Someone to Love"* is of unknown origin, but *"The Prisoner's Song"*, an American song that was a worldwide hit in the 1920s, is similar, although some of the words were changed.
95. "Fuck the dog" is a reference to goofing off.

Although Floyd was no farmer, JC convinced him that it would be a waste, given the fertile Oregon soil, not to lay in a garden. But first they would have to remove four large stumps. Sixteen was the age requirement to work for an outfit on the hill, leaving Floyd's son, fourteen-year-old Gary, whose nickname was Splice because of a knife accident, and JC's boy Virgil, who was also fourteen, on the loose. School had let out for the summer, not that they attended school anyway. One evening Floyd gave Splice and Virgil instructions: "Tomarra, I want ya fellas to go over and get Mr. Haack to help yaw blast those stumps out."

The boys could hardly contain their excitement. They had already been pulling loads apart and filling cracks in the stumps with gunpowder and setting them afire. Now the possibility of handling something much more powerful sent them beyond the light barrier. The next morning, they were gone before breakfast.

"Ya can't come with us," Virgil turned and said to Orson who was trying to tag along. "And take them dogs back with ya."

Orson, twelve, had grown at least a head taller than his older brother Virgil, and he used that fact to his advantage.

"Ya heard Virgil," Gary said. "Get on back to the house and take them dogs with ya." Then he leaned into Orson and added, "Get!"

Virgil reached down and gave his dog Randy a gentle pat on the head and said, "You too, Randy. Get on back to the house. I be back directly."

As the boys crossed the field, they occasionally checked to make sure Orson had not snuck back.

"He's a sneaky son of a bitch, ain't he?" said Gary, not looking for a reply. Then he reached out and knocked on Mr. Haack's screen door.

"Sorry, fellas, you'll have to speak up, my hearing is bad," said Mr. Haack.

The boys repeated their request. "I'd like to help you out," said Mr. Haack, "but my back is acting up so bad I can hardly stand upright."

Mr. Haack was a slender man in his forties who chain-smoked Raleighs to collect the coupons he would later redeem for fishing gear. He had been blasting since he was around twelve, now he had study job as blaster working for the state. His job was leveling out clear-cut forest and logging roads making way for functional thoroughfares to accommodate urban expansion. But when his pickup truck slid along a muddy dirt road and into a steep ravine, injuring his back, he was sent home to recuperate.

The boys silently stood and stared at Mr. Haack as though they had just dropped a dozen eggs on the blacktop in front of their mothers.

"But I'll tell you what," Mr. Haack added, "if you come out to the barn, I'll give you enough explosives to clear out half a dozen stumps."

Gary and Virgil snapped their heads and looked at each other with bug eyes. They only had four stumps to clear, and the thoughts of what they could do with the leftovers knocked around in their heads like an out-of-control Dodgem[96] bumper car.

Haack may have misread the expressions on the boy's faces, just as he had misheard the number of stumps because he said, "Don't worry, nothing to it, as long as you remember to treat these sticks with respect. They been sitting out in damp for a few years, so they may just fizzle out on you." Then, after pausing, he jokingly asked, "You're fast runners, right?" The boys assured him they were, and then they followed him to the barn.

---

96. The Stoehrer brothers were the first to patent a bumper car in 1920, creating the Dodgem Company. The cars were made of tin and often had to be nailed back together between rides, and sometimes parts came off during the rides.

Gary and Virgil followed Mr. Haack's instructions, but not quite to the letter. They drilled a deep hole in each stump with an auger bit and dropped a stick into each hole. When laying out the detonation cord, the boys decided that was their one big chance to create an explosion of epic proportions. They tied all the detonation leads into one long main cord and carefully made sure each connection was secure. After rechecking their work, they stood back to admire the possibilities.

"Reckon we otta light this sucker," said Gary. "Ya got the matches?"

"Nope, but I'll run up to the shop," answered Virgil. Then he sprinted to the mechanics shed and grabbed the box of matches that rested next to the vice he and Gary used to pull shells apart.

Gary grabbed the box from Virgil, quickly pulled out a match and began to strike it against the box. "Dang it all," he said in frustration. "They's all wet." He then tossed the box on the ground, turned, and ran into the house. He soon returned with a box of matches he had grabbed from the kitchen.

"Here, let me take a run at it," said Virgil as he reached out to grab the box from Gary.

"Let's both have a go," replied Gary as he got down on his knees. He opened the box and handed Virgil a match, then held the box so each could use the striker at the same time. They set their lit matches to the end of the detonation cord and, once they saw the flame begin its trip up the cord, they jumped and ran back toward the house until they no longer heard the hiss of the flame. Then they stopped and turned to give witness to their work. When nothing happened, they headed back toward their main detonation feed.

Virgil heard the kitchen door open and quickly turned to see Orson leaning out and hollering, "Whatcha doin'?"

"Ain't none a' yur business!" Virgil yelled back. "And pull Randy inside!"

No sooner had Virgil turned around than he felt his body lift two feet into the air and then fall flat onto the ground with a thud.

The boys heard a commotion coming from the house and quickly picked themselves up when they saw their mothers' aprons flapping around their knees as they ran to check on their boys.

"It's okay, Mamma," Virgil said. "I ain't bleedin'." And then he dusted himself off.

"Ya better have a gusher, cuz that's the only thang that's gonna keep me from beatin' the tar outta you," Martha said angrily as she pulled Virgil along by his hair.

"Daddy told us to blow these stumps out," Gary tried to explain.

"Did he tell ya to kill the fuckin' dog?" Nadene yelled as she pointed to Randy who was lying dead in the yard, impaled by a large piece of wood from the blast.

Chapter 12

Shakin' in Bakersfield

California, 1952

MONDAY, JULY 21, at 4:52 a.m., the four men, with sleep still crusted around their eyes, were driving along the Tegon Highway toward the oil field when, without warning, a wild beast in the form of a White Wolf [97] rose out of the ground with fer as sharp as a surgeon's scalpel and yellow eyes surrounded by pulsating red veins. The White Wolf carried on for forty-seven seconds. It leaped across the valley floor with such force that the ground began to liquefy under roadbeds, and then its fierce tail swung with such strength that it knocked down trees and buildings made of brick, wood, and adobe. Oil rigs shot gushers of fire over a hundred feet high, and the flames were so hot that steel turned liquid, and iron railroad tracks twisted into the shape of hairpins. Along Bear Mountain Road the ground rose to meet the car, rolling and tossing the men within.

"What in tarnation!" shouted Grady as he tried to gain control. He stomped on the brake pedal and pulled his Ford Deluxe alongside the irrigation ditch that ran parallel to the road.

---

97. The White Wolf Fault is the best known and largest fault to cut across the floor of the San Joaquin Valley. The movement along this fault on July 21, 1952, produced a 7.5 magnitude shock and over twenty aftershocks of magnitude 5.0 or greater, including a 5.8 tremblor nearly a month later on August 22.

"Feels like we got a flat on all fours," said Monroe, trying not to show fear.

"I don't thank so," said Earl in a near whisper. "Look up yonder."

Speechless, the men stared through the dusty windshield at the asphalt road that had detached itself from the soft ground beneath.

"Well, will ya look at that!" Wyatt said as he pointed to the irrigation ditch. "The water's leapin' over the sides!"

"Armageddon... gotta be!" yelled Monroe as both hands latched onto the back of the front seat. His mind exploded with a decade of flashing images on the multitude of occasions where he had lied, stolen, and fornicated.

"No, it ain't Armageddon," said Earl. "I reckon what we got here is a White Wolf[98] earthquake, boys. Better get ourselves home and check on thangs." Then he pushed the passenger door open. "I'm gonna take the wheel, Grady. I got a better feel for the road."

Their nerves were balancing on the edge of a new razor blade as the aftershocks rocked them about. On the outskirts of town they saw houses that had been pulled down. "Ain't nothin' but a burn pile now," Wyatt said under his breath. They passed other houses where people were feverishly digging through stacks of brick while a woman, still in her nightgown, looked on with tears of despair streaming down her face.

"What in the...!" Earl yelled as he swerved, just missing a woman wearing a long blue robe like an Orthodox nun who had escaped a Russian monastery. She gripped rolls of medical bandages. Close on her heels were eight more, all in long robes of

---

98. The White Wolf Fault is the best known and largest fault to cut across the floor of the San Joaquin Valley. The movement along this fault on July 21, 1952, produced a 7.5 magnitude shock and over twenty aftershocks of magnitude 5.0 or greater, including a 5.8 tremblor nearly a month later on August 22.

various colors—green, brown, yellow. They were barefooted and carrying medical supplies.

"I don't know how they done it," said Earl as he waited for the robed women to pass. "I'd be willin' to bet they got here before the ground stopped shakin'."

"Who are they?" asked Monroe.

"They's the WKFL Foundation of the World,"[99] said Earl with an emphasis on "world." "They follow a fella who thinks he's the reincarnation of Christ."

"Sounds like a crackpot!" laughed Wyatt.

"Might very well be," grinned Earl as he thought of the time Ona had dragged him to the Foundation's compound in Box Canyon one Easter to watch the group's leader, Venta, get "crucified," complete with fake blood, as part of their annual resurrection pageant. "They's oddballs for sure," continued Earl. "Anybody that thanks they come from another planet on some kinda rocket ship right next to Adam and Eve gotta be a few dogs shy of a hunt. But then I reckon that's why they so fearless. Heck, they even jump outta air-o-planes— barefoot—to bring food and bandages to firefighters!"

It was around 5:45 a.m. by the time Earl pulled onto the dirt lawn in front of their house and cut the engine. Grady bolted out of the car and yelled for his mother. Stepping over the crumbled porch, he pushed the front door with his shoulder, but it wouldn't budge. He called for Monroe and Wyatt to come help while Earl ran to the back of the house. The boys leaned hard

---

99.   Often referred to by locals as the Fountain Cult, the WKFL Foundation of the World was founded in 1948. Its leader was a man who called himself Krishna Venta. WKFL stands for Wisdom, Knowledge, Faith, Love. The organization aimed to provide spiritual upliftment, economic security, spiritual love, and scientific development for all its members. It provided communal living on twenty acres in Box Canyon. Just down the road at Spahn Ranch, Charles Manson would indoctrinate his followers a little over a decade later.

into the door and pushed. Still nothing, so they backed up a few steps and rushed at the door. But it still would not budge.

"Hold up, boys. She's right here."

They turned to see Earl with his arm around Ona, dressed in her blue moth apron and carrying an armful of cast-iron skillets.

"What yaw tryin' ta do? Pull the house clean down before I get ever'thang out?" asked Ona. "That door don't open no more, and the back one won't shut. Yaw come on, let's salvage what we can before the whole thang flattens."

After the propane tank was double checked to ensure it had been cut off, they set about emptying the contents of the house into the backyard. They separated the things that could be salvaged from those that could not. The could nots included broken jars of canned corn and shattered dishes whose pieces would never be found. The coulds included Ona's coveted green Montgomery Ward Airline tube radio that had cracked and blown its tubes.

When they had pulled everything out of the house, they stood back and laughed, realizing they had created a replica of the house: the click sofa sat across from the oil-stained upholstered chair, and the braided rag rug stretched over the dirt and under the wooden kitchen table that was surrounded by the mismatched kitchen chairs and the wooden orange crate.

"Now that we done moved in, can I get a cuppa coffee, Ma?" asked Earl as he grabbed his wife around the waist, kissed her on top of the head, and patted her butt, which prompted her to respond with a playful slap on his hand.

"Them two never quit!" laughed Wyatt. "They's the biggest kids of us all!"

"They shor is," replied Monroe as he lifted himself off the upholstered chair. "I thank I'll go check on Shelda. Be back a little later on."

Even before Monroe reached Shelda's house, he could see the fire trucks with their lights flashing, and his heart began to race. He pressed harder on the accelerator. Once he got closer, he could see that a good portion of Shelda's house was missing—the walls and the roof were torn completely off, and everything else was but smoldering ash. To his surprise, he saw two barefoot Fountain sisters in their long blue robes administering medical aid to two people on the ground, and there was a barefoot foundation brother in a long brown robe offering the firefighters and two of Shelda's sisters some coffee from a thermos.

"Where's Shelda?" yelled Monroe as he jumped out of his truck.

The firefighters and the barefoot foundation brother froze in their tracks, waiting for someone else to take the first step forward.

"Where is she?" demanded Monroe.

Slowly, one of the sisters in a blue robe rose from caring for her patient and carefully guided her bare feet around splintered wood and broken glass.

"Greetings, brother. I am Sister Ruth."

"Where is *Shelda?*" Monroe demanded again.

In his heart he already knew, like everyone does in such tragic times. He just needed to hear it said aloud.

Sister Ruth explained that the propane refrigerator had exploded. Then she tried to comfort Monroe by saying Shelda was in a better place, sitting with the Heavenly Father.

Monroe would not be consoled. He jumped back into his truck and drove toward home, banging his fist against the steering wheel over and over and over. He pressed his foot so hard on the accelerator that if there had been just a bit more rust on the undercarriage, he would have needed to resole his Red Wings. Without conscious intention, he drove to Bear Mountain and didn't even notice that the White Wolf quake had raised the land over three feet in parts of the road. His mind filled with anger at Shelda's dad for not looking out for her. He was furious at the depressed wages that forced poor folks to buy worn-out refrigerators and live in houses not fit for field mice. He was so distraught that he wanted to run his truck right over a cliff.

As he drove along the narrow road, his throat tightened, and his chest jumped like a bullfrog trying to get out of a wheelbarrow. He felt like he was drowning. Panicked, he suddenly pulled the truck alongside a trailhead. Without waiting for his dusty wake to pass, he leaped out and stumbled a few feet before leaning forward and vomiting.

Once his stomach was empty, he stood and wiped his mouth on the cuff of his khaki work shirt and trudged up the trail until he reached an outcrop of large sedimentary rocks. He climbed them like a billy goat, and then he sat down, stared at Big Bear Lake, and ruminated.

Like sharp pinpricks, painful questions surfaced, questions that could not be repudiated, questions that, if answered honestly, would uncover truths that could only point to his own culpability. Just like the relentless rolling aftershocks, the questions would not stop: *Did I love her? After going together for almost two years, why didn't I just marry her and give her somethang better? Why didn't I buy her a new fridge?* Those questions only propagated ugly thoughts about himself.

He didn't know how long he had been perched on the rocks, but the sun said it was getting around supper time, and with his new plans well baked, with or without Wyatt, he needed to escape, and the only way he knew to do that was to bolt.

A memorial service was finally held for Shelda at the Bell Tower,[100] although it was not well attended because, even a month after the quake that led to her death, the survivors were still

---

100. The First Baptist Church, aka the Bell Tower, was constructed in 1931 and was the only religious structure to survive the White Wolf earthquake of 1952.

putting their lives back together. Besides, there was not enough of her left after the explosion to put in the ground.

Monroe sat in the back of the Bell Tower alongside Ona. He had asked her not to come, but the night before the service she pin-curled her hair and pressed her best garb, a navy-and-white polka-dot, tie-waisted dress with a full swing skirt. On the day of the memorial, she stood by the newly-fixed front door, adjusting her navy Juliette cap with its small burgundy feather peeking out from a small floret. Then she gave Monroe a nod and said, "Come on, honey, it's time." She pushed the new screen door open with her elbow as she shoved her sausage-shaped fingers into a pair of shiny blue nylon gloves.

With their last paychecks cashed, Wyatt gently loaded a wooden fruit crate filled with Ona's fried chicken, a box of soda crackers, slices of pecan pie, a bag of oranges, and a few relief tins of pork and beans left over from when Ona and Earl lived in Hooverville. Ona, Earl, and Grady stood quietly in front of the leaning walls of their house and waved at the boys' newly-acquired '46 Ford as it backed off the dirt lawn and turned onto the main road.

"'Member, we'z just a hoot'n'-a-holler away!" yelled Ona as she tried to hold back her tears, halfway wishing they'd stay and halfway wishing she was riding in the back seat.

As Wyatt turned onto the Weedpatch Highway he opened it up and stretched an arm through the open window as he said so long to Bakersfield and howdy to the Northwest.

"We shoulda painted a sign in the back winder—'Oregon or Bust,'" laughed Wyatt as he merged onto Highway 99 North.

Chapter 13

Old Gray Dog

California, 1953

DORA RAISED ENOUGH courage to leave her hometown of Creswell, Oregon, albeit on a whim to support her best friend Jerrie who was on the hunt for the elusive Sledge Giddy, a much older man. Mr. Giddy had promised Jerrie everlasting love while cuddling in the backseat of a '48 Ford parked behind the Creswell High School.

Dora's bean-picking money could have taken her someplace more memorable than a dying mill town. She had visions of a matching set of Samsonite luggage and a train ticket to New York, her birthplace, or even San Francisco, but her courage would only take her as far as Crescent City. Not that she lacked gumption. She once jumped a freight train from Creswell to Roseburg, sixty miles away, just to see a schoolmate's new horse. It was more that her acumen was shrouded in doubt about her own abilities and her obligation to her God.

Before striking out for Crescent City, Dora and Jerrie spent several hours leafing through the out-of-town phone books in the Eugene Public Library, then they placed long-distance calls from the public phone booth just outside the library. Neither of their families had seen the need to install a telephone. For one thing, connecting a phone was expensive for blue-collar families, and second, since most of their friends and family were also blue-collar workers, there would be no one to receive their calls.

Jerrie and Dora finally settled on a place to stay, the Seagull Rooming House. Mrs. Flood, the proprietor, assured them she ran a clean establishment "free of drunks and suitable for young Christian women." They set the arrival date and sent a money order to secure the only available room, one with a double bed, a hot plate, and a shared bath.

It was 10:27 p.m. when Jerrie and Dora stepped off the Greyhound in Crescent City. Typically, it would have been a nine-hour trip, but the bus broke down on the way to Florence, adding another six hours to an already emotional journey. Now they stood under the yellow streetlight, waiting for the porter to pull their luggage from the underbelly of the bus. Dora peered over Jerrie's collar to double-check if her monkey bites[101] were gone. They had disappeared two months earlier, but Dora checked anyway. That was the kind of friend she was, always sending out subtle reminders of others' transgressions.

"Don't worry. We'll find him," Dora said as she tried to reassure Jerrie. "You'll feel better once you get something to eat and can rest on some clean sheets." Jerrie quietly nodded as she bent down to pick up her pitiful suitcase with the broken latch that was held together with hemp twine.

After receiving directions from the late-night stationmaster, they headed for Pacific Avenue. With their western-style Levi Strauss wool plaid shirts tucked into rolled-up jeans and stretched-out bobby socks stuffed into well-worn loafers, they barely noticed their driver leaning against the station wall in the shadows. Once they passed him with their ponytails flipping right and left, he crushed his cigarette with the sole of his shoe and kicked the butt into the street. He watched them as they turned the corner, then he tilted his gray wool flannel uniform cap back on his head and thought, *For twenty-three years I've been driving them to a dead end. Nothing changes but their getups and hairdos.*

He then turned back toward his bus and yelled, "All aboard!" to the four passengers huddling around their cups of weak vending machine coffee and filtered cigarettes. Once he was back in

---

101. Monkey bites was a popular term for "hickeys" and "love bites."

his seat, he turned the hand crank so the destination sign read "EUREKA".

Turning the heel[102] into adulthood is complicated and arduous. If that fact were more universally understood, chances are few would make the journey, opting to jump off somewhere between fifteen and eighteen. But for those two young, religious country zealots, the knowledge gained by reading the pages of *The Watchtower* was all the fortification they thought necessary for survival in the outside world, and a blind mule is never afraid of the dark.

"I didn't think it was going to be this damp and cold," Dora said to Jerrie as they reached the corner of 7th and H Streets, where she pulled on her satin-lined buckskin jacket with back and arm fringe, her one prized possession bought with her bean-picking money.

"The fog is so thick you could cut it with a knife. I can barely read the street signs," Jerrie said as she slipped into her hunter green-and-red plaid reversible carcoat.

They continued north along 7th, a hodgepodge street lined with small businesses that included an insurance office, small appliance and radio fix-it shop, and a few pawnbrokers, all of whose door signs read, "Sorry, We're Closed. Please Come Again." Sprinkled among the storefronts were a few resilient homes with shiplap siding that were doing their best to hold their ground against the onslaught of the modern age.

If the fog had been any thicker, they may not have seen the soft yellow glow of the late-night café leak out from its massive plate-glass windows across the street.

"We still have about five blocks to go," said Jerrie. "Do you want to grab a cup of hot cocoa?"

"Sure. My hands could use a warm-up."

---

102. "Turning the heal" originally described the most difficult part of knitting a sock.

They hadn't seen a car drive by since they left the bus station. Crescent City was one of those towns where the sidewalks rolled up by eight every night, except for a couple of taverns that catered to the logging and mill crowds, so neither Dora nor Jerrie bothered to look for oncoming traffic before they crossed the street toward the Blue Pelican Café.

"Might just be our lucky night!" said Dora as she pointed to the "Help Wanted" sign taped to the door.

"Look alive!" replied Jerrie as she straightened her back, sucked in her stomach, and lifted her chin.

As Jerrie pulled the door open, a large cowbell announced their arrival to the sleepy wait and kitchen staff.

"Not exactly uptown!" whispered Dora as she nodded toward a man in a red plaid flannel shirt who was slouching over the table with his right arm flung across a Seeburg Wall-O-Matic[103] commiserating with Hank Williams as though Hank had written *"Your Cheatin' Heart"*[104] especially for him.

"Sit anywhere," said the thin, middle-aged waitress as she swept her hand across the dining area like she was presenting a new 1953 Buick Roadmaster at the Detroit Auto Show. "Don't mind Chuck; he's harmless. His wife left him… again."

Chuck let out a whimper as though he was hearing about his wife's departure for the first time. After wiping his nose on his shirt sleeve, he sat back and sucked air into his diaphragm and let out a sound that could fool the most ardent Hank Williams fan.

---

103. The Seeburg Wall-O-Matic was a small tabletop unit common in diners. It was connected to the main juke box stored somewhere in the backroom. You would put in your coin and select a couple of songs that played right at your table.

104. *"Your Cheatin' Heart"* was recorded by country music singer-songwriter Hank Williams Sr. in 1952. It is still regarded as one of country music's most important standards.

Aside from Chuck, the Blue Pelican Café was empty, but for the two old hobos seated at the far end of the counter. They were dressed in threadbare coats with shoulders bent forward to surround their coffee cups like they were burn barrels. Hobos are not the same as tramps or bums. Bums are lazy drunks; tramps work to drink; but hobos work to freely ramble about.

Many would have been put off by the sight of the hobos, but Jerrie and Dora were not. Their families lived next to a Pacific Northern Railway line and often had interactions with the hobo's creed. In fact, Dora's mother would usually provide the hobos with work in the form of chopping firewood or picking fruit in exchange for a liverwurst sandwich, a slice of pie, and all the hot coffee they wanted. She found some to be learned men, and she was convinced that at least one of them was the Prophet Elijah reincarnated.

"No need to look alive," whispered Dora. "By the looks of things, this place died in the '30s, and by the smell of it, someone forgot to turn the coffee pot off."

"Tips can't be good in a joint like this," Jerrie mumbled under her breath.

They took a booth as far away from Chuck as they could, next to the large window with the big Blue Pelican Café neon sign in it, and they slid their suitcases beneath the table.

"What can I get you gals?" asked the waitress as she pulled a pencil out of her graying hair and tapped it hard on her order pad.

"A cup of hot cocoa for me, unless you have Postum," asked Dora.

"No, just regular joe," answered the waitress.

"Then I'll take a hot cocoa," replied Dora.

"Same for me but with a side of toast," said Jerrie.

"I'll get that right up," said the waitress as she tucked the pencil back into her hair without writing the order down.

"You gals just come in on the old gray dog?"[105] asked the waitress when she returned with their order.

"Ya, just got in," Dora answered, trying to make herself sound more of a world traveler than she was. "The bus broke down in Florence."

"How long you plan on staying?"

Instinctively, Jerrie's hand moved under the table and gently rested them on her stomach.

"Depends on if we can find jobs," answered Dora.

"Got any waitressing experience?"

"Some—in Creswell, Oregon," Dora told her.

"Got a place to stay?"

"Yes," said Jerrie. "We have a room at the Seagull Rooming House."

The server nodded and, after some reflection, said, "I know Mrs. Flood. If you girls want a job, I can give you each about thirty to thirty-five hours a week. I need someone on the first shift; it starts at 4 a.m. *sharp*. I also need someone for the swing shift.

"We cater to the lumber crowd. Millworkers and loggers come in fast and hungry. And some will try to talk you out of your drawers." The waitress let her gaze rest on Jerrie, who blushed and cast her eyes downward. "Others," she continued, "are just mean as hell, but they all generally tip well. First shift starts tomorrow morning, and you'll find some old uniforms hanging on the back wall. So, if you want the job, you better drink up and get tucked in." She then turned and moved behind the counter to top off a hobo's coffee.

---

105. Slang for the Greyhound Bus Line.

"I don't stand for tardiness, you understand!" she shouted over the counter.

Jerrie and Dora nodded their tired heads and quickly drank their hot cocoa while scooting off their seats. Jerrie reached over the table, wadded her uneaten toast into a paper napkin, and shoved it into the pocket of her carcoat. "Didn't realize how hungry I was," she said.

With luggage in hand, they headed for the cash register to pay for their food.

"Meals included!" shouted the waitress. "Within reason."

"Thanks!" said Jerrie and Dora, almost in unison.

"Oh, and what're your names?"

"I'm Jerrie, and this here is Dora."

"I'm Arleen. Don't be late!"

"Four o'clock—got it!" Dora said over her shoulder. "We packed an alarm clock."

The cowbell sounded again as the girls slipped back into the damp, chilly air.

"There is a dark cloud hanging over those gals, Jack. I can just feel it in my bones," Arleen told one of the hobos as she lit up a Pall Mall cigarette.

"You're seldom wrong, but you can't save them all, Arleen, not all of them."

"Hey, Chuck!" called Arleen, "hit B24."

"Oh, come on, Arleen!" Jack said as he glanced up from his cup and shook his head.

"Jack, I don't tell you how to chase your demons, and you don't tell me how to fill my emptiness," Arleen responded sharply.

Jack let it slide, turned himself around, and wrapped his hands around his coffee cup, wishing he could comfort her like a husband.

With a voice of clocked-in confidence she said, "Play it Chuck, play B24, *'Forever and Always.'*"[106] Arleen then ambled over to Chuck's table and slapped down a quarter. "Play it until I say 'quit'." Then she moved to the plate glass window, stared into the fog, took a long draw on her cigarette, and exhaled the smoke just as Lefty Frizzell began to sing. As if her full lips were searching for someone, they began to gently move to the words while her mind retraced a forlorn journey along a well-beaten path.

---

106. *"Forever and Always"* was written by Lefty Frizzell and Lisie Lyle and was recorded by Lefty Frizzell in 1952.

Chapter 14

Runnin' Money

Oregon, 1952-53

JC AND FLOYD were quick to seize an opportunity to blaze a new trail. They collected machinery thought by the big logging outfits to be too expensive and time-consuming to move when pulling out for more timber-rich hills. Other pieces were pulled off the hill under the cover of darkness. It was not long before they could cobble together a skid and assemble several hoists, chains, cables, and pullies. And to the envy of other start-ups, they even had enough parts from discarded machinery to jim-my-rig a diesel donkey[107] and a self-propelled steel tower and loader. Now all they needed was an opportunity to launch their gyppo[108] outfit known as F&J Logging.

That opportunity came just after the second of three great fires, the Tillamook Burn, when the government and lumber companies realized the stands of dead and dried-out trees had become powder kegs awaiting yet another disaster. With the larger lumber outfits focused on more substantial harvests in hopes of recouping their losses due to the big fires, the forest service turned to independent gyppos who were more risk-averse and

107. A donkey is an engine used to power a winch system. It was originally powered by steam and later converted to diesel.
108. In the Northwest there were two logging labor types, company (corporate) and gyppo (independent).

could efficiently manage the dangerous dog holes[109] with their smaller equipment.

Monroe and Wyatt arrived in West Union on the very day JC and Floyd received their first contract. With a little jingle still in their pockets, Monroe and Wyatt were not eager to get behind the mule or under their father's whip; they were more interested in showing off their car, boots, and newly-gained worldly wisdom.

The night of Monroe and Wyatt's arrival, JC pushed himself away from the supper table after barely saying a word. He was a hardheaded man, a man who chewed his own tobacco but, most of all, he was an unforgiving man with a short fuse.

Martha took a more direct approach to expressing her disappointment, a trait she had picked up from her mother-in-law Jane and then perfected.

"If ya ask me," began Martha after Monroe and Wyatt showed off a new guitar, two handguns, and a couple of pocketknives to the younger boys, "you're lookin' like yaw got too far from your raisin'."

"Ain't tryin' to be uppity. Am just sayin' that they's more to life than broke, Bible, and bent," Monroe tried to explain as he and Wyatt set their new acquisitions aside.

"Ya better hush up, boy. Ya ain't never gonna be too big or too grown to whoop," Martha scolded. "How come yaw took your sweet time gittin' here?"

"We'z workin', Mamma," answered Wyatt.

"I speck too busy livin' high on the hog to remember God... or your family."

"We sent ya money," said Monroe.

---

109. Dog hole describes the narrow and sometimes treacherous coves along the Pacific Coast.

"Yaw ain't hardly sent nothin' for the past three years." Then she changed her tone and softly added, "Yaw know how bad off we'z been."

Looking for a way to change the subject, Monroe scanned the kitchen and only then recalled that someone was missing. "Where's Lil'bit?"

"She done run off with some old coot from up in the doghouse. She's over in Forest Grove now, happy as a dead pig in sunshine... so she be tellin' ever'body."

JC and Floyd had about sixteen children between them, but there were only nine able-bodied men and women who could work on the hill. They figured they needed at least fourteen. But with Monroe and Wyatt, and if they pulled in Virgil to be the whistle punk,[110] they could add a steam donkey. Naden and Martha, the better-educated wives, took on any paperwork needed for the state and forest service while running a moveable cookhouse. The older girls became loggerettes,[111] operating ran jammers[112] and loaders, moving equipment from one hill to another, and driving trucks into the mills.

F&J Logging Co. started out salvaging damaged pecker poles[113] from clear-cuts, blowdowns, and fires. Then they started harvesting hemlock, alder, and second- and third-growth timber,

---

110. When the donkey puncher was too far from the end of the line for verbal communication, the whistle operator was known as a whistle punk. He was placed between the men attaching the cables and the donkey puncher. When the cables were attached, a series of whistle blows signaled the donkey to begin pulling and the choker setters to stay out of harm's way.

111. Women became known as loggerettes during WWI and WWII as they started taking over work that had traditionally been done by men.

112. A log jammer is a piece of equipment that was often placed on a truck frame with a boom and cables that would skid logs up to 400 yards, something like a giant version of an arcade claw machine.

113. Pecker poles are thin, straight, closely spaced young trees that grow in a clear-cut or other space where trees have been removed.

but that only brought in enough to keep a roof over their heads and keep the equipment cobbled together.

It did not take long before midsize logging companies merged to create larger operators. The mergers left the smaller outfits fighting among themselves for what few scraps were left, so they would lowball bids, sabotage a competitor's equipment, spike truck tires and trees, toss sugar into gas tanks, and fire shots across a gulch. Those who were running small family operations were soon cut out of contracts until there was pretty much nothing but harvesting blowdowns[114] for a pulp mill run by a fella who knew every dollar by its first name.

"Ya know, sometimes it's possible to stay too long at the fair," Monroe told Wyatt one night as the two of them were leaning against their car in the dark with their hands buried in their empty pockets.

"I thank this show's about over anyways," replied Wyatt, and he gave a sly glance over his shoulder to see if anyone was approaching before he continued: "I say we blow, maybe go down somewheres around Coos Bay or Crescent City."

"We need some runnin' money," said Monroe as he stared at the ground and shifted his weight to one leg. "And I got an idea," he said as he kicked the dirt with the toe of his boot.

"Alrighty, let's hear it."

"Let's just say you'd better shine up your dancin' boots come Saturday night," snickered Monroe. Then he pushed himself away from the car and headed toward the house.

It's true that all roads led to Vernonia, and on that particular Saturday night, the road was dark and wet.

"I shoulda aired up," said Wyatt as he pulled the car out of a skid after braking too hard going around a corner.

---

114. Blow downs are trees felled by wind. They are also known as wind fall.

"We'z got all night," replied Monroe as he leaned back into the seat. "Although, it sure does seem peculiar that we'z the only ones on this road."

"I was thankin' the same..." began Wyatt, but then his grip tightened around the wheel as he pumped the brakes to avoid another skid. "What in the Sam hill was that?"

A great horned owl with a five-foot wingspan had swooped down along their windshield before landing in the middle of the road about fifteen feet beyond their headlights. Wyatt and Monroe scooted up in their seats, trying to get a better look. The owl stood still with its head facing the side of the road. Then it rotated its head slowly and stared toward the car with its earlike tufts and intimidating yellow eyes. Then, without flinching a feather, it returned its attention to the side of the road.

"It don't look like it's gonna move. Flip the headlights on and off," Monroe instructed nervously.

Nothing. The owl refused to budge. Wyatt gave the horn a couple of toots, but still the owl did not flinch, so Wyatt inched the car closer and closer, like in a game of chicken. Finally, the owl took flight.

As Wyatt coaxed the car back up to full speed he said, "If that don't beat anything I ever did see," and he shook his head as though he were trying to shake himself awake. Then he asked, "Ya don't thank it's some kinda sign, do ya?"

"Like what?"

"The Cherokee thank an owl could bring on sickness as punishment."

"Why the hell you thank we got that there blue rabbit's foot danglin' off our key chain fer?" Monroe replied, and then he laughed.

They drove in silence until they reached Vernonia, where Wyatt turned the car down Bridge Street. "There it is!" shouted Monroe as he pointed to a big neon sign that read, "The Axe Handle." All the Bridge Street parking spots were taken, so Wyatt tuned up a side street and parked. As they strolled toward the door, they stopped to read the poster hanging in the tavern window announcing live music by the cover band Bobby Wonder and His Pickers.

They entered to find the bar bursting, the dance floor packed, and Bobby Wonder singing *Rub-A-Dub-Dub.*[115] They ran into a few guys they knew from up on the hill, and they bought each other beers. But it did not take Wyatt long before he had some girl pinned against the bar, trying to convince her they were made for each other. Monroe cut in on the dance floor during a slow song, and soon he was hugging and swaying like they were coming in on a high tide.

Finally, the evening wound down; the bar announced last call, and Bobby Wonder and His Pickers packed up.

"Before we cut out, I gotta see a man about a horse," Monroe told Wyatt as he headed for the bathroom in the back.

"One thang about beer; ya never own it," laughed Wyatt.

Once inside the bathroom, Monroe unlatched the window lock and rigged it so it still looked secure. Then he returned to the bar and patted the waitress on the ass as he said "Goodnight."

Wyatt moved their car a block down from The Axe Handle and, within the shadows they had a view of the front door, so they waited for the tender to lock up and leave.

Once the bar was empty, they drove the car into the alley behind the bar and parked just under the window Monroe had manipulated.

---

115. *"Rub-A-Dub-Dub"* was written and recorded by Hank Thompson, an American country and western singer whose musical style is characterized as honky-tonk western swing with a mixture of fiddles, electric guitar, and steel guitar.

Once back inside the bar, Monroe found only the back bar lights illuminated, but that was enough for him to locate the door to the secure back office. After giving the door a few powerful jolts with his shoulder, it came loose from its lock, and just as he suspected, there was a desk that he believed would hold a cash box with enough runnin' money to get him and Wyatt out of Oregon.

As he loudly jiggled, pulled, and pushed on the locked desk drawers, papers and glasses went crashing onto the floor, and he did not hear the footsteps of the large bar owner approaching until the man was in the room.

Monroe looked up with shock, darted around the desk, and ran toward the bathroom with the bar owner not far behind. Monroe pulled his chest up over the windowsill and began to lean his body out the window when a shot from behind him rang out.

"You thieving son of a bitch!" yelled the bar owner. "I'll kill you!"

Monroe pushed his body forward until he landed on the ground beneath the window.

Wyatt started the car's engine, pushed the back door open from inside and yelled, "Git in!" Monroe slid belly-first onto the backseat while Wyatt floored it, causing the back door to slam shut on its own.

The car skidded when it hit the blacktop, but Wyatt quickly got it under control. Without looking back at his brother, he asked, "Ya all right? Did he gitcha?"

"Ya, that goddamn bastard got me in the side," Monroe answered as he felt something warm and sticky oozing out.

"Gotta get ya to a hospital," Wyatt said, twisting to see Monroe in the back seat through the rearview mirror. "The closest one is in Portland; hang on!"

"Don't seem like I got much choice."

By the time they arrived at Good Samaritan Hospital, the car smelled like iron.

Wyatt assured the admissions staff that they worked for a large logging outfit and could easily cover the cost of treatment.

After an examination, the doctor asked, "How did you get shot?"

"Well, let's just say her husband come home early," Monroe lied.

"I hope it was worth it because it looks like we're going to have to remove one of your kidneys."

It took Monroe a little over a month to convalesce from his surgery, and during that time he tried to get closer to his sister Adilia. She was just out of pigtails when he last saw her. Now she was a grown, married woman. Her husband Ernest was older than she was and no longer working on the hill, but he had a good, steady job at a mill, and it was not by coincidence that Monroe's visits coincided with Ernest's Friday paychecks. But Adilia's husband was not naïve, and like everyone else, he suspected there was more to Monroe's story.

"I'll tell you what, Roe," Ernest said calmly one Friday night as he rolled his cigarette pack back into the sleeve of his white T-shirt, exposing a scar in the shape of a moth, "I'll give you your runnin' money if you leave Oregon in the next twenty-four hours and never step foot in it again."

Silently, Monroe took stock of the man who stood before him, a former Marine who had fought at Tarawa. "Well, if that's the way ya want it," he replied, feeling offended.

"And take that no-good brother of yours with ya."

Before dawn, Monroe and Wyatt were driving south along Highway 1 with one less kidney than they'd come with, and a pocketful of broke.

Chapter 15

Denying Prudence

California, 1953

THEIR PATHS CROSSED in the fall of 1953 in a small Northern California coastal town along the Smith River. Crescent City had always been a boom-and-bust town, yet that did not stop new fortune seekers from jumping off the Greyhound with a suitcase full of dreams. The area started seeing a greater number of Europeans arrive when gold was discovered in the 1800s, but the gold only lasted long enough to lay a road in and establish a new shipping lane. The town fathers put up the money to build a lighthouse, but a little too late. A year earlier the paddle steamer *Brother Jonathan* had struck a reef just off Point St. George; 244 souls were lost, and only nineteen survived. It was the postwar logging boom that brought people back, but by the time Dora and Monroe arrived, even that was running thin.

Monroe and Dora met at a farewell potluck dinner in the basement of Brother Campion, an elder of the local congregation of Jehovah's Witnesses. It was a small congregation made up mostly of seniors and families who had run out of money and could not afford to leave. Everyone who could had already journeyed to where menial jobs were more plentiful, and those who remained were left to cling onto one another like a gaggle of snow geese flying over a rod and gun club.

Brother Campion had recently retired from a local lumberyard. He wore his thin gray hair in a comb-over, and what he lacked in hair he more than made up for with forest-like eyebrows that resembled those of John L. Lewis[116] as they curved over his thick, semi-rimmed eyeglasses like awnings on an Airstream. He was fond of short-sleeved sports shirts that he wore buttoned up to the neck in such a manner that he appeared to be choking himself to death.

Now with secular work behind him, Brother Campion now focused more on God's work—and turning his basement into a showcase. He built a small kitchen in one corner and equipped it with a sink and the refrigerator he'd moved down from the central kitchen when he bought Sister Campion a new two-door Frigidaire in her favorite color of pink to match her electric stove. He also bought an apartment-size GE electric four-burner range from a family who left for Sacramento to take a janitorial job with the school district. The basement updates made his home the ideal place to host the rare social events the witnesses allowed beyond weddings, funerals, and their yearly Passover celebration, a holy celebration that falls on the first full moon after the Paschal[117] full moon. Creating this social setting gave Brother Campion an opportunity to watch for any shenanigans or heretical thinking that might worm its way into his faithful flock.

His wife, Sister Campion, stuck to the strict rules embroidered in large cursive letters across the dishtowels she inherited from her grandmother and that she proudly displayed on a multi-tiered towel bar that hung next to the sink in their upper floor kitchen. The towels advised:

Wash on Monday
Iron on Tuesday
Bake on Wednesday
Brew on Thursday
Churn on Friday
Mend on Saturday
Go to Church on Sunday

---

116. For forty years, coal miners hailed John L. Lewis, who had massive, forest-like eyebrows, as their leader. He was credited with bringing them high wages, pensions, and medical benefits.
117. Paschal means Passover in Greek.

Displaying the towels was an act of defiance by Sister Campion: it was the first time she had refused to bend to the instructions of her husband who instructed her in an authoritarian voice to pull the "Brew" and "Church" towels down. But then he reached up and pulled them off the rack and tossed them into the trash himself.

"There is nothing in the scriptures that says either of those words are evil!" she told him as she fished the towels out of the trash. Although she could defend Thursday, she could not do the same for Sunday: only pagans went to church; true believers went to the Kingdom Hall.[118]

With only a hot plate and the rooming house's community refrigerator waiting for a service call, Dora and Jerrie were limited in how far they could push their culinary skills, which were the key components to winning acceptance among the sisters and respect from the brothers, not to mention a potential husband. Dora and Jerrie pleaded with Arleen to allow them to use the café's kitchen in off-hours. Reluctantly, Arleen gave in, but not without a full measure of her womanly advice.

"I don't know why you spend time with those Bible thumpers," Arleen bluntly said with her hands firmly placed on her hips. "You will not find a rock and a frock there—only a ball and chain. Still water runs deep. You remember that," she warned as she lifted one hand to point her finger at the girls.

"Yes, madam," replied Jerrie who, despite hearing that expression dozens of times from her mother, still did not understand what was so wrong about still water running deep.

You can tell a lot about a congregation by the way it sets up its buffet tables. The sisters in the Crescent City congregation used plastic utensils to save time and work, yet they fished through garbage buckets to retrieve plastic forks, spoons, and knives, sorting and washing them after each use. Thin disposable ta-

---

118. Kingdom Hall is the name of the building in which Jehovah's Witnesses hold their services.

blecloths purchased at Woolworths could have more lives than a cat, providing Scotch tape was skillfully applied to tears and spots where hot dishes had melted the plastic. Often, a well-placed doily was the best option. If frugality was next to godliness, that congregation was close enough to rinse God's socks.

Careful not to disturb the pride of place that was generally reserved for the congregation overseer's wife, Dora and Jerrie carefully positioned their flip-top deviled eggs between a baloney cake and a tuna Jell-O mold, a recipe that most assuredly had come from Jell-O's *Man-Pleaser Salad Cookbook*.

The centerpiece, or "pride of place," was an elaborate display of skewered cubed Spam, cheese, and green olives stuffed with pimento peppers thoughtfully arranged on a giant head of cabbage with colorful plastic toothpicks that no one dare touch until every guest had a chance to marvel at its mastery.

"This is why you always bring something you like to these things," Jerrie whispered to Dora as she arranged the parsley garnish more artfully than the surrounding competition.

"Hello, Sister Ziegenfuss," called the congregation's presiding overseer,[119] Brother Squat.

Some people say owners start to look like their dogs after a while. Brother Squat looked so much like his name that folks wondered why he had never changed it. He was as wide as he was tall. The buttons on his shirt always looked as though they were under a great deal of stress, making people want to wear eye protection when speaking to him. With his big rosy cheeks, a full head of unruly white hair, and sparkling eyes he would have been the congregation's Santa Claus if only the witnesses had celebrated Christmas. Before Brother Squat found the "Truth,"[120] or rather before his wife dragged him into it, his ca-

---

119. The presiding overseer is the top-ranking member of the local congregation.

120. Jehovah's Witnesses believe they are the only ones who have the "truth" and often use the word "truth" to describe a state of enlightenment gained from following the Bible as interpreted by the governing body at the Watch Tower Bible and Tract Society.

reer was on a slow climb in the county offices. First, he had been an assistant microfiche technician, then a deputy country recorder where his excellent penmanship landed him the sworn duty of handwriting each land and mining transaction in Del Norte County's massive land ledgers that dated back to the 1800s. He often credited that lateral move to his reputation for trustworthiness that came with being a member of the Witnesses. But the job became somewhat of a punishment. Unlike his microfiche position where he sat all day, the recorder's job required him to stand and lift weighty ledgers, leaving him to complain that his ankles were starting to turn inward.

"I hope I didn't butcher your name," Brother Squat said. "What is its origin? Does it have a meaning?" "You did better than most," Dora said before smiling reassuringly. "It's German and means 'goat's feet.' My dad immigrated just before the war."

"Got here just in time, did he?" Brother Squat said. Not expecting a reply, he turned to Jerrie and asked, "And how are you settling in, Sister McCarthy?"

"It's colder and damper than I thought it would be, but otherwise we're settling in just fine."

"We were all hoping you gals would get the time off."

"Oh, Arleen was happy to give us the night off—saves her some money," Dora said. "And she pinches the nickel so hard the Indian comes riding out on the buffalo."

"Business is slow then?"

"Well, we like to say the Blue Pelican has two speeds—fast and stop," piped up Jerrie.

They all laughed.

"Oh, you gals are a breath of fresh air," said Brother Squat. "Say, have you met Brother Hornbeck?" he asked as he motioned to a young man leaning against an outer wall who was having a one-sided conversation with an elderly woman seated on a folding chair and doing her best to ignore him. Monroe was dressed in a pressed white dress shirt tucked into a dark pair of pleated, wide-leg trousers and a narrow, dark brown belt that matched his well-polished cowboy boots. His light-colored eyes were inviting, although upon closer inspection you would notice that one eye was blue and the other slightly green. His black hair was thick with an unruly wave dangling over his forehead that gave him an intriguing air.

"He just got here too—a real character, I'd say. Was born in Oklahoma, as I understand. Moved around Texas, Louisiana, and Arkansas before he ventured up to Portland, Oregon, by way of Bakersfield. Come out with his brother, but we don't see much of him," Squat said out of earshot of Brother Hornbeck.

"Your people," Dora whispered to Jerrie with a smirk. Jerrie rolled her eyes, annoyed by Dora's relentless derogatory references to her Southern roots.

"Brother Monroe Hornbeck," asked Squat, "have you met Sister McCarthy and Sister Ziegenfuss?"

"Heck, if that ain't a mouthful. Hope yaw don't ask me to spell it," laughed Monroe with a grin. Then he extended his arm and firmly shook their hands.

"You can just call me Dora."

"And I'm Jerrie."

"I'm Monroe. But folks call me Roe. It's a pleasure to meet yaw."

"Well, I'd better say the blessing before someone starts eating the legs off the table," said Brother Squat as he turned and called for folks to bow their heads.

When the whitewash was stripped off Brother Squat's lengthy prayer it sounded something like this:

We call upon you, our dear Heavenly Father Jehovah... and yes, we know we have no business speaking with you directly, but we are better than any other religious groups and have cut out the middleman, Jesus Christ, for the most part.

We have done terrible things, disgusting things, shameful things—basically, we are just terrible people, not at all living up to your expectations of us, which is probably why you are only allowing 144,000 into your heavenly kingdom, leaving the rest of us to clean up the carnage after Armageddon. And yes, we acknowledge and respectfully thank you for allowing us to live forever as a reward for being your "cleaners".

Please note the "forever" part will eventually bore us out of our gourds after the first 500 years, and we will most likely resort back to our default position.

We promise to be obedient so long as you keep the men in charge and the women and children submissive, and we will do our level best to continue keeping up the perfect family facade. Non-believers will not hear our wives disagreeing with us or see our sons' smoking cigarettes in the high school bathroom, nor our daughters making out under the bleachers with the local football team.

As to our international brothers, the Roman Hands and Russian Fingers, we will keep them under wraps and deal with them internally—no sense in exposing the dirty laundry.

And since we have already admitted to being lowlifes, we'll forge our salutations in someone else's name...

In Jesus' name, Amen.

★

Wyatt felt as though a rainbow had fallen from the sky the night he first laid eyes on her, and from then on he was rarely seen alongside his brother at the Kingdom Hall.

Her name was Jewells Vickers, a rockabilly girl in her early twenties who resembled the newly-discovered Bettie Page.[121]

---

121. Bettie Mae Page was an American model who was often referred

Wyatt and Jewells met in a tavern called The Mouse Trap, a place where loggers went to blow off steam and the mill workers came to get drunk. And while the two groups maintained a certain level of civility during the week, Fridays were payday, and unless the wives beat their husbands to the pay shack, pay envelopes were likely to be set on the bar to cover damages caused by someone getting a beer bottle or a chair busted alongside their head.

It was on a Friday night that Wyatt fell in love. The bartender, Max, a broken-down logger, had just put another hole in the ceiling with his PPK[122] and yelled, "Jewells, get over there and put some semblance of order back into this place!"

Jewells gently set her drink tray on the sticky bar and quietly approached the two fighting men. With her birdlike fingers she rested her hand on the men's shoulders like it was a kiss from an angel. And for a split second, the room fell deathly silent.

Jewells was well respected—even admired. She had what some might call a *je ne sais quoi*. And while men found her attractive and women found her ready smile, soothing voice, and gentle mannerisms nonthreatening. She wore her thick, shoulder-length, raven black hair pulled into a ponytail that she could control like a fly swatter to ward off unwanted attention from drunk patrons, and her deep blue eyes seemed to illuminate under her heavy bangs.

"Henry, clean that blood off the side of your head. And Larry, set that table back upright," Jewells told the two fighting men in a voice not much louder than a whisper. "I'll buy you both a beer so you can kiss and make up."

The tavern broke out in thunderous laughter that shook the floorboards as the two men bowed their heads and did as they

---

to as the "Queen of Pinups." She was known for her jet-black hair, blue eyes, and trademark bangs. She gained worldwide popularity in the early 1950s.

122. The PPK is part of a series of pistols developed by the gun manufacturer Walther PP and first released in 1930.

were told. And it was at that exact moment that Wyatt knew he was in love.

For a month after that night, although he was not a heavy drinker, Wyatt stopped by The Mouse Trap after work. He watched Jewells' small frame flit around the tavern floor, flashing her row of overlapping teeth to customers. "There ain't no beauty in perfection," Wyatt uttered to himself.

To all the regulars it was as clear as a pig sitting on a sofa that the two were made for each other. So it came as no surprise that, within a month, they were cohabitating—without the benefit of clergy—in Jewells' small trailer on the outskirts of Smith River.

Chapter 16:

Hunting Season

California, 1953

WITH WYATT SETTING up housekeeping with Jewells, Monroe filled his free time driving Dora and Jerrie around the countryside on their days off. They bounced around old logging roads, scouting abandoned mines and forgotten prospector shacks. They shared family stories and hopes for themselves and wishes for each other. Jerrie and Monroe developed a bittersweet bond built from scattered recollections of parched red dirt, lost farms, and food cravings like *cochon de lait*,[123] fried oysters, cracklins, and chowchow.

On a warm Saturday afternoon, seated in the back, Jerrie pressed her head against the soft brown mohair of Monroe's newly-bought used '48 Plymouth. She stared blindly out the open window, letting the warm wind fly through her thick ginger hair and breathed deep into her lungs the scent of the giant sequoias mixed with the ferns that sprang up to nourish themselves among the fallen trees.

What a mess I've made of things, Jerrie thought.

★

---

123. *Cochon de lait* is a French term used in Louisiana for pig pickin' (a pig roast).

Early that week she had contemplated throwing herself down the stairs of her rooming house but decided against it for fear she would just end up with a broken leg, which would only make matters worse. "This shithole doesn't even have a street-car to jump from!" she grumbled to herself as she shuffled to the drugstore and bought a douching bag, then plodded another four blocks to the hardware store. Then she returned to her rooming house, thought about her mother, and fought back her tears as she replayed the sacrifices her parents had made like a broken record.

"How could I have been so gullible?" Jerrie asked herself aloud.

She then turned her thoughts away from her mother and tried to make sense of Sledge. Maybe he was coming back to Creswell; his brother had said as much...but not in so many words. "Gone to make some fast money in Crescent City at some mill job," his brother had told her when she went looking for him. "No, he didn't leave an address."

Behind the locked door of the rooming house's shared bathroom, Jerrie sat on the edge of the claw tub, alone with her thoughts, alone with her truth. *I can't wait for him*, she realized.

In one hand she held the bottle of Thrill dish soap she had grabbed from the room she shared with Dora. In the other, she gripped the tin of turpentine she had bought from Ace Hardware. On the floor rested her new oxblood douche bag with its cord and nozzle winding around her feet. She had never used a douche bag, although her mother had one hanging from a hook on the back of the bathroom door. But she had read the advertisements in *Good Housekeeping*: "Family doctors know very often that incompatibility means ignorance of feminine hygiene."

Holding up the turpentine, she began reading the label as though it would tell her how much she should measure out to terminate an unwanted pregnancy. She grinned when she read the warning label: "Danger, flammable. May be harmful or fatal if swallowed."

As she unscrewed the metal cap on the can and took a sniff, she wondered if she would feel much pain and how much blood there would be.

Suddenly, she heard a loud knock at the door. Startled, she almost dropped the tin on the floor.

"I'll be out in a minute," she shot back in a curt voice, thinking it was the old busybody who lived at the end of the hall.

"Jerrie, you in there?" It was Dora.

"Yes," answered Jerrie weakly.

"Arleen wants you in early today," Jerrie heard Dora say as she sat frozen on the edge of the tub.

"Did you hear me?"

"Yes, yes, I'll... I'll be right out," Jerrie said as she searched for her composure. She then heard Dora slowly step away from the door, and Jerrie exhaled. Cautiously, she put the metal cap back on the can and meticulously wrapped the hose and nozzle around her douche bag. After placing the turpentine and douche bag back into the brown paper bag, she got on her knees and pushed the bag under the claw bathtub as far as she could reach, checking to make sure her secret could not be discovered from any vantage point.

"Guess I won't be takin' a bubble bath then," Jerrie told Dora upon entering their shared room. Then she set the bottle of Thrill next to their hot plate.

*

Jerrie paused that recent memory and tucked it safely back into a dark corner, reminding herself that the package she had stored under the bathtub was still available. When her courage rose high enough again, she leaned forward and rested her folded arms along the back of the front bench seat where Monroe and Dora were still talking about horses. Gently, Jerrie steered the conversation around to the mill workers, hoping to pick up some clues about Sledge, but always careful not to show her hand.

She reasoned that not only did Monroe live in a muzzleloader,[124] one of the few remaining after the Hobbs logging outfit shut down in '39, he was also known as a jack-of-all-trades, working anything from a cat skinner[125] to several two street hookers,[126] all of which would give him numerous occasions to bump into Sledge. Or he may even have met him on one of their seemingly many blowouts.[127]

"Say, Monroe, do ya ever run into any guys from Oregon in the camp or the taverns?" Jerrie asked. "My brother said a few guys he used to pal around with were headed to Crescent City."

"There's a few fellas I know come from around Vernonia."

"These guys would be from around Creswell, Cottage Grove, or Coos Bay."

"There's 'bout five outfits they coulda signed up with. Ya know if they got on with Simpson, M&M, Agnew, or one of the mills?"

"Can't exactly say."

"Did they say if they's cuttin' redwood or Doug fir?"

"No."

"Well, I don't rightly know anybody offhand, but I'll ask around for ya."

---

124. Within the context of the timber industry a "muzzle loader" refers to a bunkhouse filled well beyond a reasonable capacity.
125. A "cat skinner" is someone who operates a Caterpillar, Cletrak, or any other piece of machinery that rolls on tracks.
126. A "two street hooker" was any solid red piece of equipment such as a truck, Allis Chalmers Crawler, etc.
127. A "blowout" is a logging term for a night on the town.

"Don't ask on my account; they wouldn't know me," Jerrie said softly as she unfolded her arms and pushed herself back against the seat.

Monroe gave Jerrie a long look in his rearview mirror. "Alrighty," he said, calmly.

He turned his sedan onto another unmarked dirt road leading downhill into a small valley that gently curved along the Smith River. The valley once was home to a large stand of ancient and majestic trees, some thousands of years old and hundreds of feet tall. But the current landscape looked as though the trees had been indiscriminately cut to stubble by a drunk using a rusty razor. The lumber was needed to expand cities like San Francisco and to build houses for the rich in places like Carson, Winchester, and Whittier. In their place now came young Douglas fir volunteers fighting to reclaim their ancestral land and smother out the once vibrant sawmills whose names had long been forgotten. Prostrated at the feet of the strong young trunks were rust-covered, galvanized sheet metal that had once sheltered a large rough-cut outbuilding to protect a long carriage and giant circular saw. Just to the right of it was what remained of the debarker shed, its dry, gray, weathered boards scattered among pullies, flywheels, and cranks that had been abandoned by overly-ambitious curiosity seekers. Following the path of the river were miles of decaying cable that were being consumed by water and vegetation. Not yet concealed by overgrowth and young trees stood a large wigwam, but instead of burning a fire, long vines wound around its opening where spiders swung their threads from side to side, weaving a door of peril.

"Hope yaw don't mind bein' among these here pecker poles. A little more sunshine might do us a heap agood," said Monroe as he pulled the car off the dirt road, stopped next to the river, and pulled up on the parking brake.

"How 'bouts here—a place of solitude and contemplation. Dinner—or lunch, as yaw call it—cuz I'm so hungry my belly thinks my throat's been cut," laughed Monroe as he enthusiastically jumped out and jammed a nearby piece of wood under one of the back tires as a precaution.

Before heading out that day, they made a stop at a grocery store in Smith River and purchased the makings for a picnic: orange pops, soft bread, sliced deli meats, baloney for Monroe, salami for Jerrie, and headcheese for Dora along with a large watermelon, one Monroe and Jerrie had insisted the clerk plug[128] before they would buy it.

Dora pulled together a simple German potato salad from a recipe she had learned from her mother—boiled potatoes, lemon, oil, and salt. Jerrie stuffed a large paper bag with eating utensils and plates and yanked two quilts off their bed that she had snuck out of their room despite the watchful eye of Mrs. Flood.

With the quilts spread out along the riverbank, and the watermelon securely placed in the water of a small cove to chill, they sat and ate their lunch in the warmth of the sun and shared stories of how they had learned to drive, what their favorite movies were, and tales about their families. And, as it sometimes does in odd-numbered groups, a few people found corners to safely back themselves into and, eventually, withdraw into their own private thoughts. Such was the case with Jerrie. Stretched out on the quilt with her eyes shielded beneath her horn-rimmed sunglasses, the sun began to unravel her limbs and untie her muscles until she became aware of the many layers of sounds around her. Behind Monroe's voice she could hear the buzzing of bees. *Or was that a yellow jacket going after the meat?* she wondered. As her mind quieted further, she heard the flutter of a dragonfly and the whispers of dried leaves as they rubbed against one another. She felt the warmth of the sun cover her like a blanket, loosening her joints like oil loosens a rusty hinge until her body unfolded in slow motion, like the spring of a jack-in-the-box might.

---

128. It was a common practice for customers to ask the produce manager to cut a triangular slit, a "plug," before purchase to check for ripeness. If the customer did not accept the melon, then the triangle plug was replaced.

The scent of the natural world filled her lungs, and her breathing became deeper until she completely let go of the burden and guilt of not participating in the conversation that surrounded her, and she allowed herself to slowly move freely among the corridors of her inner mind, floating between that tiny space buried in the countless levels of consciousness. Jerrie allowed herself to be pulled into unexplored caverns. Perhaps it was because she rested upon ground that would forever belong to the Tolowa Dee-ni' Nation[129] that lured her to that place, or maybe it was her need to better understand her own journey. In any case, she ran head-on into a vision of her own ancestral people, not the Scots-Irishmen who had made wives of First Nation women, but the women themselves, her grandmothers before the Indian Removal, before Oklahoma.

"Get up, come closer," Jerrie heard a woman's voice call to her. But Jerrie did not move. She was confused. She did not recognize the voice and seemed to have lost her bearings. She was caught between two forces, each pulling her in a different direction.

"Hurry up, I don't have time to waste." Jerrie heard the voice demand. "Much work has yet to be done before the Green Corn Ceremony."[130]

Jerrie slowly opened her eyes and raised herself to a sitting position to find that she was no longer on the quilt beside the river. Instead, she was sitting on bare ground. She looked down at her hand as though it belonged to someone else and saw her fist was clutching red dirt, and she could smell the strong scent of iron. She knew where she was—Oklahoma, next to the reservation where she was raised before Oregon. Her mind was filled

---

129. The Tolowa Dee-ni' Nation, previously known as Smith River Rancheria, is a federally recognized tribe of Tolowa people in Del Norte County, California.

130. The biggest Choctaw celebration and most important spiritual event, the Green Corn Ceremony was held when the corn began to ripen. It was a time of fasting, thanksgiving, personal reflection, and stomp dancing when people forgave each other for their wrongs, extinguished the community's fires, and rekindled them.

with questions, but the woman's voice was relentless and kept pricking her.

"Stand up, stand up," said the woman. "Move closer. I want to get a better look at you."

Jerrie let the red dirt fall from her fist as she tried to steady herself into a kneeling position. Then she cast her eyes on an old woman about ten feet from her.

The old woman was using a three-foot long, hollowed-out log and a tree limb that had been stripped of its bark like they were mortar and pestle. The old woman raised the limb high above her head, then she pushed it down into the hollow log with great force. Jerrie heard a loud *crack*. Again, the old woman raised the limb and plunged it deep into the log: *crack*.

"I want to get a better look at you. Come closer. But not too close. I don't want to get the pox."

"Pox?" asked Jerrie, still kneeling on the parched earth.

"Yes, pox, smallpox," said the old woman as she continued to lift and drop her pestle. "Or religion, or whatever plague your people are now spreading."

"We have a vaccination for smallpox," said Jerrie as she struggled to come to her feet. Then she wiped the dirt from her bare knees.

"Do you have one for religion? It has killed more people than the pox."

"No, religion is still going pretty strong," Jerrie answered. It wasn't just her head that felt light, her entire body felt like it was balancing on a mound of sticky marshmallow cream.

"Figures!" scolded the old woman.

Jerrie looked at the woman dressed in a long, ruffled skirt and a long-sleeved white shirt with frayed cuffs. The hands that lifted the pestle with such determination were knotted and cracked.

Her dark hair was pulled back into a mound on the back of her head and tied with a strip of cloth. The deep crevasses on the woman's face threw dark shadows over her brow and along her cheeks, yet there was warmth in her eyes and concern in her determined voice. Jerrie could find no clue as to where the old woman was exactly, other than she seemed to be standing alone next to a mature cornfield.

"Come on. You are not the hunter, and I am not the alligator," said the old woman. "I am not going to eat you. How do they call you?"

Jerrie's eyes darted around the cornfield. She knew cornfields; she had planted corn, picked corn, canned corn, and cooked corn. But this field was different. The kernels were not hiding behind their silk and husks. They were visible and flashed the brilliant colors of rubies, amethyst, emeralds, and topaz, all highly polished and glistening in the sun. When her eyes focused closer she saw an even greater oddity: some of the ears were faces, faces of people, animals, birds, and insects, all of them wrapped in silk spun from threads of gold, and they moved in such a way as to cast the sun's reflection into Jerrie's eyes, sometimes blinding her. When she tried to escape the glare, the kernels followed her sightline. It was as though she was looking at the eyes in a portrait at a museum: no matter where she stood in the gallery, the eyes would never break their gaze.

A hundred questions rammed into each other in Jerrie's brain. Although she was naturally curious, she felt the rational thing to do was try to escape, but to where? The high corn stocks might as well have been a ten-foot-tall stockade. *If I don't know how I got here, how can I find my way back?* she reasoned.

"Come on, how do they call you?" the woman asked again.

"J-jerrie," she stuttered.

"What does it mean?"

"I don't know that it means anything; it's short for Geraldine."

"I am not surprised," scoffed the old woman. Jerrie could hear moans coming from the ears of corn and turned to see the stocks swaying their disapproval.

"Your generation gives little thought to the importance of a name. You worry more about how it will be misused or mispronounced than what it means: 'Will my baby's name make him a big chief; will it make her brave?'" continued the old woman with great sarcasm as she pounded the pestle down hard upon the mortar.

"What are you pounding?" Jerrie inquired.

"Black root mixed with cedar root.[131]"

"Why did you bring me here? And who are you?"

"*Me* bring *you* here?" snickered the old woman. "I do not have the power to bring people here." The wolf corn leaned back on its stock and released a drawn-out howl toward the sky, prompting all the other corn faces to snicker and laugh. "But it is my obligation to care for those who have found the trail back to the summer camp, even those who have forgotten their ancestral ways. I am your great, great, great grandmother Opa. It means owl, in case you want to know. What can I answer for you, granddaughter?"

Jerrie stood with her head turned to the ground in shame and silence. There were three branches in Jerrie's family tree: Scots-Irish, Choctaw,[132] and Okie. And although her hair was ginger, she had little in common with her European ancestors, and apart from her fascination with the natural world, she had noth-

---

131.   Many tribal societies used black root and cedar root as abortifacient agents as far back as the 1600s.

132.   The Choctaw were the first Native American tribe forced to relocate under the Indian Removal Act. The Choctaw were exiled because the US wanted to use their resources and sell them for settlement and agricultural development by European Americans. During World War I, Choctaw soldiers served in the US military as the first Native American code talkers by using the Choctaw language.

ing connecting her to the Choctaw Nation, so Jerrie leaned into her Okie roots.

"Hurry up, hurry up, the ceremony is coming upon us. We can't be waiting for you," said Opa impatiently.

Kicking the red dirt with the toe of her loafer, Jerrie looked up and said, "I'm in a bit of a jam."

"Yes, I know. We *all* know," Opa said as she rolled her eyes around the cornfield, which caused the stocks of corn to shake like tambourines at a church revival.

Taking a moment to collect her thoughts so as not to further humiliate herself, Jerrie looked around at the corn stocks. She did not know how she had missed seeing it before, or perhaps it had just recently appeared, but whichever the case, she now saw a baby board leaning against the base of the corn stocks.

"Is that my baby?" asked Jerrie as she nodded in the direction of the baby board.

"It has not yet been decided."

"Can I see it?"

"No, as nothing is yours to own, only to protect. Your heart has yet to open and receive such responsibility. If you choose not to be a protector, there will be nothing strapped to this board for you to see but a piece of wood bound in the skin of a deer and a softly woven blanket from the fer of a rabbit. If your heart leads you, you may choose to see and stretch your hand out to receive your ancestral duty to be its caretaker for all time, just as I am yours, for you cannot taste the corn before it has been planted."

Jerrie's eyes took in the full form of her grandmother, the rise and fall of her breast with each breath. *This must be what love sounds like,* thought Jerrie. And when their eyes locked for a few seconds, Jerrie knew *this is the look of disappointment.* It was not disappointment for what Jerrie had done but for what she had forgotten, and for what Opa had failed to keep alive.

"How do I get back to the beginning?" asked Jerrie.

"You are asking me to relate a story the tongue cannot tell," answered Opa, and with that her form began to dissolve along with the cornfield until there was nothing left but the sound of the mortar and pestle thrashing. And when Jerrie's ears focused on its rhythm, it began to sound less and less like thrashing and more like *"The Cattle Call."*[133]

Jerrie sat up on the quilt. Still shaking from her dream, she gently wiped away the tears that had fallen from her welled-up eyes and looked about her, hoping no one had noticed.

Fifty yards away, sitting on a rusted-out Dolbeer Donkey,[134] sat Monroe with his felt cowboy hat resting on the back of his head. He was singing and plucking away on the guitar he carried in the trunk of his car, and Dora was yodeling in all the right places.

The week following Jerrie's vision dream, Arleen asked her to fill in as the cashier at the Pelican Café while she dealt with a family matter in Yuba City. Besides running the register, cashiers were required to help bus tables and restock the front end of the house. To most of the other waitresses, the extra responsibilities were not worth the extra ten cents an hour. Jerrie needed the extra work, not because of the extra sixty cents but because she needed to work herself into a stupor.

Working oneself into a state of unconsciousness was how her family dealt with difficulties that seemed insurmountable. It wasn't so much that excessive work solved the problem as much as it made you so weary that you no longer cared about remedying the affliction. They worked to numb pain like a drunk drinks to forget. Jerrie put her back into it, organizing, clearing out week-old newspapers that had piled up around the regis-

---

133. "The Cattle Call" is a song written and recorded in 1934 by American songwriter and musician Tex Owens and is considered one of the Top 100 western songs of all time.
134. A Dolbeer Donkey was a steam-driven skidding unit designed and built by John Dolbeer of Crescent City, California, in the late 1800s.

ter, cleaning the glass shelves that displayed Wrigley, Chiclets, and Black Jack chewing gum, and ran up and down wiping the counters, emptying ashtrays, and filling coffee cups.

"What's the matter with you, sister?" barked Jack. "Got squirrels in your loafers? You're making me dizzy."

Now as it turned out, Jack was actually Arleen's brother. And there was some talk about town that he had once lived high on the hog in New York City, earning money on the stock exchange right around the time of the crash. Some thought Jack squirreled away bags of money that he siphoned off unsuspecting clients just before Black Thursday and that Arleen was his washerwoman while he played the part of a hobo so as not to raise suspicion. The more gullible, those who believed the popular suicide lore, thought the loss of everything made him go mad, and by the grace of God—and Arleen—he hadn't jumped to his death from a New York high-rise. The one thing Jerrie knew for sure was he was a lousy tipper, and when Arleen was not around, he served as her watchdog.

The afternoon lunch rush was over, leaving behind only those who had nowhere else to go, those whose daily ambition would comprise nothing more than free refills. Jerrie sat on the stool behind the cash register, resting her swollen feet, and focused on prying the dimes out of the cardboard display card with the metal fingernail file, ignoring the ne'er-do-well tippers who cocked their heads from side to side like turkeys when they wanted refills.

Jerrie raised the plaque in front of her face and started lip-reading its message when she heard one of the customers loudly clear his throat when he realized his waitress was not reading his signals. The plaque read:

"JOIN THE MARCH OF DIMES

"Give New Hope!

"Polio, Virus Diseases, Arthritis, Birth Defects"

As she finished reading the fine print, she prayed her baby would not follow the same fate as Dora, who had contracted polio when she was eleven. Dora's father would not allow her to wear a brace, so Dora struggled to walk on her own. There were more than a few parents who thought he was cruel but, in the end, no one would ever suspect Dora had fought a bout with polio, except that one foot was a half-size smaller than the other.

"Hey, can I get a refill here!" wailed an annoyed customer.

Jack twisted around on his stool and barked, "This ain't rehab. Go find yourself a fuckin' meeting."

The customer pushed his saucer hard along the Formica table-top and slid himself off the bench as he said, "You don't have to be so rude about it," then plopped his fedora on his bald head.

"Cry me a fuckin' river!" Jack yelled.

"The sign says, 'Free Refills'," replied the customer.

Jerrie, uneasy with confrontation and feeling she was responsible for the heated skirmish, quietly eased herself off her stool and made her way toward the cigarette machine with a dust-cloth in one hand and a carton of matchbooks in the other.

"Come on over here. I'll give ya a refill, you cocksucker!" shouted Jack as he jumped up and grabbed his crotch.

"I'll take my business elsewhere," the customer said as he shoved his arms into his frayed Levi's jacket and stomped toward the door.

"Oh, *please* don't. We'll have to close down without your lousy twenty-five cents!" Jack yelled.

"Ya need to take down that 'Free Refills,' Jerrie," the customer whispered as he passed the cigarette machine and then set a quarter next to the register.

"Yes, Mr. Dickerson, I will take care of that right away," Jerrie replied meekly without looking up. Hearing the cowbell, she exhaled, allowed her shoulders to relax, and slowly began to refill the small wicker matchbook basket when she saw a face reflected in the cigarette machine that startled her, causing her to drop the carton of matchbooks. Slowly, she pulled air deep into her lungs and glanced down at the matchbooks that had landed at her swollen feet. They advertised an opportunity to "Finish high school in your spare time at home – Free Booklet – See Inside," along with a reminder to close the cover before striking a match.

"Hello, Jer."

"Hi, Sledge."

Each waited in silence, each conducting an internal system check, neither wanting to tip their hand. Sledge was considering his pride and Jerrie her honor, not the pride and honor they so quickly tossed aside in the backseat of a '48 Ford, but the pride and honor they were forced to face in the light of day.

"Where did you get that busted lip and shiner?" asked Jerrie.

"Iranintoafellawhotookmeforsomebodyelse.Ithinkhecrackeda rib too," Sledge said as he rubbed the side of his red plaid flannel shirt.

Jerrie raised her eyebrows, and not to betray herself, she turned and looked out the window just as a light gray Plymouth sped by.

"Can we grab a coffee somewheres?"

"Sure," answered Jerrie, and she pointed to an empty booth.

"I mean someplace private."

"If you wanna talk, you'll hafta do it here. I'm the only waitress on the floor until the dinner shift, but I can take a short break." Jerrie then pointed to the booth in the back corner. "And that's about as private as I'm going to get."

Sledge nodded and headed toward the booth.

"Hey, Frank!" Jerrie yelled to the fry cook. "I'm goin' on break. Watch the till, will ya?" Frank gave her a salute and went back to cleaning the grill.

"Ya look good, Jer," said Sledge as he wrapped his skinned knuckles around the hot coffee cup. "Real good."

After sitting and talking long past her break, Jerrie turned her head to see what had distracted Sledge and saw a tall slender, bleached blonde with a brushed-up bob flounce into the booth next to them.

Grudgingly, Jerrie put on a slanted smile and served the woman her coffee. After emptying the sugar jar into her coffee cup, the bleached blonde plugged the Seeburg Wall-O-Matic and started banging a spoon inside her coffee mug in rhythm to Hank Lock-lin's *"Let Me Be the One"*[135].

Frank and Jack gave Jerrie a wide berth, wide enough to say the things that needed saying, yet they took it all in just the same—the low whispers, the looks, the shifting in their seats. And when it was all stitched together, the old secret and the new plans became an open book.

Monroe's two big passions were music and the picture show. He went to the movies so often that people thought he was taking acting lessons. It didn't matter what was on the screen—the Three Stooges, Alfred Hitchcock, or a Western. But it was a newly released movie that he was desperate to see: *"Courage! Gallantry! Emotion! Violence! From The Boldest Best-seller of All!"* the movie poster promised. It had been released weeks earlier in all the major cities and, at last, it had arrived in Crescent City. When Monroe invited Dora and Jerrie, he intentionally failed to mention the movie title in the event it would rub up against their sensibilities. And before he picked them up, he swung by the movie theater and purchased the tickets, thus cement-

---

135. *"Let Me Be the One"* was written by Paul Blevins, Joe Hobson, and W. S. Stevenson and made famous by up-and-coming country singer Hank Locklin.

ing their obligation. But when he arrived outside the rooming house, Dora was the only one waiting for him on the sidewalk.

"Arleen had to leave on some family business, so Jerrie had to pull a last-minute shift," Dora told Monroe as she jumped into the front seat, feeling a little uneasy that there was no chaperone.

"Ain't that a shame. We'll just hafta see it again then, I reckon."

From Here to Eternity left Monroe and Dora emotionally charged. Unlike Monroe, a man with experience, Dora had never felt such explosive sexual tension. The tiny hairs that covered her body felt like matchsticks that had been set afire. She found it difficult to make conversation as Monroe guided his car slowly along the dark streets toward her rooming house. He pulled his car to the curb just beyond the porch light, then killed the engine and turned off the headlights.

"I had a good time," he said as he turned his body toward hers and placed his right arm over the back of the bench seat.

"I did too," Dora said without making a move to open her door.

Monroe pulled Dora's neck toward him and kissed her, lightly at first. When she did not resist, he pressed harder, and she leaned in. Their hands ran through each other's hair, then moved down along their shoulders, first exploring the outer layer of clothing, then the inside of the other's coat, releasing pheromones from their warm skin. Monroe cupped his hand gently around Dora's small, firm breasts, and her body rose to meet his hand. When she realized her hand was tracing the rearing horse on Monroe's large silver belt buckle, she became alarmed and pushed herself back.

If religion makes you travel blind, then Dora lost her sight at the age of thirteen when her mother began taking up "Bible Studies" with the Witnesses. After that, there was no need to question life or labor over long-term plans. You merely had to trudge along in a trance-like state along the footpath laid down by The Watch Tower Bible and Tract Society. Up to that very moment she had carried herself as an untested backseat saint.

And as for Monroe, he had never been considered "elder material" in any congregation. But he was thought to be one of the "faithful." Like his father, he was prone to interpret the scriptures in a way that did not always fall in line with *The Watchtower*'s governing body. Even so, he was often extended a sizable latitude to operate on his own terms because he was a "good ol' boy," handy to have around, especially in poverty-stricken congregations who needed help to fix their cars in order to continue their evangelical ministry.

In return for his practical knowledge and services, Monroe found a community whose doctrines were easily understood by those devoid of secular education. But more importantly, just like his father, he reveled in belonging to a sect that considered itself above the fray, the only *true* religion, the only ones that would survive Armageddon, the only ones to be granted everlasting life in the New World. Those beliefs gave him divine permission to ridicule and judge others who had dismissed him based on his station.

"I have to check on Jerrie," Dora whispered.

"Don't fret. She's gonna be all right," Monroe said calmly.

"God, I hope so."

"Dora, honey, ain't nobody ever told ya how purty you are? Give me one more kiss before ya go."

Dora did like the way he made her feel pretty. She was aware of her physical limitations. For one, she was taller than most girls. In fact, she was a few inches taller than Monroe, her hair was mousy brown and fine, and she had inherited her family's oversized schnoz and jowl line. But her figure was well within proportion, and she had learned to work with what she had, opting for a classic look with a western flair—sensible, but with a touch of adventure.

She leaned into Monroe and pushed her lips into his before she said, "I had a great time, Roe." Then she jumped out of the car before she changed her mind.

"Pick ya up tomorrow!" yelled Monroe.

"Only if you're lucky!" she said, and then she flashed a grin.

As Dora floated toward the front door of her rooming house, she knew Monroe was watching, which made her feel both nervous and excited, but she played it coy and did not look back.

Once inside, she toggled the switch to the porch light on and off to let Monroe know she was safely inside. She then tiptoed quietly to avoid waking Mrs. Flood, whose rooms were on the ground level. Then she started climbing the stairs to the second floor when suddenly it hit her like a backhand from Jehovah himself.

What have I done? Dora asked herself as she tightly gripped the stair rail. "Oh, dear God!" she whispered, and she sat on the steps to gather her composure before she confronted Jerrie. Dora replayed the abstinence messages the congregation brothers preached from their pulpits. To the brothers, there was no difference between petting and full-blown sexual intercourse. She thought about how she had berated Jerrie for getting herself into her present condition, telling her that she never should have associated with someone not in the "truth," that it was bound to come to a sad end.

The thought of having to admit her own failings overwhelmed Dora. Apologizing for her quick and harsh judgment of Jerrie was out of the question. She came from proud, hardworking German stock, teetering between arrogance and self-righteousness. They were the keepers of grudges that isolated them from the fatherland, and launched a hasty move across the country. They buried family history behind a shroud of secrecy and created isolation until the only relatives Dora knew were the few who rested in the black leather-bound photo album that was only pulled out during rare moments of late-night episodes of melancholy and served with a slice of Dutch apple cake *mit schlagsahne* (with whipped cream) and a hot cup of tea, but not an ounce of forgiveness.

Pulling herself up, Dora climbed the remaining steps to her room and quietly opened the door. On the bedside table sat a small glass lamp with a pink ruffle shade that cast a soft glow. Dora was puzzled by the made bed. The café had closed over an hour earlier. Jerrie would have been exhausted after her shift and should have been in bed asleep. Yet, there was no sign of her. Only then did Dora notice the note lying under the glow of the lamp.

> *Dear Dora,*
>
> *I found Sledge, or rather he found me. We're taking the 10:43 bus to Reno. I know it's a fast decision, and I wanted to tell you in person, but Sledge said we had to go tonight. I know it may not work out, but I have to try.*
>
> *Thank you so much for sticking by me. I could not have made it this far without you and hope you understand and forgive me.*
>
> *I'll send you a postcard when we get settled. I'll also post one c/o your mom just in case you've decided to go back to Creswell.*
>
> *I hope something becomes of you and Roe; I think he's a swell guy.*
>
> *Your faithful friend,*
> *Jer*

Dora set the note on the bedside table. The room looked empty without Jerrie's blue bathrobe hanging from the hook on the back of the door. The starched white linen runner that ran across the top of their shared burrow seemed bare without her jar of radiation-tested Dorothy Gray Salon Cold Cream, bores hair bush, and her well-guarded bottle of Estée Lauder Youth Dew. The closest thing to a sister Dora had ever known was gone.

She fell back onto the bed, her mind sitting on the edge of a feather, not wanting to move away from childhood, yet not quite ready to fall into the infinite sky of adulthood. She closed her eyes and gently cupped her hand around her breast.

Chapter 17

Ye Be Damned

California, 1954

MONROE AND DORA'S first child arrived early, as many first babies do. They confessed their transgressions of the flesh at the feet of Brother Squat and the other elders. After construing an interpretation of the Holy Scriptures and consulting with their earthly mystics who spoke through the pages of *The Watchtower*, the elders concluded they were in the pulpit business, not the mercy business.

Monroe and Dora's punishment was a year's probation, providing they got married at once and in a government building by the justice of the peace rather than in the sanctuary of the Kingdom Hall. After buying a five-dollar marriage license, they were joined together before a county judge. Without a bridal bouquet or a new groom's suit, they entered their marital contract void of best wishes from family or congregation. There would be no celebration. Monroe and Dora would not receive matching bed sheets, a toaster, or a set of Melmac. Instead, they would attend the required five meetings per week, sitting toward the back of the Kingdom Hall, knowing the congregation was beating their gums to death when Monroe and Dora were out of earshot.

As Dora's belly and feet swelled, the sisters of the congregation avoided making eye contact for fear of betraying the darkness in their own hearts. Dora was no stranger to such conduct, for she herself was capable of pulling the same nastiness from her deepest self and had hurled fragments of it toward her spiritual brothers and sisters who had stumbled—sometimes even toward her best friend Jerrie, whom she so desperately needed.

After a hard delivery, Monroe and Dora's baby was born on July 10 at the Seaside Hospital atop a cliff that overlooked the Pacific Ocean.

"Why's there bruises up along the side of her head?" asked Monroe as he held his daughter for the first time, examining her as though he were on a car lot searching for a reason he should not pay the full sticker price. Then he smiled as he ran his fingers along the tiny bracelet the nurses had made from pink glass block beads that spelled "SHELDA."

"We had to use forceps," said Dr. J. Lloyd Wilder, who had stopped by to check on the family.

"Well, you pulled too dang hard!" Monroe shouted at the doctor. "And look at that left eye. Don't it look a bit off?"

"Sometimes you have to pull a little hard to get them out. And as for the eye, just give it a few months. It should settle into its proper place," explained Dr. Wilder.

"I ain't stupid!" Monroe yelled back. "My mamma's had a dozen, and nar one of 'em had to be pulled out with a hook, even when one of 'em come out backwards."

Dr. Wilder realized there was no reasoning with Monroe, so he quickly made his excuses and left the room.

"If brains was lard, that doctor couldn't grease up a skillet," Monroe said.

"No, I suppose not," replied Dora calmly as she reached over and placed her hand on his knee. "But he did say he threw in an extra stitch[136] for you, whatever that means."

---

136. The extra stitch, aka the husband stitch, is sometimes added post-birth solely to please the husband, and often without the mother's knowledge or consent.

"That might be all fine and good, but it don't make up fer what he done to this here baby."

"You have to drop it, Roe. It'll drive you crazy if you keep thinkin' about it." But she knew that once he got hold of a notion, he rarely let it go. That was one of the things she loved about him—his determination. In fact, his hellbent disposition was what she was counting on to procure the life she had fashioned for herself, an explicit promise to all postwar women, a life free of lugging wash water from the pump, taking sponge baths at the edge of the kitchen sink to save water for the vegetable garden... a life unlike her mother's. She wanted the blissful life that was praised from the pulpit and promoted through the religious literature she read daily. She wanted a husband who went to work every morning and took care of all the manly responsibilities, while she, the submissive wife, fluffed the nest with the help of a new Electrolux, a matching set of Maytags, and enough yardage and notions to make her Christian sisters marvel at her needlework.

The congregation sisters did not visit Dora during her four days in the hospital like other religious do-gooders may have done. They did not pass along their womanly wisdom on the subject of pumping breast milk, managing diaper rash or colic, nor did they provide hints about when it was safe to resume her "wifely" duties. Dora's only visitor was a nonbeliever, a pagan.

"Hey, you awake?" asked Arleen as she poked her head through the door of Dora's hospital room.

Dora dropped the newly-released *Cosmopolitan* that featured a sexy Esther Williams in a one-piece jungle print swimsuit on its cover. The nurse who brought it in had reassured her, "Don't you worry, Mrs. Hornbeck, you'll get your figure back in no time." Dora was not so confident.

"Ya, come in," replied Dora as she set the magazine on her still swollen belly.

"I stopped by the nursery and took a peek. I will say, Dora, once those bruises fade completely, she's gonna be a pretty little thing."

"Thanks, Arleen," said Dora as she pushed herself higher on the bed, careful not to rip open her vaginal stitches.

"I see you named her Shelda. Wherever did you come up with that name?"

Dora slowly answered. "Well, it was the name of Monroe's former girlfriend who died in an explosion." Dora paused before she continued. "He said he always really liked the name."

Arleen pulled a chair up closer to Dora and sat in silence a few moments. Finally, she extended her hand and placed it on Dora's arm.

"I know what you're going to say, Arleen."

"Well, maybe you need to hear it out loud then because you know I'm not going to leave until it's said."

Dora held a deep breath; she knew there was nothing she could do. Arleen would have her say, even if she had to yell it from the parking lot.

"Dora, you're a smart girl," began Arleen as she got up from the chair and walked over to the woman in the adjacent bed and asked to borrow her ashtray. Then she lit a cigarette before she continued: "Sure, maybe you didn't graduate from high school, but you have a brightness about you that you're throwin' away. You may not see it now, but it'll hurt like hell later, and there won't be a goddamn thing you'll be able to do about it then."

"But don't you see, Arleen. I'm a wife and a mother now, and I have responsibilities."

"Of course you do," Arleen said as she returned to the chair next to Dora and leaned in on her crossed legs. "I'm not suggesting you shuck your responsibilities. I'm only saying you have a responsibility to yourself too. You have a bright future if you want it. You're barely twenty-one, for Christ's sake!"

"Arleen," began Dora as she leaned over in her bed. "I never noticed that tattoo on your ankle. What is it, a moth?"

"Don't change the subject, Dora," demanded Arleen as she quickly uncrossed her legs. "I'm being serious."

"I know you mean well, Arleen, but this old world will be destroyed, and we will soon be living in peace—*forever*. Don't you want that for yourself too—to live forever?"

"We are meant to die, all of us, even the stars and planets will die someday, Dora. It's the law of the universe—live, die, live. This notion of living in heaven or hell is just a made-up story to keep you trapped in somebody else's narrative. Break away while you still can.

"Look around you," Arleen continued. "Where are those crazy people you're so fond of, your spiritual brothers and sisters, the ones who have you so wrapped up in fear that you're looking for Armageddon in every shadow, and a sinner behind every set of eyes? And don't forget the one who got you into this mess in the first place. His sweet talk my ass! I don't see one card or bouquet of flowers. Where is all this peace and love, Dora?" Then Arleen paused, scanned the room, and asked, "When does the love show up?"

Dora sat in silence, afraid to look Arleen in the eye, fearing she might uncloak the hurt and disappointment she felt because her religious brothers and sisters had abandoned her, just as Arleen said. Dora squeezed her mind shut and wrapped it like a walnut shell encloses its meat, not allowing so much as a ray of light to leak through the cracks of her spiritual weakness.

Arleen leaned back in her chair knowing in her heart of hearts that her case was lost, yet she felt obligated to continue: "Look, Dora, raising a baby is not the end of the world. There are thousands of women whose husbands have not returned and have to raise children on their own. Nowadays, there are all kinds of opportunities opening up to women."

"Are you speaking from experience?" asked Dora sharply.

Arleen bit her lower lip so hard that the taste of iron permeated her thick layer of Fire and Ice lipstick. She turned her face away from Dora as the image of her late husband Glen popped up like a hologram, the husband whose arms and lips she still felt in the small hours of the morning.

It had been nine years and two months since the Battle of Nuremberg, and yet she still could not move forward like most other women who had lost husbands and lovers in the war. As newlyweds, they had laid in bed late into the morning, smoking cigarettes and planning their future. After he served his tour of duty for Uncle Sam, he was going to buy a new fishing boat, and she was going to buy the café where they met to help hold them over in the offseason. They decided they would have four children, two to raise as future fishermen, and two to raise as restaurateurs. They were going to plant the seed of a great "we catch 'em, we cook 'em" empire.

The war was about to end. Everyone thought so. It would be a matter of days, maybe a week at most. There was no question that the Allies were winning. Although Glen's letters home were sometimes infrequent, his recent ones seemed more optimistic than ever. Rather than being focused on the next military engagement, he was thinking of baby names and fishing boats that he wanted to "name after each of our kids."

Glen served in the US Seventh Army that had pushed its way from Normandy deep into the Rhineland. The Seventh Army was battle-hardened and, with the smell of final victory, the soldiers pressed even harder into Nuremberg, a city enshrined to the Nazi cause. For five days the 3rd Infantry Division fought in urban combat, street by street, until it penetrated a fanatical resistance around the Nazi Rally Grounds.

Arleen shook the image loose from her head and thought, *What's wrong with me? Am I this desperate that I need to reach into*

*the bottom of the barrel to fill this hole in my gut? Look at me, grov-
eling to someone whose radical relative was probably directly responsible for killing Glen.* She felt as though she would throw up. She
crushed her cigarette, leaned forward, and placed her head in
her hands. She thought there must be something inherently
wrong with the genetic disposition of Germans to make them
both stubborn and prone to fanaticism when she heard Dora
calling to her.

"Arleen? Arleen? Did you hear me? I said I was sorry. I know you
lost your husband in the war. It must be terrible for you. I know
you have a huge heart, and you mean well. Really, I do. Look
how you took Jerrie and me in, and no one can deny how you
watch over Jack." Dora paused before she continued: "He's not
been around for over three months; he usually stops in at least
once a month. Where is he? Do you think he's okay?"

"He's on another one of his walkabouts."

"Where does he go? My mother regularly feeds hobos, but
something is different about Jack. He doesn't look or act like he
lives as rough as most."

Arleen recognized that Dora was deflecting from herself, but
she answered, "I've learned never to ask unless I'm willing to
hear the most heinous answers, and once heard, well, that's a
bell you can't un-ring."

"There is talk around town..."

"Oh, yes," interrupted Arleen, "there's always people with their
tongues wagging while their brains are resting."

"Well, I mean, when you take a good, long look at him..."

"Leave it alone, Dora," Arleen interrupted. "It can only get you
into trouble. And Lord knows you don't need more of that.
What you need to be focused on is getting out from under those
Bible thumpers. They are fanatics, and they have you completely brainwashed."

Arleen, realizing her words were pointless, slowly rose from her chair and smoothed Dora's baby-fine hair. "Take care. Maybe someday you'll realize you don't have to follow the bit." They each sank into a quiet space, that grain of silence that holds two musical notes together, but each to a different song.

Arleen broke the silence by reaching down, pulling up a box, and handing it to Dora. "Here's a small gift for the baby. I know those do-gooders are all gums and no hands."

Inside the box was a soft pink baby blanket trimmed in shiny satin. "I figured you could use it to help pad that dresser drawer she will no doubt be sleeping in for God-only-knows how many months."

Monroe picked mother and baby up and drove them back to their small apartment in a converted garage on the outskirts of Smith River. The previous tenants had already left for another mill town, leaving behind most of the furnishings, including a large bureau that was missing one of its four drawers. Monroe removed one of the remaining drawers, rested it across the seats of two slat back chairs, and draped a woolen blanket along its bottom and sides, making sure there were no splinters, nails, or screws poking through the wool. Now dressed in the gown Dora had embroidered with little blue butterflies, the baby girl slept just as content as a child sleeping in a mahogany cradle and wrapped in a fancy new blanket.

That evening, with his young wife sleeping, Monroe sat beside the bureau drawer turned bassinet. On his lap he held Dora's scrapbook full of pictures from women's magazines—electric can openers, mixers, percolators, and "just set the dial" automatic washing machines. It was as though he was seeing Dora for the first time. He suddenly realized that his wife's dreams picked up where her Mother Josephine's aspirations had crumbled in that broken-down trailer alongside a Nebraska cornfield on the family's way to Oregon. Sprawled out along the roadway were Josephine's precious ancestral artifacts and treasured books of poetry by Longfellow, Wordsworth, and her beloved

Poe. And as Josephine walked away from the heap, the desire to build a home out of a house was forever destroyed.

As Monroe continued to turn the pages, it was clear Dora's aspirations extended well beyond electric appliances. She also had clipped floor plans of a three-bedroom rambler furnished with a kidney-shaped sectional where smiling women in swing skirts sat with delicate fingers wrapped around stemmed glasses filled with a green liquid. Standing behind the society ladies were two neatly-groomed men who were leaning into each other and wearing smirks as though one of them had just told a dirty joke.

Monroe closed the scrapbook, leaned back in his chair, and tried to envision himself in that last picture, wondering which of the men he would be: the one with the tweed sports jacket with the leather patches on the elbows or the fella with the black-and-white tie holding a glass of whiskey. He shook his head. *No,* he said to himself, *nair one of 'em.*

Then he questioned Dora's attraction to high-falutin' living and was puzzled as to why she had kept her aspirations hidden. A rush of fear fell over him like someone had stepped on his grave. He set Dora's scrapbook on the floor and leaned over his sleeping child. Gently stroking her dark hair, he whispered, "A house full of lavender and laughter, but no lullabies? Well, we'z gonna see 'bout that. But right now, we'z gotta bitta climbin' ahead of us, baby girl, cuz we done run outta headroom in this here town."

Chapter 17

Boontling

California, 1954

THE CHATTER AMONG the mill workers did not surprise Monroe or Wyatt; gypsy workers[137] knew there was little money in shake.[138] It was Oregon all over again. And they knew if they didn't make a quick move, the choice jobs would be gobbled up quickly, and they could not afford to be left scrambling for nickels in a pile of sawdust.

Once the decision was made, Wyatt and Jewells packed up and were on the road before the sun broke over the horizon. They were following a dozen or so Oakies but were still ahead of a pack of Arkies down into the Anderson Valley, where even a relatively sober man who could hold his own as a bucker, feller, or a bolt puncher could get signed on by one of the more than fifty lumber outfits, or one of a dozen mills strewn across the valley. Wyatt quickly landed on his feet because the outfit he and Monroe worked with in Crescent City had a stake in another mill on the valley floor.

Jewells found work in a jukebox tavern, a local watering hole called The Comatose, a place where the locals gathered to drink

---

137. Gypsy workers were those who jumped from one mill job to another to keep working.
138. Generally, after the prime timber had been harvested, the remaining logs would be cut into rounds about three feet long and then split into shakes for roofs and siding.

and become somebody. A man named Luster Perkins had inherited the tavern from his father and his father before. It was mostly a beer joint because, like his father, Luster watered down the liquor so much that even the fruit flies couldn't get a buzz.

In one of the back corners stood a large cast iron wood stove surrounded by a half-dozen wobbly wooden chairs held together by a few screws and rusty baling wire. Those who wanted to keep warm carried in their own wood, which was usually the old-timers who liked to do some stove logging about their stories of blow-ins in Choker town, which bored the shit out of the young whistle punks.

Along an outer wall stood the tavern's crown jewel, a 1941 Wurlitzer 85 Peacock jukebox that Luster won off a sales distributor in a back-room card game at the Stateline Country Club on his way back from a trip to Reno, Nevada. When in use, the marbleized plastic that decorated its front lit up and created a light show so beautiful that some patrons said it reminded them of the northern lights they saw while mining in Alaska.

The jukebox was about the only thing Luster maintained, and anyone who tried to put a fist to it was immediately shown the sidewalk, headfirst. Luster stocked music by Patti Page, Eddy Arnold, and Red Foley, but it was the early releases of Luster Perkins' longtime friend Buzz Martin[139] whose logging songs got overplayed to the point of skipping so much so that Luster had to keep extra copies on hand. He may have been cheap with the liquor, but he knew the value of sappy songs, especially when night approached the witching hours.

It was at The Comatose that Jewells sent out feelers in search of a rental that she and Wyatt could afford, something better than the small, roach-infested motel along Highway 128. And it was Vernon, one of the regulars, a local apple farmer, who said he had something that might work. And soon, Wyatt struck a deal

---

139. Known as "The Singing Logger," Buzz Martin was the poet laureate of the timber industry, exploring through song the trials and tribulations of the brave men who risked their lives to work the Pacific Northwest forests.

with him to rent the Spartan Imperial Mansion that sat along-side a barn not far from the four-block town of Bloomville. The Spartan Imperial Mansion was a marvel of modern living with matching birch paneling and cabinets, an apartment-size cook-stove, and a porthole window in the door.

"You know who built these, don'tcha?" Vernon asked Wyatt and Jewells as he showed them the layout.

Wyatt sucked air through his teeth while he thought about it, then answered, "Don't rightly thank I do."

"Why, it was J. Paul Getty, that's who," replied Vernon as he extended his massive arm, exposing a faded tattoo of a knot-ted rope, pushed the trailer's doorbell, and stood silently to let everyone marvel at the chime. Then he let out a deep, raspy sound that made them wonder if he was laughing or coughing up a lung.

"He spared no expense; built them the same way he built his airplanes—strong as the USS *Missouri*. Damn good quality!"

"Just so he didn't forget to put in a bathroom," said Jewells as she peeked her head into a space that might have been exactly that.

"Well... that's where it gets a little tricky. You see, we don't have it plumbed into the septic. Now, it's okay to let the gray water run out into the orchard, but we can't have any black water run-off. Don't want anyone coming down with typhoid, do we?" Vernon said, and then he laughed.

"We have to have a toilet," insisted Wyatt.

"Yes, no doubt about it. Now, what I was thinking is that we (meaning Wyatt) could dig a pit some little ways out and build a cover over it. Wouldn't take more than half a day at most."

"You mean an outhouse!" yelled Jewells as she gave Wyatt a look that said, "We're being hornswoggled!"

"Do you mind if we have a private word?" Wyatt asked Vernon as he gently took hold of Jewells' elbow and politely led her out of the Spartan Imperial Mansion and around to his truck.

"Look, sugar," Wyatt calmly whispered. "We can parlay this into a better situation."

"It's bad enough we have to bunk with Roe and Dora," pleaded Jewells, "but to not have a toilet!"

"Baby, you know I love ya," Wyatt whispered as he reached out and grabbed her hand. "Do ya trust me?"

"I suppose," Jewells answered, and she gave Wyatt a faint smile that exposed her overlapping canine tooth that Wyatt had fallen in love with, a smile that quickly faded as she saw Vernon heading toward them.

"You got yourself a deal!" replied Wyatt as he extended his arm to shake hands with the farmer. Neither of them paid heed to Jewells' heavy exhale.

"We done brung every thang with us, so let's get 'er started."

Vernon had taken the trailer in as collateral on a Mack NM-3[140] that he had picked up at a military auction and converted into a self-loading log truck. The guy blew the Mack EY,[141] then skipped town. Wyatt had, indeed, seized an additional opportunity and agreed to rebuild the engine in exchange for nine months of free rent.

Monroe was hellbent to put a fire under Dora, even if it meant he had to bring up Ephesians.[142]

---

140. Mack developed a number of trucks to military specifications for WWII. The NM-3 had an enclosed cab and was uniquely designed to carry artillery pieces.

141. The Mack EY was 707 cu. inch (11.6 L) overhead valve inline six-cycle gas engine.

142. "Wives, submit to your own husbands, as to the Lord." Ephesians 5:22, King James Version.

"It's a whole lot easier travelin' when they's young," Monroe insisted.

"But she's just a few weeks old and due for her first doctor's check-up!" Dora pleaded.

"These dang doctors don't know nothin' nohow. Look what they done to her already. That lazy eye might never go straight."

Monroe put his arm around Dora as she sighed. "Look, honey, they got doctors everywheres—better ones in a better place."

"But we'll be leaving the congregation."

"Gotta tell ya, baby, they ain't never gonna be givin' us no goin' away party in Brother Campion's dagum basement. That I can tell ya for sure."

Dora didn't need to be hit over the head with a two-by-four—or Ephesians, for that matter. She knew if they were going to regain any amount of respect, they would need to make a fresh start. Besides, leaving under the cloak of a job relocation would help save face.

With Dora on board, they headed out of Crescent City faster than a trampoline in a hurricane. In a little more than an hour, Monroe and Dora had packed up and pointed the Plymouth south down Highway 101 with the bureau drawer securely placed on the tattered mohair back seat.

They were counting on all their geese turning into swans, they did not put stock in chipped dishes and broken furniture; they leave them behind for those coming up on the rung just below. That is the friendly and polite thing to do—even a bureau that was missing half its drawers. You take only enough to prime the pump at the next place—tools, an iron skillet, a coffee pot, and work and church clothes stuffed into a paper bag. What they left behind was meant to be forgotten. But Dora took no chances. She tucked her scrapbook into the bureau drawer under her sleeping baby.

Three hundred square feet would be a tight fit, but manageable for people who had lived with far less. Wyatt figured he and Jewells could sleep on the pullout in the living room, and Monroe, Dora, and the baby could take the only bedroom when they arrived. And by all accounts, they were arriving soon. Wyatt knew that because the brothers practiced the same United States Postal Service General Delivery system as his ancestors had for more than a hundred years. The sparse words scratched out with a graphite pencil onto a faded leaf of paper could quickly bring joy, opportunity, help, and sometimes grief. To Wyatt's relief, Monroe had sent such a letter addressed c/o General Delivery, Boonville, Calif.

> *Smith River, Calif.*
> *July 22, 1954*
>
> *Dear Wyatt,*
>
> *Shoven out 'a here Friday after I get my check. Be there sometime on Saterday er Sunday and ready to work. Leave note wheres ya at in the store.*
>
> *Leakin a bit fluid but been stoking up.*
>
> *Your brother*
> *Roe*

Although Monroe was forced to stop several times to add oil and let the engine cool down along Highway 101, he still made good time. There was something about being on the road that energized him, as though the painted center lines were somehow magnetic, and his car was attached to a rail that promised him immortality, so he punched the throttle.

"*Please,* Monroe, slow down!" Dora had pleaded as she dug her fingers into the armrest and glanced over her right shoulder to see the road drop into a rocky surf in the Pacific Ocean, where she swore she could hear seagulls screaming her name. She had hoped he would have become a more cautious driver with a baby in the car, *his* baby, but she had been wrong.

"She ain't even opened up!" he laughed, then he bent over the wheel and pounded the rods.

To Dora's relief, the Plymouth rolled into Boonville, population just over 1,000, and came to a stop in front of the general store.

"I'll run in and get a bead on Wyatt," said Monroe as he shifted into neutral, pushed down on the emergency brake, then shifted into first gear, just in case the brake didn't hold.

"I'll check if the baby needs changin'," said Dora as she drove her shoulder into the door, trying to unstick it.

She knew she had plenty of time to stretch her long legs up and down the short main street before Monroe returned. He could start a conversation with a dried-out fence post. If Wyatt was staying anywhere within fifty miles, Monroe would find him, even if he had to get acquainted with everyone in the store.

Dora carried her sleeping baby in her arms as she walked up and down the four-block town, peeking into café and pharmacy windows. And after reaching the end of the commercial section, she crossed the street and sat on the wooden bench just outside the feed and seed, breathing in the smell of oats and the familiar scent rising off the bales of alfalfa stacked alongside the building. The smells brought back girlhood memories of Sadie, her horse.

As Dora sat in the sun's late afternoon warmth, she leaned her head against the building, closed her eyes, and noticed her stomach growl. *Must be close to 5 o'clock*, she thought. She had grown up in a highly-disciplined outfit that some had referred to as a "military milieu." Even now, without a watch, she knew precisely what her parents were doing at any given hour. In her mind's eye she could see her dad marching down the lane after his shift at the Weyerhaeuser sawmill in Springfield, swinging an empty lunch pail in one hand, smoking a Raleigh cigarette with the other, and expecting dinner to be on the table by the time he hit the back door. Dora's mother would be rushing to have dinner ready precisely at 5 p.m., and not a minute after. Dora wondered if her mother had made sauerbraten or her favorite, pork-stuffed cabbage.

Her sudden nostalgic feelings set off an impulse to search for a public telephone. Her mother and she had devised a communication system whereby Dora would call a family friend to pass on a message and arrange a time when the two of them could speak by phone. Dora knew her mother hated speaking on the phone. Her limited hearing made a simple conversation frustrating for both, but Dora was desperate for her mother's voice. She stood and peered up and down the street for a public phone. Not seeing one, she entered the feed and seed to inquire.

"Excuse me, can you tell me where I can find a public phone?" she asked the heavyset old man wearing a solid blue pair of bib overalls over a filthy T-shirt.

"Won't find a bucky walker anywheres about," explained the old man as he leaned over a dirty wood plank counter.

"I'm just looking for a pay phone."

"Nope, ain't got a bucky walker here, but I do got me a burlap back there," said the old man as he gave her a wink and cocked his head toward the back of the feed store where an "Employees Only" sign hung.

"I said, a *'pay phone.'* There must be one around this godforsaken hole-in-the wall!" Dora said in a loud and condescending manner.

"So, you want to get a cock a fister on, do ya? Well, deek here, if you keep that up, there will be some ear-settin', and it ain't gonna be mine!" said the old man as he puffed out his chest, stepped out from behind the counter, and moved toward her.

Frightened, Dora turned on her heels, holding her baby tight to her chest, and pushed her way past an amply built woman in a faded housedress, almost knocking the old woman over.

"Well!" shouted the old woman.

"No use harpin', Betty. Nothin' but somebody's apple-head bright lighting in a taigey," said the old man.

"If you ask me," said Betty, "she's been a hornin' fralley all day, or else that apple-head needs to unknot her golden eagles and let in some air."

Dora looked back to see if the old man was still following her when she ran right into Monroe.

"Slow your roll there, honey!" said Monroe as he put his arm around her shoulder. "What's got ya all riled?"

"We can't stay here, Roe," Dora said in a panic. "Something's wrong with this town. They're speaking in tongues. They're demonized!"

"The *whole* dang town?" asked Monroe, trying to take her seriously.

"Roe, the town is all of four blocks. Of course it's the *whole* town. I'm telling you, they all speak in tongues."

"Good thang we got kin here to help protect us then."

"Mortal men cannot protect us from demons, Roe, and you know that. It's not safe for us here. We have to leave *now*."

Power gifts were not bestowed upon any individual Jehovah's Witness. Rather, they were reserved for the small governing body seated in the Brooklyn New York headquarters in offices just above the *Watchtower* printing presses. And even their gifts were limited to the channeling of interpretations of the Holy Scriptures. Any individuals or groups claiming spiritual faith gifts—healing, prophecy, or miracles—were considered charlatans. Those who displayed vocal gifts were considered under the direct influence of Satan himself and his myriad of demons. Those encountering them, Dora was taught, risked becoming demonized themselves.

"We'z less than a mile from Wyatt's, and I start work tomarra. I done got it all set up. Sides, we'z about run outta gas money, and the car needs lookin' after."

"You can't possibly think of staying here!"

"Only until we getta nest egg built up."

Monroe could see Dora was pushing her heels into the sidewalk by the way her back stiffened. He liked it when she got riled and would often poke her notions with a stick to see just how high he could get her to rise before he got bit.

"Honey, ain't nothin' to fret over. Here, let me carry the baby for a while," and he lifted the sleeping baby out of Dora's arms. "They's just Boontling,"[143] he continued. "It's a dialect, somethan' like my third cousins living in Alabama do, kinda like speakin' pig Latin.[144] You might just find yourself pickin' up some soon enough."

"Never! I am not some hillbilly! We need to find somewhere else to raise a family, Monroe."

---

143. Boontling was an elaborate jargon developed in and around Boonville, California, and although its roots are not agreed upon, its use spread and often confused outsiders.
"The lexicon included phonologically changed words borrowed from regional Appalachian dialect, Spanish, and the local Pomo Indian language; it later expanded to include invented figures of speech, nouns turned into verbs, onomatopoeia, and other neologisms." – "Rout the Kimmie in the Boat," Jeffery Gleaves, July 16, 2015, *On Language, a Glossary of Boontling*.
144. Pig Latin is not actually a language but a game that children (and some adults) use to speak in "code."

Chapter 18

Passel of Demons

California, 1954

IT WAS THE END OF JULY when JC and Martha pulled their flatbed truck up to the Spartan Imperial in Boonville with the divine spirit in their hearts, hope on their tongues, and just enough loose change to feed their passel of six children onion sandwiches.

Floyd and JC held out for a little more than a year after Monroe and Wyatt took out for Crescent City. Despite being shorthanded, they muscled through until one day when JC asked rhetorically, "I reckon the possum's up on the stump?"

"I reckon so," answered Floyd as he pushed away from the workbench he had been leaning on. "Competition has gotten so dang bad ain't nobody can make a livin'."

"Ya ain't wrong on that account. Some of 'em so dang crooked they can hide behind a corkscrew."

"Now that there is a *fact*! And nair one of 'em is fixin' to stay on their lily pad," Floyd said. Then he pulled out a pint of whiskey from the pocket of his black heavy wool work overcoat and took a long draw before passing it to JC.

"Least we can say we come away with all our digits," JC said, and then he laughed before putting the bottle to his lips.

"Purt near," Floyd said with a smirk as he shook his head and kicked a wrench with the toe of his boot. "All 'cept Clyde."

"That boy ain't got a licka sense no-how," said JC as he passed the pint back to Floyd. "If he weren't our sister's boy, he wouldn't be here anyways."

The men stood rocking back on their heels with their heads bent down in silence and their grease-stained hands shoved deep into their pants pockets in search of nickels. When none could be found, they looked at each other and concluded there was no place to go but down the road. There was never any question that Floyd would stay in the Northwest. It wasn't Louisiana, but he had adapted, trading wild boar for elk and humidity for wet moss. He had settled on his final resting place.

Although Monroe and Wyatt were expecting the arrival of their families, Dora and Jewells were kept in the dark. The brothers thought it best to keep the news to themselves, knowing it would be considered an unwelcome intrusion on an already crowded household.

JC and Martha insisted their stay was only a "visit," but without a pot to piss in or a window to throw it out of, Dora could not see where this would be anything but a long-term layover. The only thing that even remotely eased her anguish was that Martha insisted her brood sleep on the flatbed of their truck. It featured removable wooden sides so a canvas tarp could be strung across to create a shelter.

"They can't sleep outside in the truck, Roe," said Dora as they laid in bed the night of JC and Martha's arrival.

"They don't mind," Monroe said. "They done slept in worse." Then he shared part of the Bootheel story. "Shoot, one night when the headlights give out on the way back from Tennessee, Daddy spotted a clearin' and told us to toss out our pallets. When the sun come up, we seen we was sleepin' in a graveyard."

Dora sighed. "That's not what I'm talking about."

"Honey, come on over here," Monroe said as he threw an arm over Dora's waist and tried to pull her closer to him.

"That's not what I'm talking about, Roe, and you know it!" Dora hissed as she tried to push his hand away. "We're a family now. We need to be settin' up our own home."

"They's family too. We'z all family, Dora."

"I know, I know, but come on, Roe, sleeping in an old truck in the yard? What are people going to say?"

Monroe removed his hand from Dora's waist, laid flat on his back, and stared into the dark ceiling. Finally, he said, "They's gonna say we'z takin' care of our own."

Martha took command of the kitchen like the chief engineer of the first Benson[145] that rolled off the docks at the Bethlehem shipyard. One look at Martha's domination over a cast iron skillet, and Dora and Jewells knew they were out of her league. When moving, the kitchen was the last thing Martha loaded on the truck and the first thing she unloaded, from washtubs to the coffee pot. But it was her heirloom Griswold[146] cast-iron skillet that she considered "black gold" and, with it, she could cook corn mush on an open fire or fry up baloney for a sandwich on an exhaust manifold.

Although the living arrangement was tense, Dora did her best in the role of a subservient wife to adjust to her new in-laws. She had no experience with large families. The closest her family ever got to a visiting relation was a letter from New York three times a year. Even though her in-laws were rough around the edges, she quietly relished living differently than her parents,

---

145.   Built by Bethlehem Shipbuilding, the Benson was a class of destroyers the US Navy built between 1939 and 1943.

146. Matthew Griswold and his two cousins, brothers J C and Samuel Selden, formed a company to make door hinges in 1868. Their factory was known as the "Butt Factory," named after the type of door hinge (butt hinge) manufactured in the ironworks. In the 1870s, Griswold began to manufacture skillets, pots, grinding mills, and waffle irons.

of being part of something larger, more transparent, and less secretive. Yet, sometimes after supper when the washing-up was done and everyone had gathered in the Spartan Imperial Mansion's tiny living room around a small card table, laughing and joking as they played Rummy, she would often fall into a sullen mood with thoughts of her father bent over the coffee table he built in his wood shop, playing solitaire with a worn-out deck of red Bicycle cards in a silent room.

The sawmills were running at full capacity to keep up with the booming postwar housing industry in the Bay Area. And being out of the woods was a welcome relief to them all, especially to JC who was no longer considered a youthful man.

Monroe and Wyatt were put on a cross saw, and JC stood at the chicken coop[147] with a clipboard checking in the seemingly end-less procession of log trucks loaded down with giant redwoods headed to the dump.[148]

Virgil, eighteen, was short in stature, and while he may have lacked the full head of dark wavy hair and swagger of his el-dest brothers, he had an easy laugh and a goofy grin that people warmed to, although they were unsure if they should offer their pity or acknowledge his quick wit. He confidently accepted the persona of his new mill job with pride and donned a black, wide-brimmed felt hat that had been stretched out of shape by the heavy Northwest rains and a tattered wool jacket that made him look like the quintessential pond pig tramp.[149]

Orson looked older than his age. He was more than a head taller than his older brothers, a practical joker, and a fierce student of bobcat logic. At sixteen he had already developed a strong taste for alcohol, guns, and girls. His size and his job stoking the tee-

---

147. The chicken coop is a weigh station or scale shack.
148. The dump is where logs are loaded or unloaded.
149. Pond pig is someone who works in the mill pond and keeps the logs moving toward the bull chain that brings the logs into the head rig carriage of the mill.

pee[150] provided him a certain cache and opened backdoor access to card games.

Each morning at four-thirty, after Martha cooked a breakfast of runny eggs, grits flavored with salt pork, and a pot of cowboy coffee, Virgil and Orson crouched down in the back and pulled their coat collars up around their necks while Monroe, JC, and Wyatt settled onto the bench seat of Wyatt's green '47 GMC pickup. With Martha's lunch kits balancing on their knees, they prayed the 228-long block would turn over as Wyatt pumped the accelerator to give the carburetor a little extra gas. Martha would wave them off, knowing her family would always be a work in progress.

"Ya, Mamma?" asked Wyatt, as he rolled down his window after Martha gave it a knock.

"Yaw better come back with all your digits now, ya hear!" And she flashed a grin.

---

150. Tee-pee shaped burners were used to burn scrap wood and sawdust.

Chapter 19

Broken Bines

California, 1954

IF CHURCH TAUGHT the women anything, it was how to be on time, butts on seats, before the first note of the first hymn was struck. At 5:45 a.m. on the dot, Dora navigated the Plymouth around the ruts and potholes of the makeshift driveway and onto the main road. After getting the car up to 45 mph, she jammed the column shifter into third and let the clutch pop, causing Effie to slam her head against the back side-window, which forced her to groan.

"Sorry, Effie," apologized Dora as she glanced in the rearview mirror at the four kids seated in the back. It was still hard to imagine that those young children were her in-laws.

"Need ta get them boys ta take a look at that there clutch," said Martha as she held onto her grandbaby a bit tighter. "On a hot day, you might just lose a young'un out da windah," she said, and then she laughed.

"It's not so much the clutch I worry about; it's the oil leak. The way it runs out, we may as well put in used oil. I've about had it with this heap. I can't see why we can't get a new car!"

"We had ta pour in a heap a' used oil when we was comin' out, but we got here all the same."

Dora took in a deep breath and did not hide her disappointment that she would not receive any support from her mother-in-law.

"Well," continued Martha, "ya can't complain too much 'bout the way thangs go. Sometimes ya just gotta pull yur chair up closer to the stars, oil slick and all."

Dora rolled her eyes white and gave her mother-in-law an exasperated side glance. Martha could sense Dora was looking at her cockeyed, but she gave no heed and turned her attention to her children.

"Yaw ready to do your best pickin' today?" called Martha, but she received an unenthusiastic response from her four youngest children seated in the back, each holding a cold, jellied buttermilk biscuit in their sleepy hands.

"Cain't hear ya!" she said a little louder.

"Yes, Mamma!" they called out in unison.

"Well, that's good. Mind ya manners. Show 'em ya got some raisin', and for heaven's sakes, don't go actin' like your daddy's people, hear me?"

"Yes, Mamma."

"And don't yaw be getting' that there jelly on them seats, mind ya. Dora might just make yaw walk tamarra."

Dora again glanced into the rearview mirror at the four children and let her eyes rest on the eldest. Effie had a thick head of dark wavy hair that cascaded over her shoulders and her round cheeks. At eleven, her breast was already full, firm, and round and tugged at the seams of her favorite sleeved dress with its delicate orchid pattern which had become little more than a faded memory.

Fieldwork was one of the few times Martha thought it permissible for her girls to wear jeans. Yet Effie, no stranger to hot, dusty, dirty field work preferred to wear a dress rather than her brother's old heavy denim jeans. And in doing so, she had learned to use her femininity to conjure up small favors from the boys working beside her, boys drawn to eyes the color of deep water who were only too happy to help carry her cotton sacks or share their lunch.

On the opposite end from Effie, sat Landry, sitting quietly, he kept his gaze turned away from everyone. He was a handsome, dark-haired boy of twelve with steel-gray eyes and, although he was still very much a boy and too young to work in the mills, he was relentless in his desire to be viewed as a full-grown man, so he unintentionally alienated the two people he wanted to be closest to, Monroe and Wyatt, the brothers who had left home before he was born. He was tired of sitting at the proverbial kids' table. He would have rather sandpapered a bobcat's ass in a phone booth than be dispatched with the women.

The engine let out a loud sputter when Dora cut it off in a clearing next to the hop field. In front of her she saw a group of about twenty women clustered like a clutch of chickens, all dressed like they had just jumped out of the pages of *The Farmer's Wife*,[151] young and clear-skinned. Some were clucking with freshly-painted lips and drinking coffee poured from colorful thermos jugs. A few of the younger ones were checking out each other's feathers, Italian cuts pulled from the pages of *Photoplay* in a sorry attempt to look like Jane Wyman in *Magnificent Obsession*. One flashed what might have been an engagement ring and, although twenty yards away, Dora would swear she saw it sparkle, which only caused her stomach to tie in knots as she stared at her own fingers as they gripped the steering wheel. *Married with a baby and still no ring*, she thought. Even the older women were dressed in freshly-laundered bib overalls layered with short-sleeved gingham blouses in various shades of pink, red, and blue, all freshly-purchased from the Sears and Roebuck Spring/Summer Catalog.

---

151. *The Farmer's Wife* was a monthly women's magazine in print from 1837 to 1970. It offered advice about farming, housekeeping, and cooking. And it published fiction. At its peak, it had over a million subscribers nationally.

There was another group of about a half-dozen women, outliers, who hung quietly along the fringes of the clutch. The only thing that glistened in that small cluster in the soft early morning light was their heavy-handedness with a tube of Plush Red lipstick. With hair color from a cheap do-it-yourself bottle, they poured themselves into tight-fitting pedal pushers, and their tight midriff shirts were only a thin layer that rested over torpedo bras. One look at them and it was immediately obvious they rolled with the hot rod crowd. Most of the money they earned in the hop fields supported their duck butt[152] boyfriends for bragging rights when their best boy collected pinks.[153]

Dora, both jealous and intimidated, wanted to run, but her hands were glued to the steering wheel. She wanted to kick Martha and her four snot-nosed kids out of the car and drive as far as her old heap would take her. Then she felt her mother-in-law's hand rest upon her right shoulder, and she slowly closed her eyes and begged to be awakened from the nightmare that her life had become.

"Dora, don't pay 'em no never mind. A little powder, a little paint make a girl look what she ain't! Come on, let's grab our stuff and get on outta here," commanded Martha as she pushed Shelda into Dora's hands, then shoved her shoulder into the car door. "Come on, yaw, I spotted our people over yonder."

Dora followed Martha's line of sight and cringed.

Martha helped her youngest son Hollis out of the back seat. Hollis was a precocious, fair-haired boy of eight who had developed rickets, giving him an odd swing to his gait. With proper nutrition, the doctor believed Hollis could eventually see some improvements. JC and Martha kept their outward hopes up, but deep inside they affectionately referred to him as their "little gimp."

---

152. "Duck butt" is a greaser hairstyle where the hair in the back is combed toward the middle.
153. "Go for pinks" refers to unofficial hot rod races where the winner would take the loser's pink slip (auto registration).

While in the Northwest woods, JC carved Hollis a staff inspired by the biblical stories of Moses. The boy carried it more as a statement than as an aid. He would often use it on sidewalks as though he were parting the waves of the Red Sea to make a path for him and his family to pass.

Martha led her flock across the parking area, past the glaring eyes and chuckles of the women in bib overalls, toward a third group of pickers. If the first group looked like they had stepped out of the glossy pages of *The Farmer's Wife*, that group looked like they had escaped from a freak show.

"Ain't yaw a sight fer sore eyes!" Martha shouted to two women who could have been her bookends. "Bernice and Lavinia, I was a hopin' yaw would make it outta Or-e-gon! How yaw doin'?"

Dora cringed as she watched them squeeze shoulders and peck each other's cheeks.

"We'z in purdy good shape fer the shape we'z in," laughed Bernice.

"Come on over here, hun," called Martha as she motioned for Dora to come in closer. "Come on. Ain't no need to be shy."

Martha took a couple of steps back to gain the full attention of the entire crowd, and in a voice that sounded like a supper call to field hands said, "Howdy, yaw! I wanna introduce ya to one of the newest members of the Hornbeck clan." Martha reached out with her short but powerful arms, grabbed Dora by the waist, and pulled her close into her before she continued: "This purdy thang here's Dora. Her people comes from Or-e-gon, and she done married my oldest boy Monroe. Yaw remember him?"

"Member him?" said one woman. "Who could forget? If I was ten years younger..."

"Ten years? More like thirty years, ya mean!" responded another, which caused the whole group to roar with laughter.

It's Or-eh-GUN, Dora said to herself. *Why can't they ever get it right! Stupid people.*

"And this little thang here," continued Martha as she rolled the baby stroller up into the middle of the group, "is my first grand-baby, Shelda. Now, ain't she the purdiest thang ya ever did see?"

"Purdier than a spotted horse in a field of daisies," said Lavinia with one eye rolling around crazy in her head as she leaned over the stroller and squeezed the child's cheeks, causing Dora to lose her breath as she visualized the daughter's future.

"Your druthers is my ruthers," said Bernice, voicing her agreement with Lavinia. Then she snatched the baby out of the stroller.

And with that, everyone in the group surrounded Dora, reaching out to give her baby a quick squeeze, a peck on her cheeks, and passing her around like a side dish. The assemblage of strangers vocalized their words of welcome in a dialect that she had once found charming and witty when seated on a mohair seat of a Pontiac along an abandoned street in the small hours, now frightened her, and the harder she tried to compose herself, the louder the voices became until all she could hear was, "We accept her, we accept her—one of us, one of us, one of us!"

At 6:30 a.m. a flatbed truck with wooden siderails rolled into the middle of the three groups of pickers and came to a smooth stop. The driver jumped out of the cab and quickly hoisted himself onto the bed of the truck and motioned for the three groups to come closer.

"Good morning, 'op pickers. My name is Mr. Butler, and I am your field boss," he began, making sure to give equal eye contact to the three distinct groups. "Some of you 'ave worked here before, and some 'ave just arrived, and I wish each of you a warm welcome. The good news is that we 'ave a bumper crop this year." After he paused and fumbled with the small silver moth on the end of his fob, he continued: "The bad news is that we must work fast and put in longer hours than usual. To be sure, this will be 'ard work."

"Bet them girls never broke a sweat in their lives!" Bernadette whispered in Martha's ear as she nodded toward the farmers' wives.

"Ain't that a fact!" Martha said out of the corner of her mouth.

"We'll be running ten hours a day and six days a week to start," continued Mr. Butler. "We start at 6:30 a.m. sharp and end at 5 p.m. with a 'alf-hour for lunch. We want the cones picked while the dust is still yellow, awroigh'?"

"He talks funny!" whispered Effie to her mother.

"Hush, child," replied Martha. "Mind your manners!"

"Well, he do!" Effie mumbled under her breath.

"We pay well for hard work. And this year there has been $250[154] set aside to be divided among those pickers who stick through the harvest, providing we bring in this crop on or before the 20th of August," Mr. Butler explained over low hums and whispers of jubilation.

"Take note," he continued, "we will not tolerate any messing about, drunkenness, or fighting." Then he grinned and said, "Save that for *after* the harvest!"

Hearing that, Martha's group stepped a few feet closer to the truck to send a clear message to the other pickers that they would not be bullied or intimidated—they were there to the end and would collect the bonus, at all costs.

"Where you stand now marks the middle of the first field. Those on my left will start here and work their way to the north. Those on my roigh' will climb onto the back of this truck, and I'll drive you to the back field where you will work your way to the center. Once this field is picked, we will move to the next field. Awroigh'? Any questions?"

---

154. $250 in 1954 was equivalent in purchasing power to about $2,388 in 2020.

"When do we all get paid?" asked the young dirty blonde with the missing canine, standing next to Dora.

"Saturday afternoons, and *only* Saturday afternoons, so be sure you show up to work. Awroigh'? And don't send your 'usband or mother. This is *your* hard-earned money; *you* deserve the roigh' to pick it up," he said firmly.

Mr. Butler's comment stung Dora for she, as was the case with many mill and logging wives, had gotten into the habit of regularly going to the pay shack every Friday to pick up her husband's wages to save him from the foolishness that sometimes happens between the last whistle and the time he reached home.

"The best of luck to everyone. Now let's hop to it!" said Butler as he jumped off the back of the truck.

The hot rod girls stubbed out their cigarettes and followed the farmers' wives who were making their way to the rows of bines, where field hands had strategically placed cribs and piles of burlap sacks days before. Martha's group flung up baby strollers and hoisted the older women onto the back of the truck. The matriarchs steadied themselves by putting one hand on the side railing and the other on their hips, then belted out orders to each other like they were one family.

"Ronda, if you fall off and break your leg, don't come runnin' to me cuz I done told ya to step on back!"

"Jackson, don't ya stand there lookin' at me like a dyin' bull in a hailstorm. Get your behind on this here truck!"

"Darleen, you gonna see next week today if you don't get up off that sack. That's our lunch."

Mr. Butler popped a mint into his mouth, then walked around the truck to make sure no one was left behind before he slowly pulled onto the dirt road that led to the back field. He loved that part of the day when the early morning air was cool and damp. Once behind the steering wheel, he stuck his arm out the window and adjusted the side mirror so he could watch the pickers holding onto the siderails fill their lungs with fresh oxygen, knowing their ride back that evening would be hot, dusty, and sticky.

Mr. Butler knew it would have been easier to have the three groups leapfrog each other, but his experience in the American fields had taught him that separating the groups yielded more hops and less strife, which meant he could be home by supper almost every night.

Mr. Butler had a special fondness for internal immigrants, although he was careful not to openly reveal his preference. He could not help but feel a tug of sadness and joy when they arrived with their lunches in burlap and drank sweet tea from quart jars. The older women, dressed in their threadbare aprons and their gray strands sneaking out from under kerchiefs and flying about their round weathered faces, reminded him of his mother. Unlike the locals, the Southern migrants were worldly-wise, living in the here and now, balancing between life and death in that moment when you shed everything that is not worth caring for and strip away all but each other.

It would be an error to misjudge Hopkins Butler's experience and authority. He was a soft-spoken man in his mid-forties but "fit as a fiddle," as they say. Although he had been in the United States for a number of years, he held onto his London East End accent and his manner of dress like you might grip a flower pressed between the pages of a book of love poems.

His shirt was always crisp with sleeves rolled to the three-quarter mark, and the creases in his trousers were sharp enough to slice a loaf of stale bread. He was rarely seen without a pencil and small spiral notepad in the breast pocket of his ever-present vest. In his waist pockets he stowed his pipe and silver pocket watch connected to a well-worn leather fob connected to a small silver moth. His gray eyes were set deep, and when he spoke, his thin lips moved across a clean-shaven face like a small red rubber band. And although his English tweed flat cap provided shade for his suspected bald head, it offered only limited protection from the sun for his long, narrow nose.

The locals, most of whom counted him a friend, often said he had alpha acid[155] running through his veins, and yet they did not know the whole of his story.

★

Before his birth and throughout his childhood, Hopkins' mother Gladys, like thousands of other mothers from London's East End, made the annual thirty-eight-mile trek to the hop fields in Kent. Each year, upon receiving their invitation cards through the letterbox, excited mothers gathered in the street to start the planning for that year's pilgrimage. Cans of corned beef would have to be siphoned from already tight food rations, warm jumpers and hats were rounded up in jumble sales along with old cooking pots and blankets, but the most challenging would be the train fare if they were going to make it to the fields. And make it they must.

Hopkins' father, Frank, drank more than he earned, and it was only his mother's leadership and determination that kept a roof over the family's head. In four weeks, Gladys and her five children could bring in what Frank could not in ten and being shown up can make a drunk man nasty, vile, and angry.

On the day of their departures, Frank would angle his thin torso out the upper window of their London terrace and shout for all to hear, "Gone off for a little posh wiv your 'op 'usband, ay?"

Never giving Frank a glance back, Gladys leaned her full figure into her heavily laden cart and led her brood toward the East Indian Dock Road to catch the cheaper late-night hopper train leaving from the London Bridge Station.

"'Opkins," said Gladys, "don't give 'im the satisfaction of your acknowledgment. Keep your eyes straight ahead like a good lad,

---

155. Alpha acids are a class of chemical compounds primarily of importance to the production of beer. They are found in the resin glands of the cones (flowers) of the hop plant and are the source of hop bitterness.

awroigh'? Come along, children. Let's sing a little song now, shall we?"

Then she would lead them in a strong but off-key effort:

Oh, they say 'opping's lousy
I don't believe it's true.
We only go down 'opping
To earn a bob or two.

When the train pulled into the station, hundreds of East End hoppers pulled and pushed their carts onto the overcrowded cars, sometimes stowing the younger children on the overhead metal luggage racks above the seats. Old friends were reacquainted, and new babies were cooed.

Once the hoppers settled down and the train was in motion, someone would start the old hopping song, *"When Autumn Skies Are Blue,"*[156] and everyone would join in:

Well, it's away with all wine drinkers
And all such fickle thinkers
And may they all be shrinkers
From all good men and true.

Thus spoke the jovial Men of Kent
As through the golden hops he went,
With sturdy limb and brow unbent,
When Autumn skies are blue above,
When Autumn skies were blue.

The 'op that swings so lightly
And the 'op that glows so brightly
Will surely be honored rightly
By all good men and true.

---

156. The origin of *"When Autumn Skies Are Blue"* is largely unknown, but the lyrics are thought to be by Charles Dibdin and the tune from an old English song *"The Seven Trades"* or *"Jovial Crew"*.

Let the Frenchmen boast their straggling vine
Which gives them droughts of meager wine,
It'll never match the bine of mine
When Autumn skies are blue above,
When Autumn skies were blue.

After the songs died down and quiet returned, all that could be heard were the snorts and coughs of children trying to clear their lungs of the polluted East End. Then, and only then, would Hopkins reflect on the last words his father had yelled down to his mother, knowing they rang true. He and most of his siblings, like hundreds throughout the East End, were June babies,[157] and it was by no accident that Hopkins had become a popular name among the hoppers. As he pushed his back into the train's hard wooden seat, he took pride in thinking that Frank may not be his biological father, a man whom he had always regarded as a plonker. That hatred of his father had intensified when Frank openly referred to Hopkins as a "chicken," which resulted in being publicly ridiculed and forcing the companionship of his closest friend, Tommy, underground.

But that night on the train, with the exuberant East End hoppers surrounding him, their friendship would barely be noticed. They could sit next to each other, pant-leg to pant-leg, ankle to ankle, rocking to the motion of the train. When Tommy's sleeping head fell on Hopkins' shoulder, Hopkins could smell the faint scent of lavender in Tommy's hair, so he pulled the fragrance deep into his nostrils where he hoped it would remain forever.

It was on that particular trip in 1940 that Hopkins vowed to himself that he would never return to the East End. At almost seventeen, he put his back into the field with the same determination his mother put into pushing the cart all the way to London Bridge Station every year. Pushing their heavy cart un-

---

157. Nine months after the hop harvest there would be a flush of unplanned babies born to hop pickers. Hops have a considerable amount of phytoestrogen, a chemical that influences the hormones, thus the popularity of the name Hopkins.

der her own steam along the East Indian Road provided Gladys with the self-confidence and determination to keep the candle of hope burning.

At the end of the harvest, Hopkins readily agreed to stay on as an agricultural worker in support of the war because, unlike Tommy, Hopkins was still too young to enlist.

Soon, Hopkins was working on stilts, stretching wires on criss-crossed scaffolding and as the tallyman[158] during the harvest. He learned all he could about black root rot, gray mold, and various types of mildews that plagued hop fields. Along with his hop duties he filled sandbags that offered protection for farm buildings against air raids, and he spread rubbish and discarded cars and farm equipment that was too rusted to be melted around the fields to prevent German aircraft from landing. He dug foxholes for hoppers, imagining that each one would save the life of someone from the East End. He kept his mental fortitude by telling himself, "This trench is for Mum." The next would be for his sister Nell or the butcher—or for Tommy, whom he feared was already dead.

The war did not stop pickers from making their trek to Kent. Each season Hopkins looked forward to being reunited with his family. He spent his off-hours clearing a squalid hop hut for his mother and siblings, putting in fresh straw for their tick beds,[159] and placing a bouquet of wild heath lobelia and round leaf mint blooms in an empty corned beef tin and oiled an angle[160] for a leaky milk bucket to use as a bed stand. "She'll be sleepin' on velvet now," he would say to himself as he fluffed his mother's tick. And then he would smile.

It was an unexpected trip that changed Hopkins' life forever. He was sent on an unscheduled delivery of dried hops to a small brewery whose resources had run low due to the arrival of the USAAF on the RAF base in Ashford. It was there that he met

---

158.   The tallyman recorded how much was picked to calculate payments to pickers.
159.   Tick bed is a casing made of coarse cotton and stuffed with straw.
160.   Oil of angels is a bribe. (An *angel* was an old English coin).

a young gunner by the name of Arnold from the 406th Fighter Group. Arnold was recovering from a wound in his leg. He had caught a bullet that had pierced the side of his plane during an air attack.

While Arnold was convalescing, Hopkins would collect him at the train station and show him around the hop fields of Kent. They sat for hours, allowing Arnold's leg to rest in the shade of the bines. Lying back, they took in the pine resin scent dripping from the sticky cones in the warm summer sun, feasted on the egg sandwiches Hopkins packed, and smoked the cigarettes from Arnold's K rations.

After the war ended and Arnold had received his teaching certificate from the University of California, Berkeley, he sent for Hopkins to join him in a small community in the Anderson Valley where he was needed as a teacher and where Hopkins could work among the hop fields he had grown to love. They lived quietly as confirmed bachelors, introducing each other as 'across-the-pond cousins' who became reunited during the war. Many silently doubted it, thinking they may be light in the loafers, but no one openly questioned them. Even the staunchest churchgoer did not cast aspersions on their heroic war record and the contributions they were making to the growing community.

*

The truck came to a stop in the back field just as the warmth of a new light gently stretched its arms and beckoned the dampness sitting on the bines[161] to come closer. And when the dampness lifted, it released their scent. It would only be an hour or two before the sun pulled all the coolness from the cones, leaving nothing but stickiness.

"Start at the back row and leapfrog over teams of six to eight. I'll come around to each team to answer any questions," Mr. Butler

---

161. A bine is a plant that climbs by its shoots growing in a helix around a support, in contrast to vines, which climb using tendrils or suckers.

instructed the group. "Have any of you picked hops before?" he asked as he approached Martha and Dora on their row.

"When I was in high school," answered Dora.

"No, but done picked a lotta cotton and tobacco," answered Martha. "Can't be much harder, I 'spec'."

"You may find that it's a little like both," said Mr. Butler kindly as he eyed the group, taking special notice of the yellow duck diaper pin the family matriarch used to attach the torn bib of her apron to her faded jersey dress and the pair of old men's work boots with the burned-out toes and laces that had been knotted together. "The cones are sticky like tobacco, and the picking is more like plucking cotton.

"You would do well to work as a team with each person doing a specific job," continued Butler as he nodded toward Landry. "You can use this lad's strength to gently pull down the bines a few at a time so the others can pluck the cones." He pulled a few bines down and plucked off a few olive-green cones to show how to pull without breaking the lead wire.

And with that, Landry found his place, his purpose that summer as the lead man of the small hop-picking family.

There was no need for a watch or a noon whistle: the pickers emerged from their rows at noon like it was Groundhog Day, droopy-eyed, hungry, and bines stuck to their clothes and matted in their hair. They spread old blankets alongside the dirt road next to a single oak tree. Some pulled out sandwiches made of bread and ketchup or butter and sugar. Others had fried potato peel sandwiches neatly wrapped in used wax paper or old soft bread bags. Others ate a cold sweet potato they had wrapped in newspaper; some shared a can of pork and beans that was passed with a bent spoon and small packets of saltines that had been lifted from a café and drank sweet tea from Mason jars. They sat in the shade and got caught up on the trials and tribulations of life, where they broke down, ran out of money, gas, or both, and who had rickets, typhus, yellow fever, who died, and who ran off with who until it was time to head back into the rows.

With the two sides working against the middle, it took less than a week before Dora and Martha began to hear snippets of conversations drift over the bines. At first it was just a word, a snicker or two, but they each picked in silence, preferring to bury themselves deep within their self-made walls, sorting through a mixture of hopes and regrets like dirty clothes on wash day. Yet there was no mistaking the innuendos, criticism, and general insults that were shot over the stringers in their direction.

The rod girl clique began a recruitment campaign to enlarge its circle, and each day two or three fresh faces appeared until their numbers grew to about ten. Acting as their chief agitator was Ophelia. Her hair was bottle-dyed black, pulled back into a ponytail, and tied off with a bandana. She wore a thick layer of eyeliner that made her eyes look like a cat, and she was heavy-handed with a pencil on her brows. Along her left cheek ran a four-inch scar she wore like a Girl Scout Adventurer badge, and on her left arm and shoulder was a large burn scar. Ophie, as her friends called her, was more than a rod girl. She was a girl with an ax to grind who was on a mission to collect a long overdue debt.

After an accident killed her boyfriend and left her scarred, she became obsessed with building and racing her own rod. Observers watching her reaching down under a hood with a torque wrench got the impression she was searching for something buried in the crankcase—perhaps forgiveness. But until she could find redemption, she hated everyone and everything—but mostly herself. She was the one who insisted on riding alongside her boyfriend as he was going for pinks in Healdsburg that night.

His army buddies, mostly those who were fellow members of the Road Devils,[162] drove up from Southern California for the funeral. They commended her for her gallant effort in trying to

162. In 1946 a group of returning veterans founded the Rat Rodders in Southern California.

remove her boyfriend from his burning Model A, but she knew it was all show. She knew the truth; Lucas took his eyes off the road for a split second and gave her a look that made her breast swell. When his eyes turned back to the road, his headlights illuminated an old broken-down car on the side of the dark stretch of road. For Lucas, there was only one choice. He swerved to miss a migrant woman who was balancing a baby on her hip as she held a flashlight for her husband who was trying to fix their car.

The Model A flipped and burst into flames.

With Ophie as the ringleader, the Rod Girls became aggressive and calculating. After waiting until the Hornbecks reached the middle of their long row, the girls jumped ahead of the Farmers' Wives, then quietly entered the Hornbeck's row from each end, blocking them in. With baseball bats in hand, they marched toward Martha and Dora.

"Tryin' to take our jobs, aren't ya!" yelled Ophie as she tapped the palm of her hand with her bat. "You and your ankle-biters[163] don't belong here!"

Realizing she was trapped, Dora tried parting the bines to crawl through, but she was quickly blocked by a Rod Girl brandishing a chain.

"Yaw get on back to your patch!" Martha called.

"Ya, you and what Okie is gonna make us?" hissed Ophie. And she took a few steps closer to Martha. "It's an eye for an eye, tooth for a tooth, life for a life. *This* is your moment of truth!"

Effie tried to pull the stroller in which Shelda was fast asleep back into the hop bines as far as she could while Landry stepped forward and pointed the knife he had been using on the strings.

"Nothing but lazy white trash and thieves!" piped in a Rod Girl as she reached down and twisted the knife from Landry's hand

---

163. Ankle-biter is 1950s slang for a small child.

and pushed him to the ground. "Time for you to agitate the gravel!"

"But I'm not from the..." started Dora.

"Ya, cop a breeze, bitches!" yelled another Rod Girl.

"Get your head down, Dora... now!" insisted Martha. "The adults got this!"

Martha slowly reached under her apron, pulled out a pocket pistol, and asked, "What took yaw so long?"

The Rod Girls heard voices from behind them and quickly turned to see Bernice on one end and Lavinia at the other, each with a revolver drawn.

"Why, we waz just a-waitin' on you, Miss Martha," snickered Lavinia as she adjusted the grip on her small firearm.

With the matriarchs standing ground, Effie, Landry, and Hollis crawled through the bins.

Taking a step toward Ophie, Martha slowed her breath, then spoke in a calm and even voice: "Ya know as much about us as a hog knows about Sunday. Why, I stepped over better than you lookin' for a place to piss... And now it looks like yaw are ducks stuck in a dry pond. We can do a couple of thangs here. On the one hand, yaw can get back to your patch, or we can lay yaw out flat here." Martha paused and pulled the hammer back on her firearm. "Just in case ya need a little help with your giddy up."

The last to stand down was Ophelia who squeezed her hand around her bat so tight that her knuckles turned white.

"Come on, Ophie!" called out one of the girls. "They're not worth it!"

But Ophie wondered if *she* was worth it. She wondered what a gunshot would feel like. She asked herself if the woman standing before her with the duck diaper pin holding up her faded apron could make a clean kill. Ophie could feel her girls backing off, leaving her more exposed. She knew she should feel hurt and betrayed, but her hurt was deeper, and she just wanted it to go away. What she wanted was the courage to drop to her knees and ask for a bullet to her heart.

"Girl, whatever hurt you got," began Martha in a calm and understanding tone, "this ain't gonna help, not here, not now, not this-away."

Ophie pulled her eyes away from the duck diaper pin and slowly bent her head toward the ground.

"Go on, child," continued Martha. "Get on with your business."

At the end of each day, the pickers dragged their sacks to the end of their rows for a field hand to count and weigh. But that day the field hand was surprised to see the increase in yield from Martha and her children.

"This is almost twice as much as you had on any other day," said the field hand as he stared at Martha and her brood.

"Well, I thank the young'uns is finally gittin' the hang of it," replied Martha proudly as she extended her hand and tossed Landry's hair. "Yes, sir, they's growin' up all right!"

"Well," responded the field hand, "it's a good thing, because we had about seven girls walk off today."

"Is that a fact now?" Martha answered in a tone that dripped like warm honey on a hot biscuit.

If Effie had not remembered to pick up Dora's sack, it would have remained among the bines, for Dora took refuge in the dark and dank caverns of her mind and, in the silence, found comfort in her thoughtlessness.

"I am so sorry for knocking you over," Dora said as she extended her hand to help pull up the young dirty blonde woman who had inquired about paychecks on their first day. "I wasn't paying attention."

"Don't matter none. I shoulda pulled to the side. I'm just so dang blasted tired of pluggin' holes in these here shoes with cardboard. Might as well go without, like that little one up yonder," she said as she nodded toward Poppy, Martha's youngest.

Dora stood and watched the five-year-old Poppy fluttering her arms about, weaving between the rows in her favorite dress with its tattered hemline. She reminded Dora of a noisy butterfly with a torn wing trying to keep its balance, but only able to fly in circles until it makes itself dizzy and drops to the ground in a tiny puff of dust. But unlike a dizzy butterfly, Poppy rose again with a crown of bines in her thin, light-colored hair and continued her selection of little dances.

"Hurry on up, you two!" yelled Hollis as he ran awkwardly down the row. "Truck's a-loadin' up."

When Dora caught up to Hollis he boasted, "I done pretty good fluffing those cones today, don'tcha thank?" Then he gave her a side smile as he pulled the sticky gluten left by the cones from his thumb and index finger. "Fluffed 'em up like a feather bed, ya might say."

"Yes, you did Hollis," replied Dora, knowing full well what he and his brother had done.

Hollis stuck out his staff and gave a bine a hard whack. "You know what?"

"What?"

"I had a dream last night."

"Ya, what about?"

"I dreamt I was a muffler." Then he picked up his pace and caught up to his mother who was bent over, picking bines from the wheels of the baby stroller she pushed.

Dora stopped dead in her tracks and said to herself, "Who dreams they're a muffler? *Who?*"

The images of workers loading themselves on to the back of the truck reinforced Dora's worst fears, her reality, her plight, until she felt a burning in her chest that moved into her throat. She fell to her knees and threw up yellow bile. She could taste the bitterness of her impoverishment on her tongue and in her throat as Arleen's words echoed in her ears.

Standing tall, Dora screamed, "My dreams are bigger than a muffler!"

But the only one who heard her was Mr. Butler, standing silently in the next row.

Authors Notes:

Photo: Paul Thacker

The recipient of 9 awards from **The Society for Technical Communication**, is also a published photographer, and has produced and directed more than 40 lifestyle broadcast segments focused on eco and small space living. She directed, produced, and is the co-creator of the documentary series, *Where Small Business Grows* (Amazon Prime).

Shelah lives a life of voluntary simplicity, where she makes a mid-century modern Airstream her home on an island in the Pacific Northwest and enjoys kayaking and traveling across the country and around the world.

The Boloney Trail Continues

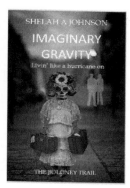

IMAGINARY GRAVITY

Coming Mid-2022

LOGLINE: Monroe fails to make financial and religious progress that match Dora's ambitions and moves his family to Mexico on a promise of financial security as a runner for the budding Sinaloa Cartel. He soon finds himself over his head, forcing his 9-year-old daughter, Shelda, to care for herself and younger siblings on the streets after Dora does a runner.

Register to get advanced pages www.theboloneytrail.com

Made in the USA
Columbia, SC
07 December 2021

50494281R00143